J. MEADE FALKNER

MOONFLEET

PUFFIN CLASSICS

PUFFIN BOOKS

UK | USA | Canada | Ireland | Australia
India | New Zealand | South Africa

Puffin Books is part of the Penguin Random House group of companies
whose addresses can be found at global.penguinrandomhouse.com.

www.penguin.co.uk
www.puffin.co.uk
www.ladybird.co.uk

First published by Edward Arnold 1898
Published in Puffin Books 1962
Reissued in this edition 2018

001

Set in 11.5/15 pt Minion
Typeset by Jouve (UK), Milton Keynes
Printed in Great Britain by Clays Ltd, St Ives plc

A CIP catalogue record for this book is available from the British Library

ISBN: 978–0–141–37762–9

All correspondence to:
Puffin Books
Penguin Random House Children's
80 Strand, London WC2R ORL

MIX
Paper from
responsible sources
FSC
www.fsc.org   FSC® C018179

Penguin Random House is committed to a
sustainable future for our business, our readers
and our planet. This book is made from Forest
Stewardship Council® certified paper.

*To All Mohunes
of Fleet and Moonfleet
in Agro Dorcestrensi
Living or Dead*

Contents

1	In Moonfleet Village	1
2	The Floods	17
3	A Discovery	33
4	In the Vault	50
5	The Rescue	73
6	An Assault	80
7	An Auction	91
8	The Landing	103
9	A Judgement	120
10	The Escape	129
11	The Sea Cave	150
12	A Funeral	162
13	An Interview	186
14	The Well House	201
15	The Well	214
16	The Jewel	229
17	At Ymeguen	258
18	In the Bay	268
19	On the Beach	286

Says the cap'n to the crew,
We have slipped the Revenue,
    I can see the cliffs of Dover on the lee:
Tip the signal to the *Swan*,
And anchor broadside on,
    And out with the kegs of eau-de-vie,
            Says the cap'n:
    Out with the kegs of eau-de-vie.

Says the lander to his men,
Get your grummets on the pin,
    There's a blue light burning out at sea.
The windward anchors creep,
And the gauger's fast asleep,
    And the kegs are bobbing one, two, three,
            Says the lander:
    The kegs are bobbing one, two, three.

But the bold preventive man
Primes the powder in his pan
    And cries to the posse, Follow me.
We will take this smuggling gang,
And those that fight shall hang
    Dingle dangle from the execution tree,
            Says the gauger:
    Dingle dangle with the weary moon to see.

1

In Moonfleet Village

So sleeps the pride of former days – Moore

The village of Moonfleet lies half a mile from the sea on the right or west bank of the Fleet stream. This rivulet, which is so narrow as it passes the houses that I have known a good jumper clear it without a pole, broadens out into salt marshes below the village, and loses itself at last in a lake of brackish water. The lake is good for nothing except sea-fowl, herons, and oysters, and forms such a place as they call in the Indies a lagoon; being shut off from the open Channel by a monstrous great beach or dike of pebbles, of which I shall speak more hereafter. When I was a child I thought that this place was called Moonfleet, because on a still night, whether in summer, or in winter frosts, the moon shone very brightly on the lagoon; but learned afterwards that 'twas but short for 'Mohune-fleet', from the Mohunes, a great family who were once lords of all these parts.

My name is John Trenchard, and I was fifteen years of age when this story begins. My father and mother had both been dead for years, and I boarded with my aunt, Miss Arnold, who was kind to me in her own fashion, but too strict and precise ever to make me love her.

I shall first speak of one evening in the fall of the year 1757. It must have been late in October, though I have forgotten the exact date, and I sat in the little front parlour reading after tea. My aunt had few books; a Bible, a Common Prayer, and some volumes of sermons are all that I can recollect now; but the Reverend Mr Glennie, who taught us village children, had lent me a storybook, full of interest and adventure, called the *Arabian Nights Entertainment*. At last the light began to fail, and I was nothing loth to leave off reading for several reasons; as, first, the parlour was a chilly room with horsehair chairs and sofa, and only a coloured-paper screen in the grate, for my aunt did not allow a fire till the first of November; second, there was a rank smell of molten tallow in the house, for my aunt was dipping winter candles on frames in the back kitchen; third, I had reached a part in the *Arabian Nights* which tightened my breath and made me wish to leave off reading for very anxiousness of expectation. It was that point in the story of the 'Wonderful Lamp', where the false uncle lets fall a stone that seals the mouth of the underground chamber; and immures the boy, Aladdin, in the darkness, because he would not give up the lamp till he stood safe on the surface again. This scene reminded me of one of those dreadful nightmares, where we dream we are shut in a little room, the walls of which are closing in upon us, and so impressed me that the memory of it served as a warning in an adventure that befell me later on.

So I gave up reading and stepped out into the street. It was a poor street at best, though once, no doubt, it had been finer. Now, there were not two hundred souls in Moonfleet, and yet the houses that held them straggled sadly over half a mile, lying at intervals along either side of the road. Nothing was ever made new in the village; if a house wanted repair badly, it was pulled down, and so there were toothless gaps in the street, and overrun gardens with broken-down walls, and many of the houses that yet stood looked as though they could stand but little longer.

The sun had set; indeed, it was already so dusk that the lower or sea-end of the street was lost from sight. There was a little fog or smoke-wreath in the air, with an odour of burning weeds, and that first frosty feeling of the autumn that makes us think of glowing fires and the comfort of long winter evenings to come. All was very still, but I could hear the tapping of a hammer farther down the street, and walked to see what was doing, for we had no trades in Moonfleet save that of fishing. It was Ratsey the sexton at work in a shed which opened on the street, lettering a tombstone with a mallet and graver. He had been mason before he became fisherman, and was handy with his tools; so that if anyone wanted a headstone set up in the churchyard, he went to Ratsey to get it done.

I lent over the half-door and watched him a minute, chipping away with the graver in a bad light from a lantern; then he looked up, and seeing me, said:

'Here, John, if you have nothing to do, come in and hold the lantern for me, 'tis but a half-hour's job to get all finished.'

Ratsey was always kind to me, and had lent me a chisel many a time to make boats, so I stepped in and held the lantern, watching him chink out the bits of Portland stone with a graver, and blinking the while when they came too near my eyes. The inscription stood complete, but he was putting the finishing touches to a little sea-piece carved at the top of the stone, which showed a schooner boarding a cutter. I thought it fine work at the time, but know now that it was rough enough; indeed, you may see it for yourself in Moonfleet churchyard to this day, and read the inscription too, though it is yellow with lichen, and not so plain as it was that night. This is how it runs:

SACRED TO THE MEMORY

OF

DAVID BLOCK

Aged 15, who was killed by a shot fired from the
Elector Schooner, 21 June 1757.

Of life bereft (by fell design),
I mingle with my fellow clay.

On God's protection I recline
To save me in the Judgement Day.

There too must you, cruel man, appear,
Repent ere it be all too late;
Or else a dreadful sentence fear,
For God will sure revenge my fate.

The Reverend Mr Glennie wrote the verses, and I knew them by heart, for he had given me a copy; indeed, the whole village had rung with the tale of David's death, and it was yet in every mouth. He was only child to Elzevir Block, who kept the Why Not? inn at the bottom of the village, and was with the contrabandiers, when their ketch was boarded that June night by the government schooner. People said that it was Magistrate Maskew of Moonfleet Manor who had put the revenue men on the track, and anyway he was on board the *Elector* as she overhauled the ketch. There was some show of fighting when the vessels first came alongside of one another, and Maskew drew a pistol and fired it off in young David's face, with only the two gunwales between them. In the afternoon of Midsummer's Day the *Elector* brought the ketch into Moonfleet, and there was a posse of constables to march the smugglers off to Dorchester jail. The prisoners trudged up through the village ironed two and two together, while people stood at their doors or followed them, the men greeting them with a kindly word, for we knew most of them as Ringstave and Monkbury men, and the women sorrowing for their wives. But they left David's body in the ketch, so the boy paid dear for his night's frolic.

'Ay, 'twas a cruel, cruel thing to fire on so young a lad,' Ratsey said, as he stepped back a pace to study the effect of a flag that he was chiselling on the Revenue schooner, 'and trouble is likely to come to the other poor fellows taken, for Lawyer Empson says three of them will surely hang at next Assize. I recollect,' he went on, 'thirty years ago, when there was a bit of a scuffle between the *Royal Sophy* and the *Marnhull*, they hanged four of the contrabandiers, and my old father caught his death of cold what with going to see the poor chaps turned off at Dorchester, and standing up to his knees in the river Frome to get a sight of them, for all the countryside was there, and such a press there was no place on land. There, that's enough,' he said, turning again to the gravestone. 'On Monday I'll line the ports in black, and get a brush of red to pick out the flag; and now, my son, you've helped with the lantern, so come down to the Why Not? and there I'll have a word with Elzevir, who sadly needs the talk of kindly friends to cheer him, and we'll find you a glass of Hollands to keep out autumn chills.'

I was but a lad, and thought it a vast honour to be asked to the Why Not? – for did not such an invitation raise me at once to the dignity of manhood? Ah, sweet boyhood,

how eager are we as boys to be quit of thee, with what regret do we look back on thee before our man's race is halfway run! Yet was not my pleasure without alloy, for I feared even to think of what Aunt Jane would say if she knew that I had been at the Why Not? – and beside that, I stood in awe of grim old Elzevir Block, grimmer and sadder a thousand times since David's death.

The Why Not? was not the real name of the inn; it was properly the Mohune Arms. The Mohunes had once owned, as I have said, the whole of the village; but their fortunes fell, and with them fell the fortunes of Moonfleet. The ruins of their mansion showed grey on the hillside above the village; their almshouses stood halfway down the street, with the quadrangle deserted and overgrown; the Mohune image and superscription was on everything from the church to the inn, and everything that bore it was stamped also with the superscription of decay. And here it is necessary that I say a few words as to this family badge; for, as you will see, I was to bear it all my life, and shall carry its impress with me to the grave. The Mohune shield was plain white or silver, and bore nothing upon it except a great black 'Y'. I call it a 'Y', though the Reverend Mr Glennie once explained to me that it was not a 'Y' at all, but what heralds call a cross pall. Cross pall or no cross pall, it looked for all the world like a black 'Y', with a broad arm ending in each of the top corners of the shield, and the tail coming down into the bottom. You might see that cognizance carved on the manor, and on the stonework and woodwork of the church, and on a score of houses in the village, and it hung on the signboard over the door of the inn. Everyone knew the Mohune 'Y' for miles around, and a former landlord having called the inn the Why Not? in jest, the name had stuck to it ever since.

More than once on winter evenings, when men were drinking in the Why Not?, I had stood outside, and listened to them singing 'Ducky-stones', or 'Kegs bobbing One, Two, Three', or some of the other tunes that sailors sing in the west. Such songs had neither beginning nor ending, and very little sense to catch hold of in the middle. One man would crone the air, and the others would crone a solemn chorus, but there was little hard drinking, for Elzevir Block never got drunk himself, and did not like his guests to get drunk either. On singing nights the room grew hot, and the steam stood so thick on the glass inside that one could not see in; but at other times, when there was no company, I have peeped through the red curtains and watched Elzevir Block and Ratsey playing backgammon at the trestle table by the fire. It was on the trestle table that Block had afterwards laid out his son's dead body, and some said they had looked through the window at night and seen the father trying to wash the blood-matting out of the boy's yellow hair, and heard him groaning and talking to the lifeless clay as if it could understand. Anyhow, there had been little drinking in the inn since that time, for Block grew more and more silent and morose. He had never courted customers, and now he scowled on any that came, so that men looked on the Why Not? as a blighted spot, and went to drink at the Three Choughs at Ringstave.

My heart was in my mouth when Ratsey lifted the latch and led me into the inn parlour. It was a low sanded room with no light except a fire of seawood on the hearth, burning clear and lambent with blue salt flames. There were tables at each end of the room, and wooden-seated chairs round the walls, and at the trestle table by the chimney sat Elzevir Block smoking a long pipe and looking at the fire. He was a man of fifty, with a shock of grizzled hair, a broad but not unkindly face of regular features, bushy eyebrows, and the finest forehead that I ever saw. His frame was thickset, and still immensely strong; indeed, the countryside was full of tales of his strange prowess or endurance. Blocks had been landlords at the Why Not? father and son for years, but Elzevir's mother came from the Low Countries, and that was how he got his outland name and could speak Dutch. Few men knew much of him, and folks often wondered how it was he kept the Why Not? on so little custom as went that way. Yet he never seemed to lack for money; and if people loved to tell stories of his strength, they would speak also of widows helped, and sick comforted with unknown gifts, and hint that some of them came from Elzevir Block for all he was so grim and silent.

He turned round and got up as we came in, and my fears led me to think that his face darkened when he saw me.

'What does this boy want?' he said to Ratsey sharply.

'He wants the same as I want, and that's a glass of Ararat milk to keep out autumn chills,' the sexton answered, drawing another chair up to the trestle table.

'Cows' milk is best for children such as he,' was Elzevir's answer, as he took two shining brass candlesticks from the mantelboard, set them on the table, and lit the candles with a burning chip from the hearth.

'John is no child; he is the same age as David, and comes from helping me to finish David's headstone. 'Tis finished now, barring the paint upon the ships, and, please God, by Monday night we will have it set fair and square in the churchyard, and then the poor lad may rest in peace, knowing he has above him Master Ratsey's best handiwork, and the parson's verses to set forth how shamefully he came to his end.'

I thought that Elzevir softened a little as Ratsey spoke of his son, and he said, 'Ay, David rests in peace. 'Tis they that brought him to his end that shall not rest in peace when their time comes. And it may come sooner than they think,' he added, speaking more to himself than to us. I knew that he meant Mr Maskew, and recollected that some had warned the magistrate that he had better keep out of Elzevir's way, for there was no knowing what a desperate man might do. And yet the two had met since in the village street, and nothing worse come of it than a scowling look from Block.

'Tush, man!' broke in the sexton, 'it was the foulest deed ever man did; but let not thy mind brood on it, nor think how thou mayest get thyself avenged. Leave that to Providence; for He whose wisdom lets such things be done, will surely see they meet their due reward. "Vengeance is Mine; I will repay, saith the Lord."' And he took his hat off and hung it on a peg.

Block did not answer, but set three glasses on the table, and then took out from a cupboard a little round long-necked bottle, from which he poured out a glass for Ratsey and himself. Then he half filled the third, and pushed it along the table to me, saying, 'There, take it, lad, if thou wilt; 'twill do thee no good, but may do thee no harm.'

Ratsey raised his glass almost before it was filled. He sniffed the liquor and smacked his lips. 'O rare milk of Ararat!' he said, 'it is sweet and strong, and sets the heart at ease. And now get the backgammon board, John, and set it for us on the table.' So they fell to the game, and I took a sly sip at the liquor, but nearly choked myself, not being used to strong waters, and finding it heady and burning in the throat. Neither man spoke, and there was no sound except the constant rattle of the dice, and the rubbing of the pieces being moved across the board. Now and then one of the players stopped to light his pipe, and at the end of a game they scored their totals on the table with a bit of chalk. So I watched them for an hour, knowing the game myself, and being interested at seeing Elzevir's backgammon board, which I had heard talked of before.

It had formed part of the furniture of the Why Not? for generations of landlords, and served perhaps to pass time for cavaliers of the Civil Wars. All was of oak, black and polished, board, dice boxes, and men, but round the edge ran a Latin inscription inlaid in light wood, which I read on that first evening, but did not understand till Mr Glennie translated it to me. I had cause to remember it afterwards, so I shall set it down here in Latin for those who know that tongue, *Ita in vita ut in lusu alae pessima jactura arte corrigenda est*, and in English as Mr Glennie translated it, *As in life, so in a game of hazard, skill will make something of the worst of throws.*

At last Elzevir looked up and spoke to me, not unkindly, 'Lad, it is time for you to go home; men say that Blackbeard walks on the first nights of winter, and some have met him face to face betwixt this house and yours.' I saw he wanted to be rid of me, so bade them both goodnight, and was off home, running all the way thither, though not from any fear of Blackbeard, for Ratsey had often told me that there was no chance of meeting him unless one passed the churchyard by night.

Blackbeard was one of the Mohunes who had died a century back, and was buried in the vault under the church, with others of his family, but could not rest there, whether, as some said, because he was always looking for a lost treasure, or as others, because of his exceeding wickedness in life. If this last were the true reason, he must have been bad indeed, for Mohunes have died before and since his day wicked enough to bear anyone company in their vault or elsewhere. Men would have it that on dark winter nights Blackbeard might be seen with an old-fashioned lantern digging for treasure in the graveyard; and those who professed to know said he was the tallest of men, with full black beard, coppery face, and such evil eyes, that any who once met their gaze must die within a year. However that might be, there were few in Moonfleet who would not rather walk ten miles round than go near the churchyard after dark; and once when Cracky Jones, a poor doited body, was found there one summer morning, lying dead on the grass, it was thought that he had met Blackbeard in the night.

Mr Glennie, who knew more about such things than anyone else, told me that Blackbeard was none other than a certain Colonel John Mohune, deceased about one hundred years ago. He would have it that Colonel Mohune, in the dreadful wars against King Charles the First, had deserted the allegiance of his house and supported the cause of the rebels. So being made governor of Carisbrooke Castle for the Parliament, he became there the king's jailer, but was false to his trust. For the king, carrying constantly hidden about his person a great diamond which had once been given him by his brother-king of

France, Mohune got wind of this jewel, and promised that if it were given him he would wink at His Majesty's escape. Then this wicked man, having taken the bribe, plays traitor again, comes with a file of soldiers at the hour appointed for the king's flight, finds His Majesty escaping through a window, has him away to a stricter ward, and reports to the Parliament that the king's escape is only prevented by Colonel Mohune's watchfulness. But how true, as Mr Glennie said, that we should not be envious against the ungodly, against the man that walketh after evil counsels. Suspicion fell on Colonel Mohune; he was removed from his governorship, and came back to his home at Moonfleet. There he lived in seclusion, despised by both parties in the State, until he died, about the time of the happy Restoration of King Charles the Second. But even after his death he could not get rest; for men said that he had hid somewhere that treasure given him to permit the king's escape, and that not daring to reclaim it, had let the secret die with him, and so must needs come out of his grave to try to get at it again. Mr Glennie would never say whether he believed the tale or not, pointing out that apparitions both of good and evil spirits are related in Holy Scripture, but that the churchyard was an unlikely spot for Colonel Mohune to seek his treasure in; for had it been buried there, he would have had a hundred chances to have it up in his lifetime. However this may be, though I was brave as a lion by day, and used indeed to frequent the churchyard, because there was the widest view of the sea to be obtained from it, yet no reward would have taken me thither at night. Nor was I myself without some witness to the tale, for having to walk to Ringstave for Dr Hawkins on the night my aunt broke her leg, I took the path along the down which overlooks the churchyard at a mile off; and thence most certainly saw a light moving to and fro about the church, where no honest man could be at two o'clock in the morning.

2

The Floods

> Then banks came down with ruin and rout,
> Then beaten spray flew round about,
> Then all the mighty floods were out,
> And all the world was in the sea – *Jean Ingelow*

On the third of November, a few days after this visit to the Why Not?, the wind, which had been blowing from the south-west, began about four in the afternoon to rise in sudden strong gusts. The rooks had been pitch-falling all the morning, so we knew that bad weather was due; and when we came out from the schooling that Mr Glennie gave us in the hall of the old almshouses, there were wisps of thatch, and even stray tiles, flying from the roofs, and the children sang:

> Blow wind, rise storm,
> Ship ashore before morn.

It is heathenish rhyme that has come down out of other and worse times; for though I do not say but that a wreck on Moonfleet beach was looked upon sometimes as little short of a godsend, yet I hope none of us were so wicked as to *wish* a vessel to be wrecked that we might share in the plunder. Indeed, I have known the men of Moonfleet risk their own lives a hundred times to save those of shipwrecked mariners, as when the *Darius*, East Indiaman, came ashore; nay, even poor nameless corpses washed up were sure of Christian burial, or perhaps of one of Master Ratsey's headstones to set forth sex and date, as may be seen in the churchyard to this day.

Our village lies near the centre of Moonfleet Bay, a great bight twenty miles across, and a deathtrap to up-channel sailors in a south-westerly gale. For with that wind blowing strong from south, if you cannot double the Snout, you must most surely come ashore; and many a good ship failing to round that point has beat up and down the bay all day, but come to beach in the evening. And once on the beach, the sea has little mercy, for the water is deep right in, and the waves curl over full on the pebbles with a weight no timbers can withstand. Then if poor fellows try to save themselves, there is a deadly undertow or rush back of the water, which sucks them off their legs, and carries them again under the thundering waves. It is that back-suck of the pebbles that you may hear for miles inland, even at Dorchester, on still nights long after the winds that caused it have sunk, and which makes people turn in their beds, and thank God they are not fighting with the sea on Moonfleet beach.

But on this third of November there was no wreck, only such a wind as I have never known before, and only once since. All night long the tempest grew fiercer, and I think no one in Moonfleet went to bed; for there was such a breaking of tiles and glass, such a banging of doors and rattling of shutters, that no sleep was possible, and we were afraid besides lest the chimneys should fall and crush us. The wind blew fiercest about five in the morning, and then some ran up the street calling out a new danger – that the sea was breaking over the beach, and that all the place was like to be flooded. Some of the women were for flitting forthwith and climbing the down; but Master Ratsey, who was going round with others to comfort people, soon showed us that the upper part of the village stood so high, that if the water was to get thither, there was no knowing if it would not cover Ridgedown itself. But what with its being a spring tide, and the sea breaking clean over the great outer beach of pebbles – a thing that had not happened for fifty years – there was so much water piled up in the lagoon, that it passed its bounds and flooded all the sea meadows, and even the lower end of the street. So when day broke, there was the churchyard flooded, though 'twas on rising ground, and the church itself standing up like a steep little island, and the water over the door sill of the Why Not?, though Elzevir Block would not budge, saying he did not care if the sea swept him away. It was but a nine-hours' wonder, for the wind fell very suddenly; the water began to go back, the sun shone bright, and before noon people came out to the doors to see the floods and talk over the storm. Most said that never had been so fierce a wind, but some of the oldest spoke of one in the second year of Queen Anne, and would have it as bad or worse. But whether worse or not, this storm was a weighty matter enough for me, and turned the course of my life, as you shall hear.

I have said that the waters came up so high that the church stood out like an island; but they went back quickly, and Mr Glennie was able to hold service on the next Sunday morning. Few enough folks came to Moonfleet church at any time; but fewer still came that morning, for the meadows between the village and the churchyard were wet and miry from the water. There were streamers of seaweed tangled about the very tombstones, and against the outside of the churchyard wall was piled up a great bank of it, from which came a salt rancid smell like a guillemot's egg that is always in the air after a south-westerly gale has strewn the shore with wrack.

This church is as large as any other I have seen, and divided into two parts with a stone screen across the middle. Perhaps Moonfleet was once a large place, and then likely enough there were people to fill such a church, but never since I knew it did anyone worship in that part called the nave. This western portion was quite empty beyond a few old tombs and a royal arms of Queen Anne; the pavement too was damp and mossy; and there were green patches down the white walls where the rains had got in. So the handful of people that came to church were glad enough to get the other side of the screen in the chancel, where at least the pew floors were boarded over, and the panelling of oak-work kept off the draughts.

Now this Sunday morning there were only three or four, I think, beside Mr Glennie and Ratsey and the half-dozen of us boys, who crossed the swampy meadows strewn with drowned shrew-mice and moles. Even my aunt was not at church, being prevented by a migraine, but a surprise waited those who did go, for there in a pew by himself sat Elzevir Block. The people stared at him as they came in, for no one had ever known him go to church before; some saying in the village that he was a Catholic, and others an infidel. However that may be, there he was this day, wishing perhaps to show a favour to the parson who had written the verses for David's headstone. He took no notice of anyone, nor exchanged greetings with those that came in, as was the fashion in Moonfleet church, but kept his eyes fixed on a prayer book which he held in his hand, though he could not be following the minister, for he never turned the leaf.

The church was so damp from the floods, that Master Ratsey had put a fire in the brazier which stood at the back, but was not commonly lighted till the winter had fairly begun. We boys sat as close to the brazier as we could, for the wet cold struck up from the flags, and besides that, we were so far from the clergyman, and so well screened by the oak backs, that we could bake an apple or roast a chestnut without much fear of being caught. But that morning there was something else to take off our thoughts; for before the service was well begun, we became aware of a strange noise under the church. The first time it came was just as Mr Glennie was finishing 'Dearly Beloved', and we heard it again before the second lesson. It was not a loud noise, but rather like that which a boat makes jostling against another at sea, only there was something deeper and more hollow about it. We boys looked at each other, for we knew what was under the church, and that the sound could only come from the Mohune vault. No one at Moonfleet had ever seen the inside of that vault; but Ratsey was told by his father, who was clerk before him, that it underlay half the chancel, and that there were more than a score of Mohunes lying there. It had not been opened for over forty years, since Gerald Mohune, who burst a blood vessel drinking at Weymouth races, was buried there; but there was a tale that one Sunday afternoon, many years back, there had come from the vault so horrible and unearthly a cry, that parson and people got up and fled from the church, and would not worship there for weeks afterwards.

We thought of these stories, and huddled up closer to the brazier, being frightened at the noise, and uncertain whether we should not turn tail and run from the church. For it was certain that something was moving in the Mohune vault, to which there was no entrance except by a ringed stone in the chancel floor, that had not been lifted for forty years.

However, we thought better of it, and did not budge, though I could see when standing up and looking over the tops of the seats that others beside ourselves were ill at ease; for Granny Tucker gave such starts when she heard the sounds, that twice her spectacles fell off her nose into her lap, and Master Ratsey seemed to be trying to mask the one noise by making another himself, whether by shuffling with his feet or by thumping down his prayer book. But the thing that most surprised me was that even Elzevir Block, who cared, men said, for neither God nor Devil, looked unquiet, and gave a quick glance at Ratsey every time the sound came. So we sat till Mr Glennie was well on with the sermon. His discourse interested me though I was only a boy, for he likened life to the letter 'Y', saying that 'in each man's life must come a point where two roads part like the arms of a "Y", and that everyone must choose for himself whether he will follow the broad and sloping path on the left or the steep and narrow path on the right. For,' said he, 'if you will look in your books, you will see that the letter "Y" is not like the Mohune's, with both arms equal, but has the arm on the left broader and more sloping than the arm on the right; hence ancient philosophers hold that this arm on the left represents the easy downward road to destruction, and the arm on the right the narrow upward path of life.' When we heard that we all fell to searching our prayer books for a capital 'Y'; and Granny Tucker, who knew not A from B, made much ado in fumbling with her book, for she would have people think that she could read. Then just at that moment came a noise from below louder than those before, hollow and grating like the cry of an old man in pain. With that up jumps Granny Tucker, calling out loud in church to Mr Glennie –

'O master, however can'ee bide there preaching when the Moons be rising from their graves?' and out from the church.

That was too much for the others, and all fled, Mrs Vining crying, 'Lordsakes, we shall all be throttled like Cracky Jones.'

So in a minute there were none left in the church, save and except Mr Glennie, with me, Ratsey, and Elzevir Block. I did not run: first, not wishing to show myself coward before the men; second, because I thought if Blackbeard came he would fall on the men rather than on a boy; and third, that if it came to blows, Block was strong enough to give account even of a Mohune. Mr Glennie went on with his sermon, making as though he neither heard any noise nor saw the people leave the church; and when he had finished, Elzevir walked out, but I stopped to see what the minister would say to Ratsey about the noise in the vault. The sexton helped Mr Glennie off with his gown, and then seeing me standing by and listening, said –

'The Lord has sent evil angels among us; 'tis a terrible thing, Master Glennie, to hear the dead men moving under our feet.'

'Tut, tut,' answered the minister, 'it is only their own fears that make such noises terrible to the vulgar. As for Blackbeard, I am not here to say whether guilty spirits sometimes cannot rest and are seen wandering by men; but for these noises, they are certainly Nature's work as is the noise of waves upon the beach. The floods have filled the vault with water, and so the coffins getting afloat, move in some eddies that we know not of, and jostle one another. Then being hollow, they give forth those sounds you hear, and these are your evil angels. 'Tis very true the dead do move beneath our feet, but 'tis because they cannot help themselves, being carried hither and thither by the water. Fie, Ratsey man, you should know better than to fright a boy with silly talk of spirits when the truth is bad enough.'

The parson's words had the ring of truth in them to me, and I never doubted that he was right. So this mystery was explained, and yet it was a dreadful thing, and made me shiver, to think of the Mohunes all adrift in their coffins, and jostling one another in the dark. I pictured them to myself, the many generations, old men and children, man and maid, all bones now, each afloat in his little box of rotting wood;

and Blackbeard himself in a great coffin bigger than all the rest, coming crashing into the weaker ones, as a ship in a heavy sea comes crashing down sometimes in the trough, on a small boat that is trying to board her. And then there was the outer darkness of the vault itself to think of, and the close air, and the black putrid water nearly up to the roof on which such sorry ships were sailing.

Ratsey looked a little crestfallen at what Mr Glennie said, but put a good face on it, and answered –

'Well, master, I am but a plain man, and know nothing about floods and these eddies and hidden workings of Nature of which you speak; but, saving your presence, I hold it a fond thing to make light of such warnings as are given us. 'Tis always said, "When the Moons move, then Moonfleet mourns"; and I have heard my father tell that the last time they stirred was in Queen Anne's second year, when the great storm blew men's homes about their heads. And as for frighting children, 'tis well that heady boys should learn to stand in awe, and not pry into what does not concern them – or they may come to harm.' He added the last words with what I felt sure was a nod of warning to myself, though I did not then understand what he meant. So he walked off in a huff with Elzevir, who was waiting for him outside, and I went with Mr Glennie and carried his gown for him back to his lodging in the village.

Mr Glennie was always very friendly, making much of me, and talking to me as though I were his equal; which was due, I think, to there being no one of his own knowledge in the neighbourhood, and so he had as lief talk to an ignorant boy as to an ignorant man. After we had passed the churchyard turnstile and were crossing the sludgy meadows, I asked him again what he knew of Blackbeard and his lost treasure.

'My son,' he answered, 'all that I have been able to gather is, that this Colonel John Mohune (foolishly called Blackbeard) was the first to impair the family fortunes by his excesses, and even let the almshouses fall to ruin, and turned the poor away. Unless report strangely belies him, he was an evil man, and besides numberless lesser crimes, had on his hands the blood of a faithful servant, whom he made away with because chance had brought to the man's ears some guilty secret of the master. Then, at the end of his life, being filled with fear and remorse (as must always happen with evil livers at the last), he sent for Rector Kindersley of Dorchester to confess him, though a Protestant, and wished to make amends by leaving that treasure so ill-gotten from King Charles (which was all that he had to leave) for the repair and support of the almshouses. He made a last will, which I have seen, to this effect, but without describing the treasure further than to call it a diamond, nor saying where it was to be found. Doubtless he meant to get it himself, sell it, and afterwards apply the profit to his good purpose, but before he could do so death called him suddenly to his account. So men say that he cannot rest in his grave, not having made even so tardy a reparation, and never will rest unless the treasure is found and spent upon the poor.'

I thought much over what Mr Glennie had said and fell to wondering where Blackbeard could have hid his diamond, and whether I might not find it some day and make myself a rich man. Now, as I considered that noise we had heard under the church, and Parson Glennie's explanation of it, I was more and more perplexed; for the noise had, as I have said, something deep and hollow-booming in it, and how was that to be made by decayed coffins? I had more than once seen Ratsey, in digging a grave, turn up pieces of coffins, and sometimes a tarnished nameplate would show that they had not been so very long underground, and yet the wood was quite decayed and rotten. And granting that such were in the earth, and so might more easily perish, yet when the top was taken off old Guy's brick grave to put his widow beside him, Master Ratsey gave me a peep in, and old Guy's coffin had cracks and warps in it, and looked as if a sound blow would send it to pieces. Yet here were the Mohune coffins that had been put away for generations, and must be rotten as tinder, tapping against each other with a sound like a drum, as if they were still sound and airtight. Still, Mr Glennie must be right; for if it was not the coffins, what should it be that made the noise?

So on the next day after we heard the sounds in church, being the Monday, as soon as morning school was over, off I ran down street and across meadows to the churchyard, meaning to listen outside the church if the Mohunes were still moving. I say outside the church, for I knew Ratsey would not lend me the key to go in after what he had said about boys prying into things that did not concern them; and besides that, I do not know that I should care to have ventured inside alone, even if I had the key.

When I reached the church, not a little out of breath, I listened first on the side nearest the village, that is the north side; putting my ear against the wall, and afterwards lying down on the ground, though the grass was long and wet, so that I might the better catch any sound that came. But I could hear nothing, and so concluded that the Mohunes had come to rest again, yet thought I would walk round the church and listen too on the south or sea side, for that their worships might have drifted over to that side, and be there rubbing shoulders with one another. So I went round, and was glad to get out of the cold shade into the sun on the south. But here was a surprise; for when I came round a great buttress which juts out from the wall, what should I see but two men, and these two were Ratsey and Elzevir Block. I came upon them unawares, and, lo and behold, there was Master Ratsey lying also on the ground with his ear to the wall, while

Elzevir sat back against the inside of the buttress with a spyglass in his hand, smoking and looking out to sea.

Now, I had as much right to be in the churchyard as Ratsey or Elzevir, and yet I felt a sudden shame as if I had been caught in some bad act, and knew the blood was running to my cheeks. At first I had it in my mind to turn tail and make off, but concluded to stand my ground since they had seen me, and so bade them 'Good morning'. Master Ratsey jumped to his feet as nimbly as a cat; and if he had not been a man, I should have thought he was blushing too, for his face was very red, though that came perhaps from lying on the ground. I could see he was a little put about, and out of countenance, though he tried to say 'Good morning, John', in an easy tone, as if it was a common thing for him to be lying in the churchyard, with his ear to the wall, on a winter's morning.

'Good morning, John,' he said; 'and what might you be doing in the churchyard this fine day?'

I answered that I was come to listen if the Mohunes were still moving.

'Well, that I can't tell you,' returned Ratsey, 'not wishing to waste thought on such idle matters, and having to examine this wall whether the floods have not so damaged it as to need underpinning; so if you have time to gad about of a morning, get you back to my workshop and fetch me a plasterer's hammer which I have left behind, so that I can try this mortar.'

I knew that he was making excuses about under-pinning, for the wall was sound as a rock, but was glad enough to take him at his word and beat a retreat from where I was not wanted. Indeed, I soon saw how he was mocking me, for the men did not even wait for me to come back with the hammer, but I met them returning in the first meadow. Master Ratsey made another excuse that he did not need the hammer now, as he had found out that all that was wanted was a little pointing with new mortar. 'But if you have such time to waste, John,' he added, 'you can come tomorrow and help me to get new thwarts in the *Petrel*, which she badly wants.'

So we three came back to the village together; but looking up at Elzevir once while Master Ratsey was making these pretences, I saw his eyes twinkle under their heavy brows, as if he was amused at the other's embarrassment.

The next Sunday, when we went to church, all was quiet as usual, there was no Elzevir, and no more noises, and I never heard the Mohunes move again.

3

A Discovery

Some bold adventurers disdain
The limits of their little reign,
And unknown regions dare descry;
Still, as they run, they look behind,
They hear a voice in every wind
And snatch a fearful joy – *Gray*

I have said that I used often in the daytime, when not at school, to go to the churchyard, because being on a little rise, there was the best view of the sea to be had from it; and on a fine day you could watch the French privateers creeping along the cliffs under the Snout, and lying in wait for an Indiaman or up-channel trader. There were at Moonfleet few boys of my own age, and none that I cared to make my companion; so I was given to muse alone, and did so for the most part in the open air, all the more because my aunt did not like to see an idle boy, with muddy boots, about her house.

For a few weeks, indeed, after the day that I had surprised Elzevir and Ratsey, I kept away from the church, fearing to meet them there again; but a little later resumed my visits, and saw no more of them. Now, my favourite seat in the churchyard was the flat top of a raised stone tomb, which stands on the south-east of the church. I have heard Mr Glennie call it an altar tomb, and in its day it had been a fine monument, being carved round with festoons of fruit and flowers; but had suffered so much from the weather, that I never was able to read the lettering on it, or to find out who had been buried beneath. Here I chose most to sit, not only because it had a flat and convenient top, but because it was screened from the wind by a thick clump of yew trees. These yews had once, I think, completely surrounded it, but had either died or been cut down on the south side, so that anyone sitting on the grave top was snug from the weather, and yet possessed a fine prospect over the sea. On the other three sides, the yews grew close and thick, embowering the tomb like the high back of a fireside chair; and many times in autumn I have seen the stone slab crimson with the fallen waxy berries, and taken some home to my aunt, who liked to taste them with a glass of sloe gin after her Sunday dinner. Others beside me, no doubt, found this tomb a comfortable seat and lookout; for there was quite a path worn to it on the south side, though all the times I had visited it I had never seen anyone there.

So it came about that on a certain afternoon in the beginning of February, in the year 1758, I was sitting on this tomb looking out to sea. Though it was so early in the year, the air was soft and warm as a May day, and so still that I could hear the drumming of turnips that Gaffer George was flinging into a cart on the hillside, near half a mile away. Ever since the floods of which I have spoken, the weather had been open, but with high winds, and little or no rain. Thus as the land dried after the floods there began to open cracks in the heavy clay soil on which Moonfleet is built, such as are usually only seen with us in the height of summer. There were cracks by the side of the path in the sea meadows between the village and the church, and cracks in the churchyard itself, and one running right up to this very tomb.

It must have been past four o'clock in the afternoon, and I was for returning to tea at my aunt's, when underneath the stone on which I sat I heard a rumbling and crumbling, and on jumping off saw that the crack in the ground had still further widened, just where it came up to the tomb, and that the dry earth had so shrunk and settled that there was a hole in the ground a foot or more across. Now this hole reached under the big stone that formed one side of the tomb, and falling on my hands and knees and looking down it, I perceived that there was under the monument a larger cavity, into which the hole opened. I believe there never was boy yet who saw a hole in the ground, or a cave in a hill, or much more an underground passage, but longed incontinently to be into it and discover whither it led. So it was with me; and seeing that the earth had fallen enough into the hole to open a way under the stone, I slipped myself in feet foremost, dropped down on to a heap of fallen mould, and found that I could stand upright under the monument itself.

Now this was what I had expected, for I thought that there had been below this grave a vault, the roof of which had given way and let the earth fall in. But as soon as my eyes were used to the dimmer light, I saw that it was no such thing, but that the hole into which I had crept was only the mouth of a passage, which sloped gently down in the direction of the church. My heart fell to thumping with eagerness and surprise, for I thought I had made a wonderful discovery, and that this hidden way would certainly lead to great things, perhaps even to Blackbeard's hoard; for ever since Mr Glennie's tale I had constantly before my eyes a vision of the diamond and the wealth it was to bring me. The passage was two paces broad, as high as a tall man, and cut through the soil, without bricks or any other lining; and what surprised me most was that it did not seem deserted nor mouldy and cobwebbed, as one would expect such a place to be, but rather a well-used thoroughfare; for I could see the soft clay floor was trodden with the prints of many boots, and marked with a trail as if some heavy thing had been dragged over it.

So I set out down the passage, reaching out my hand before me lest I should run against anything in the dark, and sliding my feet slowly to avoid pitfalls in the floor. But before I had gone half a dozen paces, the darkness grew so black that I was frightened, and so far from going on was glad to turn sharp about, and see the glimmer of light that came in through the hole under the tomb. Then a horror of the darkness seized me, and before I well knew what I was about I found myself wriggling my body up under the tombstone on to the churchyard grass, and was once more in the low evening sunlight and the soft sweet air.

Home I ran to my aunt's, for it was past teatime, and beside that I knew I must fetch a candle if I were ever to search out the passage; and to search it I had well made up my mind, no matter how much I was scared for this moment. My aunt gave me but a sorry greeting when I came into the kitchen, for I was late and hot. She never said much when displeased, but had a way of saying nothing, which was much worse; and would only reply yes or no, and that after an interval, to anything that was asked of her. So the meal was silent enough, for she had finished before I arrived, and I ate but little myself being too much occupied with the thought of my strange discovery, and finding, beside, the tea lukewarm and the victuals not enticing.

You may guess that I said nothing of what I had seen, but made up my mind that as soon as my aunt's back was turned I would get a candle and tinderbox, and return to the churchyard. The sun was down before Aunt Jane gave thanks for what we had received, and then, turning to me, she said in a cold and measured voice –

'John, I have observed that you are often out and about of nights, sometimes as late as half past seven or eight. Now, it is not seemly for young folk to be abroad after dark, and I do not choose that my nephew should be called a gadabout. "What's bred in the bone will come out in the flesh", and 'twas with such loafing that your father began his wild ways, and afterwards led my poor sister such a life as never was, till the mercy of Providence took him away.'

Aunt Jane often spoke thus of my father, whom I never remembered, but believe him to have been an honest man and good fellow to boot, if something given to roaming and to the contraband.

'So understand,' she went on, 'that I will not have you out again this evening, no, nor any other evening, after dusk. Bed is the place for youth when night falls, but if this seem to you too early you can sit with me for an hour in the parlour, and I will read you a discourse of Doctor Sherlock that will banish vain thoughts, and leave you in a fit frame for quiet sleep.'

So she led the way into the parlour, took the book from the shelf, put it on the table within the little circle of light cast by a shaded candle, and began. It was dull enough, though I had borne such tribulations before, and the drone of my aunt's voice would have sent me to sleep, as it had done at other times, even in a straight-backed chair, had I not been so full of my discovery, and chafed at this delay. Thus all the time my aunt read of spiritualities and saving grace, I had my mind on diamonds and all kinds of mammon, for I never doubted that Blackbeard's treasure would be found at the end of that secret passage. The sermon finished at last, and my aunt closed the book with a stiff 'goodnight' for me. I was for giving her my formal kiss, but she made as if she did not see me and turned away; so we went upstairs each to our own room, and I never kissed Aunt Jane again.

There was a moon three-quarters full, already in the sky, and on moonlight nights I was allowed no candle to show me to bed. But on that night I needed none, for I never took off my clothes, having resolved to wait till my aunt was asleep, and then, ghosts or no ghosts, to make my way back to the churchyard. I did not dare to put off that visit even till the morning, lest some chance passer-by should light upon the hole, and so forestall me with Blackbeard's treasure.

Thus I lay wide awake on my bed watching the shadow of the tester post against the whitewashed wall, and noting how it had moved, by degrees, as the moon went farther round. At last, just as it touched the picture of the Good Shepherd which hung over the mantelpiece, I heard my aunt snoring in her room, and knew that I was free. Yet I waited a few minutes so that she might get well on with her first sleep, and then took off my boots, and in stockinged feet slipped past her room and down the stairs. How stair, handrail, and landing creaked that night, and how my feet and body struck noisily against things seen quite well but misjudged in the effort not to misjudge them! And yet there was the note of safety still sounding, for the snoring never ceased, and the sleeper woke not, though her waking then might have changed all my life. So I came safely to the kitchen, and there put in my pocket one of the best winter candles and the tinderbox, and as I crept out of the room heard suddenly how loud the old clock was ticking, and looking up saw the bright brass hand marking half past ten on the dial.

Out in the street I kept in the shadow of the houses as far as I might, though all was silent as the grave; indeed, I think that when the moon is bright a great hush falls always upon Nature, as though she was taken up in wondering at her own beauty. Everyone was fast asleep in Moonfleet and there was no light in any window; only when I came opposite the Why Not? I saw from the red glow behind the curtains that the bottom room was lit up, so Elzevir was not yet gone to bed. It was strange, for the Why Not? had been shut up early for many a long night past, and I crossed over cautiously to see if I could make out what was going forward. But that was not to be done, for the panes were thickly steamed over; and this surprised me more as showing that there was a good company inside. Moreover, as I stood and listened I could hear a mutter of deep voices inside, not as of roisterers, but of sober men talking low.

Eagerness would not let me wait long, and I was off across the meadows towards the church, though not without sad misgivings as soon as the last house was left well behind me. At the churchyard wall my courage had waned somewhat: it seemed a shameless thing to come to rifle Blackbeard's treasure just in the very place and hour that Blackbeard loved; and as I passed the turnstile I half expected that a tall figure, hairy and evil-eyed, would spring out from the shadow on the north side of the church. But nothing stirred, and the frosty grass sounded crisp under my feet as I made across the churchyard, stepping over the graves and keeping always out of the shadows, towards the black clump of yew trees on the far side.

When I got round the yews, there was the tomb standing out white against them, and at the foot of the tomb was the hole like a patch of black velvet spread upon the ground, it was so dark. Then, for a moment, I thought that Blackbeard might be lying in wait in the bottom of the hole, and I stood uncertain whether to go on or back. I could catch the rustle of the water on the beach – not of any waves, for the bay was smooth as glass, but just a lipper at the fringe; and wishing to put off with any excuse the descent into the passage, though I had quite resolved to make it, I settled with myself that I would count the water wash twenty times, and at the twentieth would let myself down into the hole.

Only seven wavelets had come in when I forgot to count, for there, right in the middle of the moon's path across the water, lay a lugger moored broadside to the beach. She was about half a mile out, but there was no mistake, for though her sails were lowered her masts and hull stood out black against the moonlight. Here was a fresh reason for delay, for surely one must consider what this craft could be, and what had brought her here. She was too small for a privateer, too large for a fishing smack, and could not be a Revenue boat by her low freeboard in the waist; and 'twas a strange thing for a boat to cast anchor in the midst of Moonfleet Bay even on a night so fine as this. Then while I watched I saw a blue flare in the bows, only for a moment, as if a man had lit a squib and flung it overboard, but I knew from it she was a contrabandier, and signalling either to the shore or to a mate in the offing. With that, courage came back, and I resolved to make this flare my signal for getting down into the hole, screwing my heart up with the thought that if Blackbeard was really waiting for me there, 'twould be little good to turn tail now, for he would be after me and could certainly run much faster than I. Then I took one last look round, and down into the hole forthwith, the same way as I had got down earlier in the day. So on that February night John Trenchard found himself standing in the heap of loose fallen mould at the bottom of the hole, with a mixture of courage and cowardice in his heart, but overruling all a great desire to get at Blackbeard's diamond.

Out came tinderbox and candle, and I was glad indeed when the light burned up bright enough to show that no one, at any rate, was standing by my side. But then there was the passage, and who could say what might be lurking there? Yet I did not falter, but set out on this adventurous journey, walking very slowly indeed – but that was from fear of pitfalls – and nerving myself with the thought of the great diamond which surely would be found at the end of the passage. What should I not be able to do with such wealth? I would buy a nag for Mr Glennie, a new boat for Ratsey, and a silk gown for Aunt Jane, in spite of her being so hard with me as on this night. And thus I would make myself the greatest man in Moonfleet, richer even than Mr Maskew, and build a stone house in the sea meadows with a good prospect of the sea, and marry Grace Maskew and live happily, and fish. I walked on down the passage, reaching out the candle as far as might be in front of me, and whistling to keep myself company, yet saw neither Blackbeard nor anyone else. All the way there were footprints on the floor, and the roof was black as with smoke of torches, and this made me fear lest some of those who had been there before might have made away

43

with the diamond. Now, though I have spoken of this journey down the passage as though it were a mile long, and though it verily seemed so to me that night, yet I afterwards found it was not more than twenty yards or thereabouts; and then I came upon a stone wall which had once blocked the road, but was now broken through so as to make a ragged doorway into a chamber beyond. There I stood on the rough sill of the door, holding my breath and reaching out my candle arm's length into the darkness, to see what sort of a place this was before I put foot into it. And before the light had well time to fall on things, I knew that I was underneath the church, and that this chamber was none other than the Mohune vault.

It was a large room, much larger, I think, than the schoolroom where Mr Glennie taught us, but not near so high, being only some nine feet from floor to roof. I say floor, though in reality there was none, but only a bottom of soft wet sand; and when I stepped down on to it my heart beat very fiercely, for I remembered what manner of place I was entering, and the dreadful sounds which had issued from it that Sunday morning so short a time before. I satisfied myself that there was nothing evil lurking in the dark corners, or nothing visible at least, and then began to look round and note what was to be seen. Walls and roof were stone, and at one end was a staircase closed by a great flat stone at top – that same stone which I had often seen, with a ring in it, in the floor of the church above. All round the sides were stone shelves, with divisions between them like great bookcases, but instead of books there were the coffins of the Mohunes. Yet these lay only at the sides, and in the middle of the room was something very different, for here were stacked scores of casks, kegs, and rundlets, from a storage butt that might hold thirty gallons down to a breaker that held only one. They were marked all of them in white paint on the end with figures and letters, that doubtless set forth the quality to those that understood. Here indeed was a discovery, and instead of picking up at the end of the passage a little brass or silver casket, which had only to be opened to show Blackbeard's diamond gleaming inside, I had stumbled on the Mohune's vault, and found it to be nothing but a cellar of gentlemen of the contraband, for surely good liquor would never be stored in so shy a place if it ever had paid the excise.

As I walked round this stack of casks my foot struck sharply on the edge of a butt, which must have been near empty, and straightway came from it the same hollow, booming sound (only fainter) which had so frightened us in church that Sunday morning. So it was the casks, and not the coffins, that had been knocking one against another; and I was pleased with myself, remembering how I had reasoned that coffin wood could never give that booming sound.

It was plain enough that the whole place had been under water: the floor was still muddy, and the green and sweating walls showed the flood mark within two feet of the roof; there was a wisp or two of fine seaweed that had somehow got in, and a small crab was still alive and scuttled across the corner, yet the coffins were but little disturbed. They lay on the shelves in rows, one above the other, and numbered twenty-three in all: most were in lead, and so could never float, but of those in wood some were turned slantways in their niches, and one had floated right away and been left on the floor upside down in a corner when the waters went back.

First I fell to wondering as to whose cellar this was, and how so much liquor could have been brought in with secrecy; and how it was I had never seen anything of the contraband men, though it was clear that they had made this flat tomb the entrance to their storehouse, as I had made it my seat. And then I remembered how Ratsey had tried to scare me with talk of Blackbeard; and how Elzevir, who had never been seen at church before, was there the Sunday of the noises; and how he had looked ill at ease whenever the noise came, though he was bold as a lion; and how I had tripped upon him and Ratsey in the churchyard; and how Master Ratsey lay with his ear to the wall: and putting all these things together and casting them up, I thought that Elzevir and Ratsey knew as much as any about this hiding place. These reflections gave me more courage, for I considered that the tales of Blackbeard walking or digging among the graves had been set afloat to keep those that were not wanted from the place, and guessed now that when I saw the light moving in the churchyard that night I went to fetch Dr Hawkins, it was no corpse-candle, but a lantern of smugglers running a cargo.

Then, having settled these important matters, I began to turn over in my mind how to get at the treasure; and herein was much cast down, for in this place was neither casket nor diamond, but only coffins and double-Hollands. So it was that, having no better plan, I set to work to see whether I could learn anything from the coffins themselves; but with little success, for the lead coffins had no names upon them, and on such of the wooden coffins as bore plates I found the writing to be Latin, and so rusted over that I could make nothing of it.

Soon I wished I had not come at all, considering that the diamond had vanished into air, and it was a sad thing to be cabined with so many dead men. It moved me, too, to see pieces of banners and funeral shields, and even shreds of wreaths that dear hearts had put there a century ago, now all ruined and rotten – some still clinging, water-sodden, to the coffins, and some trampled in the sand of the floor. I had spent some time in this bootless search, and was resolved to give up further enquiry and foot it home, when the clock in the tower struck midnight. Surely never was ghostly hour sounded in more ghostly place. Moonfleet peal was known over half the county, and the finest part of it was the clock bell. 'Twas said that in times past (when, perhaps, the chimes were rung more often than now) the voice of this bell had led safe home boats that were lost in the fog; and this night its clangour, mellow and profound, reached even to the vault. Bim-bom it went, bim-bom, twelve heavy thuds that shook the walls, twelve resonant echoes that followed, and then a purring and vibration of the air, so that the ear could not tell when it ended.

I was wrought up, perhaps, by the strangeness of the hour and place, and my hearing quicker than at other times, but before the tremor of the bell was quite passed away I knew there was some other sound in the air, and that the awful stillness of the vault was broken. At first I could not tell what this new sound was, nor whence it came, and now it seemed a little noise close by, and now a great noise in the distance. And then it grew nearer and more defined, and in a moment I knew it was the sound of voices talking. They must have been a long way off at first, and for a minute, that seemed as an age, they came no nearer. What a minute was that to me! Even now, so many years after, I can recall the anguish of it, and how I stood with ears pricked up, eyes starting, and a clammy sweat upon my face, waiting for those speakers to come. It was the anguish of the rabbit at the end of his burrow, with the ferret's eyes gleaming in the dark, and gun and lurcher waiting at the mouth of the hole. I was caught in a trap, and knew beside that contraband men had a way of sealing prying eyes and stilling babbling tongues; and I remembered poor Cracky Jones found dead in the churchyard, and how men *said* he had met Blackbeard in the night.

These were but the thoughts of a second, but the voices were nearer, and I heard a dull thud far up the passage, and knew that a man had jumped down from the churchyard into the hole. So I took a last stare round, agonizing to see if there was any way of escape; but the stone walls and roof were solid enough to crush me, and the stack of casks too closely packed to hide more than a rat. There was a man speaking now from the bottom of the hole to others in the churchyard, and then my eyes were led as by a loadstone to a great wooden coffin that lay by itself on the top shelf, a full six feet from the ground. When I saw the coffin I knew that I was respited, for, as I judged, there was space between it and the wall behind enough to contain my little carcass; and in a second I had put out the candle, scrambled up the shelves, half stunned my senses with dashing my head against the roof, and squeezed my body betwixt wall and coffin. There I lay on one side with a thin and rotten plank between the dead man and me, dazed with the blow to my head, and breathing hard; while the glow of torches as they came down the passage reddened and flickered on the roof above.

4

In the Vault

Let us hob and nob with Death – *Tennyson*

Though nothing of the vault except the roof was visible from where I lay, and so I could not see these visitors, yet I heard every word spoken, and soon made out one voice as being Master Ratsey's. This discovery gave me no surprise but much solace, for I thought that if the worst happened and I was discovered, I should find one friend with whom I could plead for life.

'It is well the earth gave way,' the sexton was saying, 'on a night when we were here to find it. I was in the graveyard myself after midday, and all was snug and tight then. 'Twould have been awkward enough to have the hole stand open through the day, for any passer-by to light on.'

There were four or five men in the vault already, and I could hear more coming down the passage, and guessed from their heavy footsteps that they were carrying burdens. There was a sound, too, of dumping kegs down on the ground, with a swish of liquor inside them, and then the noise of casks being moved.

'I thought we should have a fall there ere long,' Ratsey went on, 'what with this drought parching the ground, and the trampling at the edge when we move out the side stone to get in, but there is no mischief done beyond what can be easily made good. A gravestone or two and a few spades of earth will make all sound again. Leave that to me.'

'Be careful what you do,' rejoined another man's voice that I did not know, 'lest someone see you digging, and scent us out.'

'Make your mind easy,' Ratsey said; 'I have dug too often in this graveyard for any to wonder if they see me with a spade.'

Then the conversation broke off, and there was little more talking, only a noise of men going backwards and forwards, and of putting down of kegs and the hollow gurgle of good liquor being poured from breakers into the casks. By and by fumes of brandy began to fill the air, and climb to where I lay, overcoming the mouldy smell of decayed wood and the dampness of the green walls. It may have been that these fumes mounted to my head, and gave me courage not my own, but so it was that I lost something of the stifling fear that had gripped me, and could listen with more ease to what was going forward. There was a pause in the carrying to and fro; they were talking again now, and someone said –

'I was in Dorchester three days ago, and heard men say it will go hard with the poor chaps who had the brush with the *Elector* last summer. Judge Barentyne comes on Assize next week, and that old fox Maskew has driven down to Taunton to get at him before and coach him back; making out to him that the law's arm is weak in these parts against the contraband, and must be strengthened by some wholesome hangings.'

'They are a cruel pair,' another put in, 'and we shall have new gibbets on Ridgedown for leading lights. Once I get even with Maskew, the other may go hang, ay, and they may hang me too.'

'The devil send him to meet me one dark night on the down alone,' said someone else, 'and I will give him a pistol's mouth to look down, and spoil his face for him.'

'No, thou wilt not,' said a deep voice, and then I knew that Elzevir was there too; 'none shall lay hand on Maskew but I. So mark that, lad, that when his day of reckoning comes, 'tis *I* will reckon with him.'

Then for a few minutes I did not pay much heed to what was said, being terribly straitened for room, and cramped with pain from lying so long in one place. The thick smoke from the pitch torches too came curling across the roof and down upon me, making me sick and giddy with its evil smell and taste; and though all was very dim, I could see my hands were black with oily smuts. At last I was able to wriggle myself over without making too much noise, and felt a great relief in changing sides, but gave such a start as made the coffin creak again at hearing my own name.

'There is a boy of Trenchard's,' said a voice that I thought was Parmiter's, who lived at the bottom of the village – 'there is a boy of Trenchard's that I mistrust; he is forever wandering in the graveyard, and I have seen him a score of times sitting on this tomb and looking out to sea. This very night, when the wind fell at sundown, and we were hung up with sails flapping, three miles out, and waited for the dark to get the sweeps, I took my glass to scan the coastline, and lo, here on the tomb top sits Master Trenchard. I could not see his face, but knew him by his cut, and fear the boy sits there to play the spy and then tells Maskew.'

'You're right,' said Greening of Ringstave, for I knew his slow drawl; 'and many a time when I have sat in the wood, and watched the manor to see Maskew safe at home before we ran a cargo, I have seen this boy too go round about the place with a hangdog look, scanning the house as if his life depended on't.'

'Twas very true what Greening said; for of a summer evening I would take the path that led up Weatherbeech Hill, behind the manor; both because 'twas a walk that had a good prospect in itself, and also a sweet charm for me, namely, the hope of seeing Grace Maskew. And there I often sat upon the stile that ends the path and opens on the down, and watched the old half-ruined house below; and sometimes saw white-frocked Gracie walking on the terrace in the evening sun, and sometimes in returning passed her window near enough to wave a greeting. And once, when she had the fever, and Dr Hawkins came twice a day to see her, I had no heart for school, but sat on that stile the livelong day, looking at the gabled house where she was lying ill. And Mr Glennie never rated me for playing truant, nor told Aunt Jane, guessing, as I thought afterwards, the cause, and having once been young himself. 'Twas but boy's love, yet serious for me; and on the day she lay near death, I made so bold as to stop Dr Hawkins on his horse and ask him how she did; and he bearing with me for the eagerness that he read in my face, bent down over his saddle and smiled, and said my playmate would come back to me again.

So it was quite true that I had watched the house, but not as a spy, and would not have borne tales to old Maskew for anything that could be offered. Then Ratsey spoke up for me and said –

''Tis a false scent. The boy is well enough, and simple, and has told me many a time he seeks the churchyard because there is a fine view to be had there of the sea, and 'tis the sea he loves. A month ago, when the high tide set, and this vault was so full of water that we could not get in, I came with Elzevir to make out if the floods were going down inside, or what eddy 'twas that set the casks tapping one against another. So as I lay on the ground with my ear glued close against the wall, who should march round the church but John Trenchard, Esquire, not treading delicately like King Agag, or spying, but just come on a voyage of discovery for himself. For in the church on Sunday, when we heard the tapping in the vault below, my young gentleman was scared enough; but afterwards, being told by Parson Glennie – who should know better – that such noises were not made by ghosts, but by the Mohunes at sea in their coffins, he plucks up heart, and comes down on the Monday to see if they are still afloat. So there he caught me lying like a zany on the ground. You may guess I stood at attention soon enough, but told him I was looking at the founds to see if they wanted underpinning from the floods. And so I set his mind at ease, for 'tis a simple child, and packed him off to get my dubbing hammer. And I think the boy will not be here so often now to frighten honest Parmiter, for I have weaved him some pretty tales of Blackbeard, and he has a wholesome scare of meeting the Colonel. But after dark I pledge my life that neither he nor any other in the town would pass the churchyard wall, no, not for a thousand pounds.'

I heard him chuckling to himself, and the others laughed loudly too, when he was telling how he palmed me off; but 'he laughs loudest who laughs last', thought I, and should have chuckled too, were it not for making the coffin creak.

And then, to my surprise, Elzevir spoke: 'The lad is a brave lad; I would he were my son. He is David's age, and will make a good sailor later on.'

They were simple words, yet pleasing to me; for Elzevir spoke as if he meant them, and I had got to like him a little in spite of all his grimness; and beside that, was sorry for his grief over his son. I was so moved by what he said, that for a moment I was for jumping up and calling out to him that I lay here and liked him well, but then thought better of it, and so kept still.

The carrying was over, and I fancy they were all sitting on the ends of kegs or leaning up against the pile; but could not see, and was still much troubled with the torch smoke, though now and then I caught through it a whiff of tobacco, which showed that some were smoking.

Then Greening, who had a singing voice for all his drawl, struck up with –

'Says the cap'n to the crew,
We have slipped the Revenue,'

but Ratsey stopped him with a sharp 'No more of that; the words aren't to our taste tonight, but come as wry as if the parson called "Old Hundred" and I tuned up with "*Veni*".' I knew he meant the last verse with a hanging touch in it; but Greening was for going on with the song, until some others broke in too, and he saw that the company would have none of it.

'Not but what the labourer is worthy of his hire,' went on Master Ratsey; 'so spile that little breaker of Schiedam, and send a rummer round to keep off midnight chills.'

He loved a glass of the good liquor well, and with him 'twas always the same reasoning, namely, to keep off chills; though he chopped the words to suit the season, and now 'twas autumn, now winter, now spring, or summer chills.

They must have found glasses, though I could not remember to have seen any in the vault, for a minute later fugleman Ratsey spoke again –

'Now, lads, glasses full and bumpers for a toast. And here's to Blackbeard, to Father Blackbeard, who watches over our treasure better than he did over his own; for were it not the fear of him that keeps off idle feet and prying eyes, we should have the gaugers in, and our store ransacked twenty times.'

So he spoke, and it seemed there was a little halting at first, as of men not liking to take Blackbeard's name in Blackbeard's place, or raise the devil by mocking at him. But then some of the bolder shouted 'Blackbeard', and so the more timid chimed in, and in a minute there were a score of voices calling 'Blackbeard, Blackbeard', till the place rang again.

Then Elzevir cried out angrily, 'Silence. Are you mad, or has the liquor mastered you? Are you revenue men that you dare shout and roister? Or contrabandiers with the lugger in the offing, and your life in your hand. You make noise enough to wake folk in Moonfleet from their beds.'

'Tut, man,' retorted Ratsey testily, 'and if they waked, they would but pull the blankets tight about their ears, and say 'twas Blackbeard piping his crew of lost Mohunes to help him dig for treasure.'

Yet for all that 'twas plain that Block ruled the roost, for there was silence for a minute, and then one said, 'Ay, Master Elzevir is right; let us away, the night is far spent, and we have nothing but the sweeps to take the lugger out of sight by dawn.'

So the meeting broke up, and the torchlight grew dimmer, and died away as it had come in a red flicker on the roof, and the footsteps sounded fainter as they went up the passage, until the vault was left to the dead men and me. Yet for a very long time – it seemed hours – after all had gone I could hear a murmur of distant voices, and knew that some were talking at the end of the passage, and perhaps considering how the landslip might best be restored. So while I heard them thus conversing I dared not descend from my perch, lest someone might turn back to the vault, though I was glad enough to sit up, and ease my aching back and limbs. Yet in the awful blackness of the place even the echo of these human voices seemed a kindly and blessed thing, and a certain shrinking loneliness fell on me when they ceased at last and all was silent. Then I resolved I would be off at once, and get back to the moonlight bed that I had left hours ago, having no stomach for more treasure hunting, and being glad indeed to be still left with the treasure of life.

Thus, sitting where I was, I lit my candle once more, and then clambered across that great coffin which, for two hours or more, had been a mid-wall of partition between me and danger. But to get out of the niche was harder than to get in; for now that I had a candle to light me, I saw that the coffin, though sound enough to outer view, was wormed through and through, and little better than a rotten shell. So it was that I had some ado to get over it, not daring either to kneel upon it or to bring much weight to bear with my hand, lest it should go through. And now having got safely across, I sat for an instant on that narrow ledge of the stone shelf which projected beyond the coffin on the vault side, and made ready to jump forward on to the floor below. And how it happened I know not, but there I lost my balance, and as I slipped the candle flew out of my grasp. Then I clutched at the coffin to save myself, but my hand went clean through it, and so I came to the ground in a cloud of dust and splinters; having only got hold of a wisp of seaweed, or a handful of those draggled funeral trappings which were strewn about this place. The floor of the vault was sandy; and so, though I fell crookedly, I took but little harm beyond a shaking; and soon, pulling myself together, set to strike my flint and blow the match into a flame to search for the fallen candle. Yet all the time I kept in my fingers this handful of light stuff; and when the flame burned up again I held the thing against the light, and saw that it was no wisp of seaweed, but something black and wiry. For a moment, I could not gather what I had hold of, but then gave a start that nearly sent the candle out, and perhaps a cry, and let it drop as if it were red-hot iron, for I knew that it was a man's beard.

Now when I saw that, I felt a sort of throttling fright, as though one had caught hold of my heartstrings; and so many and such strange thoughts rose in me, that the blood went pounding round and round in my head, as it did once afterwards when I was fighting with the sea and near drowned. Surely to have in hand the beard of any dead man in any place was bad enough, but worse a thousand times in such a place as this, and to know on whose face it had grown. For, almost before I fully saw what it was, I knew it was that black beard which had given Colonel John Mohune his nickname, and this was his great coffin I had hid behind.

I had lain, therefore, all that time, cheek by jowl with Blackbeard himself, with only a thin shell of tinderwood to keep him from me, and now had thrust my hand into his coffin and plucked away his beard. So that if ever wicked men have power to show themselves after death, and still to work evil, one would guess that he would show himself now and fall upon me. Thus a sick dread got hold of me, and had I been a woman or a girl I think I should have swooned; but being only a boy, and not knowing how to swoon, did the next best thing, which was to put myself as far as might be from the beard, and make for the outlet. Yet had I scarce set foot in the passage when I stopped, remembering how once already this same evening I had played the coward, and run home scared with my own fears. So I was brought up for very shame, and beside that thought how I had come to this place to look for Blackbeard's treasure, and might have gone away without knowing even so much as where he lay, had not chance first led me to lie down by his side, and afterwards placed my hand upon his beard. And surely this could not be chance alone, but must rather be the finger of Providence guiding me to that which I desired to find. This consideration somewhat restored my courage, and after several feints to return, advances, stoppings, and panics, I was in the vault again, walking carefully round the stack of barrels, and fearing to see the glimmer of the candle fall upon that beard. There it was upon the sand, and holding the candle nearer to it with a certain caution, as though it would spring up and bite me, I saw it was a great full black beard, more than a foot long, but going grey at the tips; and had at the back, keeping it together, a thin tissue of dried skin, like the false parting which Aunt Jane wore under her cap on Sundays. This I could see as it lay before me, for I did not handle or lift it, but only peered into it, with the candle, on all sides, busying myself the while with thoughts of the man of whom it had once been part.

In returning to the vault, I had no very sure purpose in mind; only a vague surmise that this finding of Blackbeard's coffin would somehow lead to the finding of his treasure. But as I looked at the beard and pondered, I began to see that if anything was to be done, it must be by searching in the coffin itself, and the clearer this became to me, the greater was my dislike to set about such a task. So I put off the evil hour, by feigning to myself that it was necessary to make a careful scrutiny of the beard, and thus wasted at least ten minutes. But at length, seeing that the candle was burning low, and could certainly last little more than half an hour, and considering that it must now be getting near dawn, I buckled to the distasteful work of rummaging the coffin. Nor had I any need to climb up on to the top shelf again, but standing on the one beneath, found my head and arms well on a level with the search. And beside that, the task was not so difficult as I had thought; for in my fall I had broken off the head-end of the lid, and brought away the whole of that side that faced the vault. Now, any lad of my age, and perhaps some men too, might well have been frightened to set about such a matter as to search in a coffin; and if any had said, a few hours before, that I should ever have courage to do this by night in the Mohune vault, I would not have believed him. Yet here I was, and had advanced along the path of terror so gradually, and as it were foot by foot in the past night, that when I came to this final step I was not near so scared as when I first felt my way into the vault. It was not the first time either that I had looked on death; but had, indeed, always a leaning to such sights and matters, and had seen corpses washed up from the *Darius* and other wrecks, and besides that had helped Ratsey to case some poor bodies that had died in their beds.

The coffin was, as I have said, of great length, and the side being removed, I could see the whole outline of the skeleton that lay in it. I say the outline, for the form was wrapped in a woollen or flannel shroud, so that the bones themselves were not visible. The man that lay in it was little short of a giant, measuring, as I guessed, a full six and a half feet, and the flannel having sunk in over the belly, the end of the breastbone, the hips, knees, and toes were very easy to be made out. The head was swathed in linen bands that had been white, but were now stained and discoloured with damp, but of this I shall not speak more, and beneath the chin cloth the beard had once escaped. The clutch which I had made to save myself in falling had torn away this chin band and let the lower jaw drop on the breast; but little else was disturbed, and there was Colonel John Mohune resting as he had been laid out a century ago. I lifted that portion of the lid which had been left behind, and reached over to see if there was anything hid on the other side of the body; but had scarce let the light fall in the coffin when my heart gave a great bound, and all fear left me in the flush of success, for there I saw what I had come to seek.

On the breast of this silent and swathed figure lay a locket, attached to the neck by a thin chain, which passed inside the linen bandages. A whiter portion of the flannel showed how far the beard had extended, but locket and chain were quite black, though I judged that they were made of silver. The shape of this locket was not unlike a crown-piece, only three times as thick, and as soon as I set eyes upon it I never doubted but that inside would be found the diamond.

It was then that a great pity came over me for this thin shadow of man; thinking rather what a fine, tall gentleman Colonel Mohune had once been, and a good soldier no doubt besides, than that he had wasted a noble estate and played traitor to the king. And then I reflected that it was all for the bit of flashing stone, which lay as I hoped within the locket, that he had sold his honour; and wished that the jewel might bring me better fortune than had fallen to him, or at any rate, that it might not lead me into such miry paths. Yet such thoughts did not delay my purpose, and I possessed myself of the locket easily enough, finding a hasp in the chain, and so drawing it out from the linen folds. I had expected as I moved the locket to hear the jewel rattle in the inside, but there was no sound, and then I thought that the diamond might cleave to the side with damp, or perhaps be wrapped in wool. Scarcely was the locket well in my hand before I had it undone, finding a thumb-nick whereby, after a little persuasion, the back, though rusted, could be opened on a hinge. My breath came very fast, and I shook so that I had a difficulty to keep my thumbnail in the nick, yet hardly was it opened before exalted expectation gave place to deepest disappointment.

For there lay all the secret of the locket disclosed, and there was no diamond, no, nor any other jewel, and nothing at all except a little piece of folded paper. Then I felt like a man who has played away all his property and stakes his last crown – heavy-hearted, yet hoping against hope that luck may turn, and that with this piece he may win back all his money. So it was with me; for I hoped that this paper might have written on it directions for the finding of the jewel, and that I might yet rise from the table a winner. It was but a frail hope, and quickly dashed; for when I had smoothed the creases and spread out the piece of paper in the candlelight, there was nothing to be seen except a few verses from the Psalms of David. The paper was yellow, and showed a lattice of folds where it had been pressed into the locket; but the handwriting, though small, was clear and neat, and there was no mistaking a word of what was there set down. 'Twas so short, I could read it at once:

> The days of our age are threescore years and ten;
> And though men be so strong that they come
> To fourscore years, yet is their strength then
> But labour and sorrow, so soon passeth it
> Away, and we are gone.
>
> Psalm 90, 21

> And as for me, my feet are almost gone;
> My treadings are wellnigh slipped.
> 73, 6

> But let not the waterflood drown me; neither let
> The deep swallow me up.
> 69, 11

> So, going through the vale of misery, I shall
> Use it for a well, till the pools are filled
> With water.
> 84, 14

> For thou hast made the North and the South:
> Tabor and Hermon shall rejoice in thy name.
>
> 89, 6

So here was an end to great hopes, and I was after all to leave the vault no richer than I had entered it. For look at it as I might, I could not see that these verses could ever lead to any diamond; and though I might otherwise have thought of ciphers or secret writing, yet, remembering what Mr Glennie had said, that Blackbeard after his wicked life desired to make a good end, and sent for a parson to confess him, I guessed that such pious words had been hung round his neck as a charm to keep the spirits of evil away from his tomb. I was disappointed enough, but before I left picked up the beard from the floor, though it sent a shiver through me to touch it, and put it back in its place on the dead man's breast. I restored also such pieces of the coffin as I could get at, but could not make much of it; so left things as they were, trusting that those who came there next would think the wood had fallen to pieces by natural decay. But the locket I kept, and hung about my neck under my shirt; both as being a curious thing in itself, and because I thought that if the good words inside it were strong enough to keep off bad spirits from Blackbeard, they would be also strong enough to keep Blackbeard from me.

When this was done the candle had burned so low, that I could no longer hold it in my fingers, and was forced to stick it on a piece of the broken wood, and so carry it before me. But, after all, I was not to escape from Blackbeard's clutches so easily; for when I came to the end of the passage, and was prepared to climb up into the churchyard, I found that the hole was stopped, and that there was no exit.

I understood now how it was that I had heard talking so long after the company had left the vault; for it was clear that Ratsey had been as good as his word, and that the falling in of the ground had been repaired before the contraband men went home that night. At first I made light of the matter, thinking I should soon be able to dislodge this new work, and so find a way out. But when I looked more narrowly into the business, I did not feel so sure; for they had made a sound job of it, putting one very heavy burial slab at the side to pile earth against till the hole was full, and then covering it with another. These were both of slate, and I knew whence they came; for there were a dozen or more of such disused and weather-worn covers laid up against the north side of the church, and every one of them a good burden for four men. Yet I hoped by grouting at the earth below it to be able to dislodge the stone at the side; but while I was considering how best to begin, the candle flickered, the wick gave a sudden lurch to one side, and I was left in darkness.

Thus my plight was evil indeed, for I had nothing now to burn to give me light, and knew that 'twas no use setting to grout till I could see to go about it. Moreover, the darkness was of that black kind that is never found beneath the open sky, no, not even on the darkest night, but lurks in close and covered places and strains the eyes in trying to see into it. Yet I did not give way, but settled to wait for the dawn, which must, I knew, be now at hand;

for then I thought enough light would come through the chinks of the tomb above to show me how to set to work. Nor was I even much scared, as one who having been in peril of life from the contraband men for a spy, and in peril from evil ghosts for rifling Blackbeard's tomb, deemed it a light thing to be left in the dark to wait an hour till morning. So I sat down on the floor of the passage, which, if damp, was at least soft, and being tired with what I had gone through, and not used to miss a night's rest, fell straightway asleep.

How long I slept I cannot tell, for I had nothing to guide me to the time, but woke at length, and found myself still in darkness. I stood up and stretched my limbs, but did not feel as one refreshed by wholesome sleep, but sick and tired with pains in back, arms, and legs, as if beaten or bruised. I have said I was still in darkness, yet it was not the blackness of the last night; and looking up into the inside of the tomb above, I could see the faintest line of light at one corner, which showed the sun was up. For this line of light was the sunlight, filtering slowly through a crevice at the joining of the stones; but the sides of the tomb had been fitted much closer than I reckoned for, and it was plain there would never be light in the place enough to guide me to my work. All this I considered as I rested on the ground, for I had sat down again, feeling too tired to stand. But as I kept my eye on the narrow streak of light I was much startled, for I looked at the south-west corner of the tomb, and yet was looking towards the sun. This I gathered from the tone of the light; and although there was no direct outlet to the air, and only a glimmer came in, as I have said, yet I knew certainly that the sun was low in the west and falling full upon this stone.

Here was a surprise, and a sad one for me, for I perceived that I had slept away a day, and that the sun was setting for another night. And yet it mattered little, for night or daytime there was no light to help me in this horrible place; and though my eyes had grown accustomed to the gloom, I could make out nothing to show me where to work. So I took out my tinderbox, meaning to fan the match into a flame, and to get at least one moment's look at the place, and then to set to digging with my hands. But as I lay asleep the top had been pressed off the box, and the tinder got loose in my pocket; and though I picked the tinder out easily enough, and got it in the box again, yet the salt damps of the place had soddened it in the night, and spark by spark fell idle from the flint.

And then it was that I first perceived the danger in which I stood; for there was no hope of kindling a light, and I doubted now whether even in the light I could ever have done much to dislodge the great slab of slate. I began also to feel very hungry, as not having eaten for twenty-four hours; and worse than that, there was a parching thirst and dryness in my throat, and nothing with which to quench it. Yet there was no time to be lost if I was ever to get out alive, and so I groped with my hands against the side of the grave until I made out the bottom edge of the slab, and then fell to grubbing beneath it with my fingers. But the earth, which the day before had looked light and loamy to the eye, was stiff and hard enough when one came to tackle it with naked hands, and in an hour's time I had done little more than further weary myself and bruise my fingers.

Then I was forced to rest; and, sitting down on the ground, saw that the glimmering streak of light had faded, and that the awful blackness of the previous night was creeping up again. And now I had no heart to face it, being cowed with hunger, thirst, and weariness; and so flung myself upon my face, that I might not see how dark it was, and groaned for very lowness of spirit. Thus I lay for a long time, but afterwards stood up and cried aloud, and shrieked if anyone should haply hear me, calling to Mr Glennie and Ratsey, and even Elzevir, by name, to save me from this awful place. But there came no answer, except the echo of my own voice sounding hollow and far off down in the vault. So in despair I turned back to the earth wall below the slab, and scrabbled at it with my fingers, till my nails were broken and the blood ran out; having all the while a sure knowledge, like a cord twisted round my head, that no effort of mine could ever dislodge the great stone. And thus the hours passed, and I shall not say more here, for the remembrance of that time is still terrible, and besides, no words could ever set forth the anguish I then suffered, yet did slumber come sometimes to my help; for even while I was working at the earth, sheer weariness would overtake me, and I sank on to the ground and fell asleep.

And still the hours passed, and at last I knew by the glimmer of light in the tomb above that the sun had risen again, and a maddening thirst had hold of me. And then I thought of all the barrels piled up in the vault and of the liquor that they held; and stuck not because 'twas spirit, for I would scarce have paused to sate that thirst even with molten lead. So I felt my way down the passage back to the vault, and recked not of the darkness, nor of Blackbeard and his crew, if only I could lay my lips to liquor. Thus I groped about the barrels till near the top of the stack my hand struck on the spile of a keg, and drawing it, I got my mouth to the hold.

What the liquor was I do not know, but it was not so strong but that I could swallow it in great gulps and found it less burning than my burning throat. But when I turned to get back to the passage, I could not find the outlet, and fumbled round and round until my brain was dizzy, and I fell senseless to the ground.

5

The Rescue

Shades of the dead, have I not heard your voices
Rise on the night-rolling breath of the gale? – *Byron*

When I came to myself I was lying, not in the outer
blackness of the Mohune vault, not on a floor of
sand; but in a bed of sweet clean linen, and in a little
whitewashed room, through the window of which the
spring sunlight streamed. Oh, the blessed sunshine, and
how I praised God for the light! At first I thought I was in
my own bed at my aunt's house, and had dreamed of the
vault and the smugglers, and that my being prisoned in
the darkness was but the horror of a nightmare. I was for
getting up, but fell back on my pillow in the effort to rise,
with a weakness and sick languor which I had never
known before. And as I sunk down, I felt something swing
about my neck, and putting up my hand, found 'twas
Colonel John Mohune's black locket, and so knew that
part at least of this adventure was no dream.

Then the door opened, and to my wandering thought it seemed that I was back again in the vault, for in came Elzevir Block. Then I held up my hands, and cried –

'O Elzevir, save me, save me; I am not come to spy.'

But he, with a kind look on his face, put his hand on my shoulder, and pushed me gently back, saying –

'Lie still, lad, there is none here will hurt thee, and drink this.'

He held out to me a bowl of steaming broth, that filled the room with a savour sweeter, ten thousand times, to me than every rose and lily of the world; yet would not let me drink it at a gulp, but made me sip it with a spoon like any baby. Thus while I drank, he told me where I was, namely, in an attic at the Why Not?, but would not say more then, bidding me get to sleep again, and I should know all afterwards. And so it was ten days or more before youth and health had their way, and I was strong again; and all that time Elzevir Block sat by my bed, and nursed me tenderly as a woman. So piece by piece I learned the story of how they found me.

'Twas Mr Glennie who first moved to seek me; for when the second day came that I was not at school, he thought that I was ill, and went to my aunt's to ask how I did, as was his wont when any ailed. But Aunt Jane answered him stiffly that she could not say how I did.

'For,' says she, 'he is run off I know not where, but as he makes his bed, must he lie on't; and if he run away for his pleasure, may stay away for mine. I have been pestered with this lot too long, and only bore with him for poor sister Martha's sake; but 'tis after his father that the graceless lad takes, and thus rewards me.'

With that she bangs the door in the parson's face and off he goes to Ratsey, but can learn nothing there, and so concludes that I have run away to sea, and am seeking ship at Poole or Weymouth.

But that same day came Sam Tewkesbury to the Why Not? about nightfall, and begged a glass of rum, being, as he said, 'all of a shake', and telling a tale of how he passed the churchyard wall on his return from work, and in the dusk heard screams and wailing voices, and knew 'twas Blackbeard piping his lost Mohunes to hunt for treasure. So, though he saw nothing, he turned tail and never stopped running till he stood at the inn door. Then, forthwith, Elzevir leaves Sam to drink at the Why Not? alone, and himself sets off running up the street to call for Master Ratsey; and they two make straight across the sea meadows in the dark.

'For as soon as I heard Tewkesbury tell of screams and wailings in the air, and no one to be seen,' said Elzevir, 'I guessed that some poor soul had got shut in the vault, and was there crying for his life. And to this I was not guided by mother wit, but by a surer and a sadder token. Thou wilt have heard how thirteen years ago a daft body we called Cracky Jones was found one morning in the churchyard dead. He was gone missing for a week before, and twice within that week I had sat through the night upon the hill behind the church, watching to warn the lugger with a flare she could not put in for the surf upon the beach. And on those nights, the air being still though a heavy swell was running, I heard thrice or more a throttled scream come shivering across the meadows from the graveyard. Yet beyond turning my blood cold for a moment, it gave me little trouble, for evil tales have hung about the church; and though I did not set much store by the old yarns of Blackbeard piping up his crew, yet I thought strange things might well go on among the graves at night. And so I never budged, nor stirred hand or foot to save a fellow creature in his agony.

'But when the surf fell enough for the boats to get ashore, and Greening held a lantern for me to jump down into the passage, after we had got the side out of the tomb, the first thing the light fell on at the bottom was a white face turned skyward. I have not forgot that, lad, for 'twas Cracky Jones lay there, with his face thin and shrunk, yet all the doited look gone out of it. We tried to force some brandy in his mouth, but he was stark and dead; with knees drawn up towards his head, so stiff we had to lift him doubled as he was, and lay him by the churchyard wall for some of us to find next day. We never knew how he got there, but guessed that he had hung about the landers some night when they ran a cargo, and slipped in when the watchman's back was turned. Thus when Sam Tewkesbury spoke of screams and wailings, and no one to be seen, I knew what 'twas, but never guessed who might be shut in there, not knowing thou wert gone amissing. So ran to Ratsey to get his help to slip the side stone off, for by myself I cannot stir it now, though once I did when I was younger; and from him learned that thou wert lost, and knew whom we should find before we got there.'

I shuddered while Elzevir talked, for I thought how Cracky Jones had perhaps hidden behind the self-same coffin that sheltered me, and how narrowly I had escaped his fate. And that old story came back into my mind, how, years ago, there once arose so terrible a cry from the vault at service-time, that parson and people fled from the church; and I doubted not now that some other poor soul had got shut in that awful place, and was then calling for help to those whose fears would not let them listen.

'There we found thee,' Elzevir went on, 'stretched out on the sand, senseless and far gone; and there was something in thy face that made me think of David when he lay stretched out in his last sleep. And so I put thee on my shoulder and bore thee back, and here thou art in David's room, and shalt find board and bed with me as long as thou hast mind to.'

We spoke much together during the days when I was getting stronger, and I grew to like Elzevir well, finding his grimness was but on the outside, and that never was a kinder man. Indeed, I think that my being with him did him good; for he felt that there was once more someone to love him, and his heart went out to me as to his son David. Never once did he ask me to keep my counsel as to the vault and what I had seen there, knowing, perhaps, he had no need, for I would have died rather than tell the secret to any. Only, one day Master Ratsey, who often came to see me, said –

'John, there is only Elzevir and I who know that you have seen the inside of our bond-cellar; and 'tis well, for if some of the landers guessed, they might have ugly ways to stop all chance of prating. So keep our secret tight, and we'll keep yours, for "he that refraineth his lips is wise".'

I wondered how Master Ratsey could quote scripture so pat, and yet cheat the Revenue; though, in truth, 'twas thought little sin at Moonfleet to run a cargo; and, perhaps, he guessed what I was thinking, for he added –

'Not that a Christian man has aught to be ashamed of in landing a cask of good liquor, for we read that when Israel came out of Egypt, the chosen people were bid trick their oppressors out of jewels of silver and jewels of gold; and among those cruel taskmasters, some of the worst must certainly have been the tax gatherers.'

The first walk I took when I grew stronger and was able to get about was up to Aunt Jane's, notwithstanding she had never so much as been to ask after me all these days. She knew, indeed, where I was, for Ratsey had told her I lay at the Why Not?, explaining that Elzevir had found me one night on the ground famished and half dead, yet not saying where. But my aunt greeted me with hard words, which I need not repeat here; for, perhaps, she meant them not unkindly, but only to bring me back again to the right way. She did not let me cross the threshold, holding the door ajar in her hand, and saying she would have no tavern-loungers in her house, but that if I liked the Why Not? so well, I could go back there again for her. I had been for begging her pardon for playing truant; but when I heard such scurvy words, felt the devil rise in my heart, and only laughed, though bitter tears were in my eyes. So I turned my back upon the only home that I had ever known, and sauntered off down the village, feeling very lone, and am not sure I was not crying before I came again to the Why Not?

Then Elzevir saw that my face was downcast, and asked what ailed me, and so I told him how my aunt had turned me away, and that I had no home to go to. But he seemed pleased rather than sorry, and said that I must come now and live with him, for he had plenty for both; and that since chance had led him to save my life, I should be to him a son in David's place. So I went to keep house with him at the Why Not? and my aunt sent down my bag of clothes, and would have made over to Elzevir the pittance that my father left for my keep, but he said it was not needful, and he would have none of it.

6

An Assault

Surely after all,
The noblest answer unto such
Is perfect stillness when they brawl – *Tennyson*

I have more than once brought up the name of Mr
Maskew; and as I shall have other things to tell of him
later on, I may as well relate here what manner of man he
was. His stature was but medium, not exceeding five feet
four inches, I think; and to make the most of it, he flung
his head far back, and gave himself a little strut in walking.
He had a thin face with a sharp nose that looked as if it
would peck you, and grey eyes that could pierce a millstone
if there was a guinea on the far side of it. His hair, for he
wore his own, had been red, though it was now grizzled;
and the colour of it was set down in Moonfleet to his
being a Scotchman, for we thought all Scotchmen were
red-headed. He was a lawyer by profession, and having
made money in Edinburgh, had gone so far south as
Moonfleet to get quit, as was said, of the memories of

rascally deeds. It was about four years since he bought a parcel of the Mohune estate, which had been breaking up and selling piecemeal for a generation; and on his land stood the manor house, or so much of it as was left. Of the mansion I have spoken before. It was a very long house of two storeys, with a projecting gable and doorway in the middle, and at each end gabled wings running out crosswise. The Maskews lived in one of these wings, and that was the only habitable portion of the place; for as to the rest, the glass was out of the windows, and in some places the roofs had fallen in. Mr Maskew made no attempt to repair house or grounds, and the bough of the great cedar which the snows had brought down in '49 still blocked the drive. The entrance to the house was through the porchway in the middle, but more than one tumble-down corridor had to be threaded before one reached the inhabited wing; while fowls and pigs and squirrels had possession of the terrace lawns in front. It was not for want of money that Maskew let things remain thus, for men said that he was rich enough, only that his mood was miserly; and perhaps, also, it was the lack of woman's company that made him think so little of neatness and order. For his wife was dead; and though he had a daughter, she was young, and had not yet weight enough to make her father do things that he did not choose.

Till Maskew came there had been none living in the manor house for a generation, so the village children used the terrace for a playground, and picked primroses in the woods; and the men thought they had a right to snare a rabbit or shoot a pheasant in the chase. But the new owner changed all this, hiding gins and spring-guns in the coverts, and nailing up boards on the trees to say he would have the law of any that trespassed. So he soon made enemies for himself, and before long had everyone's hand against him. Yet he preferred his neighbour's enmity to their goodwill, and went about to make it more bitter by getting himself posted for magistrate, and giving out that he would put down the contraband thereabouts. For no one round Moonfleet was for the Excise; but farmers loved a glass of Schnapps that had never been gauged, and their wives a piece of fine lace from France. And then came the affair between the *Elector* and the ketch, with David Block's death; and after that they said it was not safe for Maskew to walk at large, and that he would be found some day dead on the down; but he gave no heed to it, and went on as if he had been a paid exciseman rather than a magistrate.

When I was a little boy the manor woods were my delight, and many a sunny afternoon have I sat on the terrace edge looking down over the village, and munching red quarantines from the ruined fruit gardens. And though this was now forbidden, yet the manor had still a sweeter attraction to me than apples or bird-batting, and that was Grace Maskew. She was an only child, and about my own age, or little better, at the time of which I am speaking. I knew her, because she went every day to the old almshouses to be taught by the Reverend Mr Glennie, from whom I also received my schooling. She was tall for her age, and slim, with a thin face and a tumble of tawny hair, which flew about her in a wind or when she ran. Her frocks were washed and patched and faded, and showed more of her arms and legs than the dressmaker had ever intended, for she was a growing girl, and had none to look after her clothes. She was a favourite playfellow with all, and an early choice for games of 'prisoner's base', and she could beat most of us boys at speed. Thus, though we all hated her father, and had for him many jeering titles among ourselves, yet we never used an evil nickname nor a railing word against him when she was by, because we liked her well.

There were a half-dozen of us boys, and as many girls, whom Mr Glennie used to teach; and that you may see what sort of man Maskew was, I will tell you what happened one day in school between him and the parson. Mr Glennie taught us in the almshouses; for though there were now no bedesmen, and the houses themselves were fallen to decay, yet the little hall in which the inmates had once dined was still maintained, and served for our schoolroom. It was a long and lofty room, with a high wainscot all round it, a carved oak screen at one end, and a broad window at the other. A very heavy table, polished by use, and sadly besmirched with ink, ran down the middle of the hall with benches on either side of it for us to use; and a high desk for Mr Glennie stood under the window at the end of the room. Thus we were sitting one morning with our summing slates and grammars before us when the door in the screen opens and Mr Maskew enters.

I have told you already of the verses which Mr Glennie wrote for David Block's grave; and when the floods had gone down Ratsey set up the headstone with the poetry carved on it. But Maskew, through not going to church, never saw the stone for weeks, until one morning, walking through the churchyard, he lighted on it, and knew the verses for Mr Glennie's. So 'twas to have it out with the parson that he had come to school this day; and though we did not know so much then, yet guessed from his presence that something was in the wind, and could read in his face that he was very angry. Now, for all that we hated Maskew, yet were we glad enough to see him there, as hoping for something strange to vary the sameness of school, and scenting a disturbance in the air. Only Grace was ill at ease for fear her father should say something unseemly, and kept her head down with shocks of hair falling over her book, though I could see her blushing between them. So in vapours Maskew, and with an angry glance about him, makes straight for the desk where our master sits at the top of the room.

For a moment Mr Glennie, being shortsighted, did not see who 'twas; but as his visitor drew near, rose courteously to greet him.

'Good day to you, Mister Maskew,' says he, holding out his hand.

But Maskew puts his arms behind his back and bubbles out, 'Hold not out your hand to me lest I spit on it. 'Tis like your snivelling cant to write sweet psalms for smuggling rogues and try to frighten honest men with your judgements.'

At first Mr Glennie did not know what the other would be at, and afterwards understanding, turned very pale; but said as a minister he would never be backward in reproving those whom he considered in the wrong, whether from the pulpit or from the gravestone.

Then Maskew flies into a great passion, and pours out many vile and insolent words, saying Mr Glennie is in league with the smugglers and fattens on their crimes; that the poetry is a libel; and that he, Maskew, will have the law of him for calumny.

After that he took Grace by the arm, and bade her get hat and cape and come with him. 'For,' says he, 'I will not have thee taught any more by a psalm-singing hypocrite that calls thy father murderer.' And all the while he kept drawing up closer to Mr Glennie, until the two stood very near each other.

There was a great difference between them; the one short and blustering, with a red face turned up; the other tall and craning down, ill-clad, ill-fed, and pale. Maskew had in his left hand a basket, with which he went marketing of mornings, for he made his own purchases, and liked fish, as being cheaper than meat. He had been chaffering with the fishwives this very day, and was bringing back his provend with him when he visited our school.

Then he said to Mr Glennie: 'Now, Sir Parson, the law has given into your fool's hands a power over this churchyard, and 'tis your trade to stop unseemly headlines from being set up within its walls, or once set up, to turn them out forthwith. So I give you a week's grace, and if tomorrow sennight yon stone be not gone, I will have it up and flung in pieces outside the wall.'

Mr Glennie answered him in a low voice, but quite clear, so that we could hear where we sat: 'I can neither turn the stone out myself, nor stop you from turning it out if you so mind; but if you do this thing, and dishonour the graveyard, there is One stronger than either you or I that must be reckoned with.'

I knew afterwards that he meant the Almighty, but thought then that 'twas of Elzevir he spoke; and so, perhaps, did Mr Maskew, for he fell into a worse rage, thrust his hand in the basket, whipped out a great sole he had there, and in a twinkling dashes it in Mr Glennie's face, with a 'Then, take that for an unmannerly parson, for I would not foul my fist with your mealy chops.'

86

But to see that stirred my choler, for Mr Glennie was weak as wax, and would never have held up his hand to stop a blow, even were he strong as Goliath. So I was for setting on Maskew, and being a stout lad for my age, could have had him on the floor as easy as a baby; but as I rose from my seat, I saw he held Grace by the hand, and so hung back for a moment, and before I got my thoughts together he was gone, and I saw the tail of Grace's cape whisk round the screen door.

A sole is at the best an ugly thing to have in one's face, and this sole was larger than most, for Maskew took care to get what he could for his money, so it went with a loud smack on Mr Glennie's cheek, and then fell with another smack on the floor. At this we all laughed, as children will, and Mr Glennie did not check us, but went back and sat very quiet at his desk; and soon I was sorry I had laughed, for he looked sad, with his face sanded and a great red patch on one side, and beside that the fin had scratched him and made a blood-drop trickle down his cheek. A few minutes later the thin voice of the almshouse clock said twelve, and away walked Mr Glennie without his usual 'Good day, children', and there was the sole left lying on the dusty floor in front of his desk.

It seemed a shame so fine a fish should be wasted, so I picked it up and slipped it in my desk, sending Fred Burt to get his mother's gridiron that we might grill it on the schoolroom fire. While he was gone I went out to the court to play, and had not been there five minutes when back comes Maskew through our playground without Grace, and goes into the schoolroom. But in the screen at the end of the room was a chink, against which we used to hold our fingers on bright days for the sun to shine through, and show the blood pink; so up I slipped and fixed my eye to the hole, wanting to know what he was at. He had his basket with him, and I soon saw he had come back for the sole, not having the heart to leave so good a bit of fish. But look where he would, he could not find it, for he never searched my desk, and had to go off with a sour countenance; but Fred Burt and I cooked the sole, and found it well flavoured, for all it had given so much pain to Mr Glennie.

After that Grace came no more to school, both because her father had said she should not, and because she was herself ashamed to go back after what Maskew had done to Mr Glennie. And then it was that I took to wandering much in the manor woods, having no fear of mantraps, for I knew their place as soon as they were put down, but often catching sight of Grace, and sometimes finding occasion to talk with her. Thus time passed, and I lived with Elzevir at the Why Not?, still going to school of mornings, but spending the afternoons in fishing, or in helping him in the garden, or with the boats. As soon as I got to know him well, I begged him to let me help run the cargoes, but he refused, saying I was yet too young, and must not come into mischief. Yet, later, yielding to my importunity, he consented; and more than one dark night I was in the landing boats that unburdened the lugger, though I could never bring myself to enter the Mohune vault again, but would stand as sentry at the passage-mouth. And all the while I had round my neck Colonel John Mohune's locket, and at first wore it next myself, but finding it blacked the skin, put it between shirt and body-jacket. And there by dint of wear it grew less black, and showed a little of the metal underneath, and at last I took to polishing it at odd times, until it came out quite white and shiny, like the pure silver that it was. Elzevir had seen this locket when he put me to bed the first time I came to the Why Not? and afterwards I told him whence I got it; but though we had it out more than once of an evening, we could never come at any hidden meaning. Indeed, we scarce tried to, judging it to be certainly a sacred charm to keep evil spirits from Blackbeard's body.

7

An Auction

What if my house be troubled with a rat,
And I be pleased to give ten thousand ducats
To have it baned – *Shakespeare*

One evening in March, when the days were lengthening fast, there came a messenger from Dorchester, and brought printed notices for fixing to the shutters of the Why Not? and to the church door, which said that in a week's time the bailiff of the duchy of Cornwall would visit Moonfleet. This bailiff was an important person, and his visits stood as events in village history. Once in five years he made a perambulation, or journey, through the whole duchy, inspecting all the royal property, and arranging for new leases. His visits to Moonfleet were generally short enough, for owing to the Mohunes owning all the land, the only duchy estate there was the Why Not? and the only duty of the bailiff to renew that five-year lease, under which Blocks had held the inn, father and son, for generations. But for all that, the business was not performed without ceremony, for there was a solemn show of putting up the lease of the inn to the highest bidder, though it was well understood that no one except Elzevir would make an offer.

So one morning, a week later, I went up to the top end of the village to watch for the bailiff's postchaise, and about eleven of the forenoon saw it coming down the hill with four horses and two postillions. Presently it came past, and I saw there were two men in it – a clerk sitting with his back to the horses, and in the seat opposite a little man in a periwig, whom I took for the bailiff. Then I ran down to my aunt's house, for Elzevir had asked me to beg one of her best winter candles for a purpose which I will explain presently. I had not seen Aunt Jane, except in church, since the day that she dismissed me, but she was no stiffer than usual, and gave me the candle readily enough. 'There,' she said, 'take it, and I wish it may bring light into your dark heart, and show you what a wicked thing it is to leave your own kith and kin and go to dwell in a tavern.' I was for saying that it was kith and kin that left me, and not I them; and as for living in a tavern, it was better to live there than nowhere at all, as she would wish me to do in turning me out of her house; but did not, and only thanked her for the candle, and was off.

When I came to the inn, there was the postchaise in front of the door, the horses being led away to bait, and a little group of villagers standing round; for though the auction of the Why Not? was in itself a trite thing with a foregone conclusion, yet the bailiff's visit always stirred some show of interest. There were a few children with their noses flattened against the windows of the parlour, and inside were Mr Bailiff and Mr Clerk hard at work on their dinner. Mr Bailiff, who was, as I guessed, the little man in the periwig, sat at the top of the table, and Mr Clerk sat at the bottom, and on chairs were placed their hats, and travelling cloaks, and bundles of papers tied together with green tape. You may be sure that Elzevir had a good dinner for them, with hot rabbit pie and cold round of brawn, and a piece of blue vinny, which Mr Bailiff ate heartily, but his clerk would not touch, saying he had as lief chew soap. There was also a bottle of Ararat milk, and a flagon of ale, for we were afraid to set French wines before them, lest they should fall to wondering how they were come by.

Elzevir took the candle, chiding me a little for being late, and set it in a brass candlestick in the middle of the table. Then Mr Clerk takes a little rule from his pocket, measures an inch down on the candle, sticks into the grease at that point a scarf pin with an onyx head that Elzevir lent him, and lights the wick. Now the reason of this was, that the custom ran in Moonfleet when either land or lease was put up to bidding, to stick a pin in a candle; and so long as the pin held firm, it was open to any to make a better offer, but when the flame burned down and the pin fell out, then land or lease fell to the last bidder. So after dinner was over and the table cleared, Mr Clerk takes out a roll of papers and reads a legal description of the Why Not?, calling it the Mohune Arms, an excellent messuage or tenement now used as a tavern, and speaking of the convenient paddocks or parcels of grazing land at the back of it, called Moons'-lease, amounting to sixteen acres more or less. Then he invites the company to make an offer of rent for such a desirable property under a five years' lease, and as Elzevir and I are the only company present, the bidding is soon done; for Elzevir offers a rent of £12 a year, which has always been the value of the Why Not? The clerk makes a note of this; but the business is not over yet, for we must wait till the pin drops out of the candle before the lease is finally made out. So the men fell to smoking to pass the time, till there could not have been more than ten minutes' candle to burn, and Mr Bailiff, with a glass of Ararat milk in his hand, was saying, ''Tis a curious and fine tap of Hollands you keep here, Master Block,' when in walked Mr Maskew.

A thunderbolt would not have astonished me so much as did his appearance, and Elzevir's face grew black as night; but the bailiff and clerk showed no surprise, not knowing the terms on which persons in our village stood to one another, and thinking it natural that someone should come in to see the pin drop, and the end of an ancient custom. Indeed, Maskew seemed to know the bailiff, for he passed the time of day with him, and was then for sitting down at the table without taking any notice of Elzevir or me. But just as he began to seat himself, Block shouted out, 'You are no welcome visitor in my house, and I would sooner see your back than see your face, but sit at this table you shall not.' I knew what he meant; for on that table they had laid out David's body, and with that he struck his fist upon the board so smart as to make the bailiff jump and nearly bring the pin out of the candle.

'Heyday, sirs,' says Mr Bailiff, astonished, 'let us have no brawling here, the more so as this worshipful gentleman is a magistrate and something of a friend of mine.' Yet Maskew refrained from sitting, but stood by the bailiff's chair, turning white, and not red, as he did with Mr Glennie; and muttered something, that he had as lief stand as sit, and that it should soon be Block's turn to ask sitting-room of *him*.

I was wondering what possibly could have brought Maskew there, when the bailiff, who was ill at ease, said –

'Come, Mr Clerk, the pin hath but another minute's hold; rehearse what has been done, for I must get this lease delivered and off to Bridport, where much business waits.'

So the clerk read in a singsong voice that the property of the duchy of Cornwall, called the Mohune Arms, an inn or tavern, with all its land, tenements, and appurtenances, situate in the Parish of St Sebastian, Moonfleet, having been offered on lease for five years, would be let to Elzevir Block at a rent of £12 per annum, unless anyone offered a higher rent before the pin fell from the candle.

There was no one to make another offer, and the bailiff said to Elzevir, 'Tell them to have the horses round, the pin will be out in a minute, and 'twill save time.' So Elzevir gave the order, and then we all stood round in silence, waiting for the pin to fall. The grease had burned down to the mark, or almost below it, as it appeared; but just where the pin stuck in there was a little lump of harder tallow that held bravely out, refusing to be melted. The bailiff gave a stamp of impatience with his foot under the table as though he hoped thus to shake out the pin, and then a little dry voice came from Maskew, saying –

'I offer £13 a year for the inn.'

This fell upon us with so much surprise, that all looked round, seeking as it were some other speaker, and never thinking that it could be Maskew. Elzevir was the first, I believe, to fully understand 'twas he; and without turning to look at bailiff or Maskew, but having his elbows on the table, his face between his hands, and looking straight out to sea, said in a sturdy voice, 'I offer £20.'

The words were scarce out of his mouth when Maskew caps them with £21, and so in less than a minute the rent of the Why Not? was near doubled. Then the bailiff looked from one to the other, not knowing what to make of it all, nor whether 'twas comedy or serious, and said –

'Kind sir, I warn ye not to trifle; I have no time to waste in April fooling, and he who makes offers in sport will have to stand to them in earnest.'

But there was no lack of earnest in one at least of the men that he had before him, and the voice with which Elzevir said £30 was still sturdy. Maskew called £31 and £41, and Elzevir £40 and £50, and then I looked at the candle, and saw that the head of the pin was no longer level, it had sunk a little – a very little. The clerk awoke from his indifference, and was making notes of the bids with a squeaking quill, the bailiff frowned as being puzzled, and thinking that none had a right to puzzle him. As for me, I could not sit still, but got on my feet, if so I might better bear the suspense; for I understood now that Maskew had made up his mind to turn Elzevir out, and that Elzevir was fighting for his home. *His* home, and had he not made it my home too, and were we both to be made outcasts to please the spite of this mean little man?

There were some more bids, and then I knew that Maskew was saying £91, and saw the head of the pin was lower; the hard lump of tallow in Aunt Jane's candle was thawing. The bailiff struck in: 'Are ye mad, sirs, and you, Master Block, save your breath, and spare your money; and if this worshipful gentleman must become innkeeper at any price, let him have the place in the devil's name, and I will give thee the Mermaid, at Bridport, with a snug parlour, and ten times the trade of this.'

Elzevir seemed not to hear what he said, but only called out £100, with his face still looking out to sea, and the same sturdiness in his voice. Then Maskew tried a spring, and went to £120, and Elzevir capped him with £130, and £140, £150, £160, £170 followed quick. My breath came so fast that I was almost giddy, and I had to clench my hands to remind myself of where I was, and what was going on. The bidders too were breathing hard, Elzevir had taken his head from his hands, and the eyes of all were on the pin. The lump of tallow was worn down now; it was hard to say why the pin did not fall. Maskew gulped out £180, and Elzevir said £190, and then the pin gave a lurch, and I thought the Why Not? was saved, though at the price of ruin. No; the pin had not fallen, there was a film that held it by the point, one second, only one second. Elzevir's breath, which was ready to outbid whatever Maskew said, caught in his throat with the catching pin, and Maskew sighed out £200, before the pin pattered on the bottom of the brass candlestick.

The clerk forgot his master's presence and shut his notebook with a bang, 'I congratulate you, sir,' says he, quite pert to Maskew; 'you are the landlord of the poorest pothouse in the duchy at £200 a year.'

The bailiff paid no heed to what his man did, but took his periwig off and wiped his head. 'Well, I'm hanged,' he said; and so the Why Not? was lost.

Just as the last bid was given, Elzevir half rose from his chair, and for a moment I expected to see him spring like a wild beast on Maskew; but he said nothing, and sat down again with the same stolid look on his face. And, indeed, it was perhaps well that he thus thought better of it, for Maskew stuck his hand into his bosom as the other rose; and though he withdrew it again when Elzevir got back to his chair, yet the front of his waistcoat was a little bulged, and, looking sideways, I saw the silver-shod butt of a pistol nestling far down against his white shirt. The bailiff was vexed, I think, that he had been betrayed into such strong words; for he tried at once to put on as indifferent an air as might be, saying in dry tones, 'Well, gentlemen, there seems to be here some personal matter into which I shall not attempt to spy. Two hundred pounds more or less is but a flea bite to the duchy; and if you, sir,' turning to Maskew, 'wish later on to change your mind, and be quit of the bargain, I shall not be the man to stand in your way. In any case, I imagine 'twill be time enough to seal the lease if I send it from London.'

I knew he said this, and hinted at delay as wishing to do Elzevir a good turn; for his clerk had the lease already made out pat, and it only wanted the name and rent filled in to be sealed and signed. But, 'No,' says Maskew, 'business is business, Mr Bailiff, and the post uncertain to parts so distant from the capital as these; so I'll thank you to make out the lease to me now, and on May Day place me in possession.'

'So be it then,' said the bailiff a little testily, 'but blame me not for driving hard bargains; for the duchy, whose servant I am,' and he raised his hat, 'is no daughter of the horseleech. Fill in the figures, Mr Scrutton, and let us away.'

So Mr Scrutton, for that was Mr Clerk's name, scratches a bit with his quill on the parchment sheet to fill in the money, and then Maskew scratches his name, and Mr Bailiff scratches his name, and Mr Clerk scratches again to witness Mr Bailiff's name, and then Mr Bailiff takes from his mails a little shagreen case, and out from the case comes sealing wax and the travelling seal of the duchy.

There was my aunt's best winter candle still burning away in the daylight, for no one had taken any thought to put it out; and Mr Bailiff melts the wax at it, till a drop of sealing wax falls into the grease and makes a gutter down one side, and then there is a sweating of the parchment under the hot wax, and at last on goes the seal.

'Signed, sealed, and delivered,' says Mr Clerk, rolling up the sheet and handing it to Maskew; and Maskew takes and thrusts it into his bosom underneath his waistcoat front – all cheek by jowl with that silver-hafted pistol, whose butt I had seen before.

The postchaise stood before the door, the horses were stamping on the cobblestones, and the harness jingled. Mr Clerk had carried out his mails, but Mr Bailiff stopped for a moment as he flung the travelling cloak about his shoulders to say to Elzevir, 'Tut, man, take things not too hardly. Thou shalt have the Mermaid at £20 a year, which will be worth ten times as much to thee as this dreary place; and canst send thy son to Bryson's school, where they will make a scholar of him, for he is a brave lad;' and he touched my shoulder, and gave me a kindly look as he passed.

'I thank your worship,' said Elzevir, 'for all your goodness; but when I quit this place, I shall not set up my staff again at any inn door.'

Mr Bailiff seemed nettled to see his offer made so little of, and left the room with a sniff. 'Then I wish you good day.'

Maskew had slipped out before him, and the children's noses left the windowpane as the great man walked down the steps. There was a little group to see the start, but it quickly melted; and before the clatter of hoofs died away, the report spread through the village that Maskew had turned Elzevir out of the Why Not?

For a long time after all had gone, Elzevir sat at the table with his head between his hands, and I kept quiet also, both because I was myself sorry that we were to be sent adrift, and because I wished to show Elzevir that I felt for him in his troubles. But the young cannot enter fully into their elders' sorrows, however much they may wish to, and after a time the silence palled upon me. It was getting dusk, and the candle which bore itself so bravely through auction and lease-sealing burned low in the socket. A minute later the light gave some flickering flashes, failings, and sputters, and then the wick tottered, and out popped the flame, leaving us with the chilly grey of a March evening creeping up in the corners of the room. I could bear the gloom no longer, but made up the fire till the light danced ruddy across pewter and porcelain on the dresser. 'Come, Master Block,' I said, 'there is time enough before May Day to think what we shall do, so let us take a cup of tea, and after that I will play you a game of backgammon.' But he still remained cast down, and would say nothing; and as chance would have it, though I wished to let him win at backgammon, that so, perhaps, he might get cheered, yet do what I would that night I could not lose. So as his luck grew worse his moodiness increased, and at last he shut the board with a bang, saying, in reference to that motto that ran round its edge, 'Life is like a game of hazard, and surely none ever flung worse throws, or made so little of them as I.'

8

The Landing

Let my lamp at midnight hour
Be seen in some high lonely tower – *Milton*

Maskew got ugly looks from the men, and sour words from the wives, as he went up through the village that afternoon, for all knew what he had done, and for many days after the auction he durst not show his face abroad. Yet Damen of Ringstave and some others of the landers' men, who made it their business to keep an eye upon him, said that he had been twice to Weymouth of evenings, and held converse there with Mr Luckham of the Excise, and with Captain Henning, who commanded the troopers then in quarters on the Nothe. And by degrees it got about, but how I do not know, that he had persuaded the Revenue to strike hard at the smugglers, and that a strong posse was to be held in readiness to take the landers in the act the next time they should try to run a cargo. Why Maskew should so put himself about to help the Revenue I cannot tell, nor did anyone ever certainly find out; but some said 'twas out of sheer wantonness, and a desire to hurt his neighbours; and others, that he saw what an apt place this was for landing cargoes, and wished first to make a brave show of zeal for the Excise, and afterwards to get the whole of the contraband trade into his own hands. However that may be, I think he was certainly in league with the revenue men, and more than once I saw him on the manor terrace with a spyglass in his hand, and guessed that he was looking for the lugger in the offing. Now, word was mostly given to the lander, by safe hands, of the night on which a cargo should be run, and then in the morning or afternoon the lugger would come just near enough the land to be made out with glasses, and afterwards lie off again out of sight till nightfall. The nights chosen for such work were without moon, but as still as might be, so long as there was wind enough to fill the sails; and often the lugger could be made out from the beach, but sometimes 'twas necessary to signal with flares, though they were used as little as might be. Yet after there had been a long spell of rough weather, and a cargo had to be run at all hazards, I have known the boats come in even on the bright moonlight and take their risk, for 'twas said the Excise slept sounder round us than anywhere in all the Channel.

These tales of Maskew's doings failed not to reach Elzevir, and for some days he thought best not to move, though there was a cargo on the other side that wanted landing badly. But one evening when he had won at backgammon, and was in an open mood, he took me into confidence, setting down the dice box on the table, and saying –

'There is word come from the shippers that we must take a cargo, for that they cannot keep the stuff by them longer at St Malo. Now with this devil at the manor prowling round, I dare not risk the job on Moonfleet beach, nor yet stow the liquor in the vault; so I have told the *Bonaventure* to put her nose into this bay tomorrow afternoon that Maskew may see her well, and then to lie out again to sea, as she has done a hundred times before. But instead of waiting in the offing, she will make straight off up Channel to a little strip of shingle underneath Hoar Head.' I nodded to show I knew the place, and he went on – 'Men used to choose that spot in good old times to beach a cargo before the passage to the vault was dug; and there is a worked-out quarry they called Pyegrove's Hole, not too far off up the down, and choked with brambles where we can find shelter for a hundred kegs. So we'll be under Hoar Head at five tomorrow morn with the packhorses. I wish we could be earlier, for the sun rises thereabout, but the tide will not serve before.'

It was at that moment that I felt a cold touch on my shoulders, as of the fresh air from outside, and thought beside I had a whiff of salt seaweed from the beach. So round I looked to see if door or window stood ajar. The window was tight enough, and shuttered to boot, but the door was not to be seen plainly for a wooden screen, which parted it from the parlour, and was meant to keep off draughts. Yet I could just see a top corner of the door above the screen and thought it was not fast. So up I got to shut it, for the nights were cold; but coming round the corner of the screen, found that 'twas closed, and yet I could have sworn I saw the latch fall to its place as I walked towards it. Then I dashed forward, and in a trice had the door open, and was in the street. But the night was moonless and black, and I neither saw nor heard aught stirring, save the gentle sea-wash on Moonfleet beach beyond the salt meadows.

Elzevir looked at me uneasily as I came back.

'What ails thee, boy?' said he.

'I thought I heard someone at the door,' I answered; 'did you not feel a cold wind as if it was open?'

'It is but the night is sharp, the spring sets in very chill; slip the bolt, and sit down again,' and he flung a fresh log on the fire, that sent a cloud of sparks crackling up the chimney and out into the room.

'Elzevir,' I said, 'I think there was one listening at the door, and there may be others in the house, so before we sit again let us take candle and go through the rooms to make sure none are prying on us.'

He laughed and said, ''Twas but the wind that blew the door open,' but that I might do as I pleased. So I lit another candle, and was for starting on my search; but he cried,

'Nay, thou shalt not go alone;' and so we went all round the house together, and found not so much as a mouse stirring.

He laughed the more when we came back to the parlour.

''Tis the cold has chilled thy heart and made thee timid of that skulking rascal of the manor; fill me a glass of Ararat milk, and one for thyself, and let us to bed.'

I had learned by this not to be afraid of the good liquor, and while we sat sipping it, Elzevir went on –

'There is a fortnight yet to run, and then you and I shall be cut adrift from our moorings. It is a cruel thing to see the doors of this house closed on me, where I and mine have lived a century or more, but I must see it. Yet let us not be too cast down, but try to make something even of this worst of throws.'

I was glad enough to hear him speak in this firmer strain, for I had seen what a sore thought it had been for these days past that he must leave the Why Not?, and how it often made him moody and downcast.

'We will have no more of innkeeping,' he said; 'I have been sick and tired of it this many a day, and care not now to see men abuse good liquor and addle their silly pates to fill my purse. And I have something, boy, put snug away in Dorchester town that will give us bread to eat and beer to drink, even if the throws run still deuce-ace. But we must seek a roof to shelter us when the Why Not? is shut, and 'tis best we leave this Moonfleet of ours for a season, till Maskew finds a rope's end long enough to hang himself withal. So, when our work is done tomorrow night, we will walk out along the cliff to Worth, and take a look at a cottage there that Damen spoke about, with a walled orchard at the back, and fuchsia hedge in front – 'tis near the Lobster Inn, and has a fine prospect of the sea; and if we live there, we will leave the vault alone awhile and use this Pyegrove's Hole for storehouse, till the watch is relaxed.'

I did not answer, having my thoughts on other things, and he tossed off his liquor, saying, 'Thou'rt tired; so let's to bed, for we shall get little sleep tomorrow night.'

It was true that I was tired, and yet I could not get to sleep, but tossed and turned in my bed for thinking of many things, and being vexed that we were to leave Moonfleet. Yet mine was a selfish sorrow; for I had little thought for Elzevir and the pain that it must be to him to quit the Why Not?: nor yet was it the grief of leaving Moonfleet that so troubled me, although that was the only place I ever had known, and seemed to me then – as now – the only spot on earth fit to be lived in; but the real care and canker was that I was going away from Grace Maskew. For since she had left school I had grown fonder of her; and now that it was difficult to see her, I took the more pains to accomplish it, and met her sometimes in Manor Woods, and more than once, when Maskew was away, had walked with her on Weatherbeech Hill. So we bred up a boy-and-girl affection, and must needs pledge ourselves to be true to one another, not knowing what such silly words might mean. And I told Grace all my secrets, not even excepting the doings of the contraband, and the Mohune vault and Blackbeard's locket, for I knew all was as safe with her as with me, and that her father could never rack aught from her. Nay, more, her bedroom was at the top of the gabled wing of the manor house, and looked right out to sea; and one clear night, when our boat was coming late from fishing, I saw her candle burning there, and next day told her of it. And then she said that she would set a candle to burn before the panes on winter nights, and be a leading light for boats at sea. And so she did, and others beside me saw and used it, calling it 'Maskew's Match', and saying that it was the attorney sitting up all night to pore over ledgers and add up his fortune.

So this night as I lay awake I vexed and vexed myself for thinking of her, and at last resolved to go up next morning to the manor woods and lie in wait for Grace, to tell her what was up, and that we were going away to Worth.

Next day, the 16th of April – a day I have had cause to remember all my life – I played truant from Mr Glennie, and by ten in the forenoon found myself in the woods.

There was a little dimple on the hillside above the house, green with burdocks in summer and filled with dry leaves in winter – just big enough to hold one lying flat, and not so deep but that I could look over the lip of it and see the house without being seen. Thither I went that day, and lay down in the dry leaves to wait and watch for Grace.

The morning was bright enough. The chills of the night before had given way to sunlight that seemed warm as summer, and yet had with it the soft freshness of spring. There was scarce a breath moving in the wood, though I could see the clouds of white dust stalking up the road that climbs Ridgedown, and the trees were green with buds, yet without leafage to keep the sunbeams from lighting up the ground below, which glowed with yellow kingcups. So I lay there for a long, long while; and to make time pass quicker, took from my bosom the silver locket, and opening it, read again the parchment, which I had read times out of mind before, and knew indeed by heart.

'The days of our age are threescore years and ten,' and the rest.

Now, whenever I handled the locket, my thoughts were turned to Mohune's treasure; and it was natural that it should be so, for the locket reminded me of my first journey to the vault; and I laughed at myself, remembering how simple I had been, and had hoped to find the place littered with diamonds, and to see the gold lying packed in heaps. And thus for the hundredth time I came to rack my brain to know where the diamond could be hid, and thought at last it must be buried in the churchyard, because of the talk of Blackbeard being seen on wild nights digging there for his treasure. But then, I reasoned, that very like it was the contrabandiers whom men had seen with spades when they were digging out the passage from the tomb to the vault, and set them down for ghosts because they wrought at night. And while I was busy with such thoughts, the door opened in the house below me, and out came Grace with a hood on her head and a basket for wild flowers in her hand.

I watched to see which way she would walk; and as soon as she took the path that leads up Weatherbeech, made off through the dry brushwood to meet her, for we had settled she should never go that road except when Maskew was away. So there we met and spent an hour together on the hill, though I shall not write here what we said, because it was mostly silly stuff. She spoke much of the auction and of Elzevir leaving the Why Not?, and though she never said a word against her father, let me know what pain his doing gave her. But most she grieved that we were leaving Moonfleet, and showed her grief in such pretty ways, as made me almost glad to see her sorry. And from her I learned that Maskew was indeed absent from home, having been called away suddenly last night. The evening was so fine, he said (and this surprised me, remembering how dark and cold it was with us), that he must needs walk round the policies; but about nine o'clock came back and told her he had got a sudden call to business, which would take him to Weymouth then and there. So to saddle, and off he went on his mare, bidding Grace not to look for him for two nights to come.

I know not why it was, but what she said of Maskew made me thoughtful and silent, and she too must be back home lest the old servant that kept house for them should say she had been too long away, and so we parted. Then off I went through the woods and down the village street, but as I passed my old home saw Aunt Jane standing on the doorstep. I bade her 'Good day', and was for running on to the Why Not?, for I was late enough already, but she called me to her, seeming in a milder mood, and said she had something for me in the house. So left me standing while she went off to get it, and back she came and thrust into my hand a little prayer book, which I had often seen about the parlour in past days, saying, 'Here is a Common Prayer which I had meant to send thee with thy clothes. It was thy poor mother's, and I pray may some day be as precious a balm to thee as it once was to that godly woman.' With that she gave me the 'Good day', and I pocketed the little red leather book, which did indeed afterwards prove precious to me, though not in the way she meant, and ran down street to the Why Not?

That same evening Elzevir and I left the Why Not?, went up through the village, climbed the down, and were at the brow by sunset. We had started earlier than we fixed the night before, because word had come to Elzevir that morning that the tide called Gulder would serve for the beaching of the *Bonaventure* at three instead of five. 'Tis a strange thing the Gulder, and not even sailors can count closely with it; for on the Dorset coast the tide makes four times a day, twice with the common flow, and twice with the Gulder, and this last being shifty and uncertain as to time, flings out many a sea-reckoning.

It was about seven o'clock when we were at the top of the hill, and there were fifteen good miles to cover to get to Hoar Head. Dusk was upon us before we had walked half an hour; but when the night fell, it was not black as on the last evening, but a deep sort of blue, and the heat of the day did not die with the sun, but left the air still warm and balmy. We trudged on in silence, and were glad enough when we saw by a white stone here and there at the side of the path that we were nearing the cliff; for the Preventive men mark all the footpaths on the cliff with whitewashed stones, so that one can pick up the way without risk on a dark night. A few minutes more, and we reached a broad piece of open sward, which I knew for the top of Hoar Head.

Hoar Head is the highest of that line of cliffs, which stretches twenty miles from Weymouth to St Alban's Head, and it stands up eighty fathoms or more above the water. The seaward side is a great sheer of chalk, but falls not straight into the sea, for three parts down there is a lower ledge or terrace, called the undercliff.

'Twas to this ledge that we were bound; and though we were now straight above, I knew we had a mile or more to go before we could get down to it. So on we went again, and found the bridle path that slopes down through a deep dip in the cliff line; and when we reached this under-ledge, I looked up at the sky, the night being clear, and guessed by the stars that 'twas past midnight. I knew the place from having once been there for blackberries; for the brambles on the undercliff being sheltered every way but south, and open to the sun, grow the finest in all those parts.

We were not alone, for I could make out a score of men, some standing in groups, some resting on the ground, and the dark shapes of the packhorses showing larger in the dimness. There were a few words of greeting muttered in deep voices, and then all was still, so that one heard the browsing horses trying to crop something off the turf. It was not the first cargo I had helped to run, and I knew most of the men, but did not speak with them, being tired, and wishing to rest till I was wanted. So cast myself down on the turf, but had not lain there long when I saw someone coming to me through the brambles, and Master Ratsey said, 'Well, Jack, so thou and Elzevir are leaving Moonfleet, and I fain would flit myself, but then who would be left to lead the old folk to their last homes, for dead do not bury their dead in these days.'

I was half asleep, and took little heed of what he said, putting him off with, 'That need not keep you, master; they will find others to fill your place.' Yet he would not let me be, but went on talking for the pleasure of hearing his own voice.

'Nay, child, you know not what you say. They may find men to dig a grave, and perhaps to fill it, but who shall toss the mould when Parson Glennie gives the "earth to earth"? It takes a mort of knowledge to make it rattle kindly on the coffin lid.'

I felt sleep heavy on my eyelids, and was for begging him to let me rest, when there came a whistle from below, and in a moment all were on their feet. The drivers went to the packhorses' heads, and so we walked down to the strand, a silent moving group of men and horses mixed; and before we came to the bottom, heard the first boat's nose grind on the beach, and the feet of the seamen crunching in the pebbles. Then all fell to the business of landing, and a strange enough scene it was, what with the medley of men, the lanterns swinging, and a frothy lipper from the sea running up till sometimes it was over our boots; and all the time there was a patter of French and Dutch, for most of the *Bonaventure*'s men were foreigners. But I shall not speak more of this; for, after all, one landing is very like another, and kegs come ashore in much the same way, whether they are to pay excise or not.

It must have been three o'clock before the lugger's boats were off again to sea, and by that time the horses were well laden, and most of the men had a keg or two to carry beside. Then Elzevir, who was in command, gave the word, and we began to file away from the beach up to the undercliff. Now, what with the cargo being heavy, we were longer than usual in getting away; and though there was no sign of sunrise, yet the night was greyer, and not so blue as it had been.

We reached the undercliff, and were moving across it to address ourselves to the bridle path, and so wind sideways up the steep; when I saw something moving behind one of the plumps of brambles with which the place is beset. It was only a glimpse of motion that I had perceived, and could not say whether 'twas man or animal, or even frightened bird behind the bushes. But others had seen it as well; there was some shouting, half a dozen flung down their kegs and started in pursuit.

All eyes were turned to the bridle path, and in a twinkling hunters and hunted were in view. The greyhounds were Damen and Garrett, with some others, and the hare was an older man, who leapt and bounded forward, faster than I should have thought any but a youth could run; but then he knew what men were after him, and that 'twas a race for life. For though it was but a moment before all were lost in the night, yet this was long enough to show me that the man was none other than Maskew, and I knew that his life was not worth ten minutes' purchase.

Now I hated this man, and had myself suffered something at his hand, besides seeing him put much grievous suffering on others; but I wished then with all my heart he might escape, and had a horrible dread of what was to come. Yet I knew all the time escape was impossible; for though Maskew ran desperately, the way was steep and stony, and he had behind him some of the fleetest feet along that coast. We had all stopped with one accord, as not wishing to move a step forward till we had seen the issue of the chase; and I was near enough to look into Elzevir's face, but saw there neither passion nor bloodthirstiness, but only a calm resolve, as if he had to deal with something well expected.

We had not long to wait, for very soon we heard a rolling of stones and trampling of feet coming down the path, and from the darkness issued a group of men, having Maskew in the middle of them. They were hustling him along fast, two having hold of him by the arms, and a third by the neck of his shirt behind. The sight gave me a sick qualm, like an overdose of tobacco, for it was the first time I had ever seen a man manhandled, and a fellow creature abused. His cap was lost, and his thin hair tangled over his forehead, his coat was torn off, so that he stood in his waistcoat alone; he was pale, and gasped terribly, whether from the sharp run, or from violence, or fear, or all combined.

There was a babel of voices when they came up of desperate men who had a bitterest enemy in their clutch;

and some shouted, 'Club him', 'Shoot him', 'Hang him', while others were for throwing him over the cliff. Then someone saw under the flap of his waistcoat that same silver-hafted pistol that lay so lately next the lease of the Why Not? and snatching it from him, flung it on the grass at Block's feet.

But Elzevir's deep voice mastered their contentions –

'Lads, ye remember how I said when this man's reckoning day should come 'twas I would reckon with him, and had your promise to it. Nor is it right that any should lay hand on him but I, for is he not sealed to me with my son's blood? So touch him not, but bind him hand and foot, and leave him here with me and go your ways; there is no time to lose, for the light grows apace.'

There was a little muttered murmuring, but Elzevir's will overbore them here as it had done in the vault; and they yielded the more easily, because every man knew in his heart that he would never see Maskew again alive. So within ten minutes all were winding up the bridle path, horses and men, all except three; for there were left upon the brambly greensward of the undercliff Maskew and Elzevir and I, and the pistol lay at Elzevir's feet.

9

A Judgement

Let them fight it out, friend. Things have gone too far,
God must judge the couple: leave them as they are

– Browning

I made as if I would follow the others, not wishing to see
what I must see if I stayed behind, and knowing that I
was powerless to bend Elzevir from his purpose. But he
called me back and bade me wait with him, for that I
might be useful by and by. So I waited, but was only able
to make a dreadful guess at how I might be of use, and
feared the worst.

Maskew sat on the sward with his hands lashed tight
behind his back, and his feet tied in front. They had set
him with his shoulders against a great block of weather-
worn stone that was half buried and half stuck up out of
the turf. There he sat keeping his eyes on the ground, and
was breathing less painfully than when he was first
brought, but still very pale. Elzevir stood with the lantern
in his hand, looking at Maskew with a fixed gaze, and we

could hear the hoofs of the heavy-laden horses beating up the path, till they turned a corner, and all was still.

The silence was broken by Maskew: 'Unloose me, villain, and let me go. I am a magistrate of the county, and if you do not, I will have you gibbeted on this clifftop.'

They were brave words enough, yet seemed to me but bad play-acting; and brought to my remembrance how, when I was a little fellow, Mr Glennie once made me recite a battlepiece of Mr Dryden before my betters; and how I could scarce get out the bloody threats for shyness and rising tears. So it was with Maskew's words; for he had much ado to gather breath to say them, and they came in a thin voice that had no sting of wrath or passion in it.

Then Elzevir spoke to him, not roughly, but resolved; and yet with melancholy, like a judge sentencing a prisoner: 'Talk not to me of gibbets, for thou wilt neither hang nor see men hanged again. A month ago thou satst under my roof, watching the flame burn down till the pin dropped and gave thee right to turn me out from my old home. And now this morning thou shalt watch that flame again, for I will give thee one inch more of candle, and when the pin drops, will put this thine own pistol to thy head, and kill thee with as little thought as I would kill a stoat or other vermin.'

Then he opened the lantern slide, took out from his neckcloth that same pin with the onyx head which he had used in the Why Not? and fixed it in the tallow a short inch from the top, setting the lantern down upon the sward in front of Maskew.

As for me, I was dismayed beyond telling at these words, and made giddy with the revulsion of feeling; for, whereas, but a few minutes ago, I would have thought nothing too bad for Maskew, now I was turned round to wish he might come off with his life, and to look with terror upon Elzevir.

It had grown much lighter, but not yet with the rosy flush of sunrise; only the stars had faded out, and the deep blue of the night given way to a misty grey. The light was strong enough to let all things be seen, but not to call the due tints back to them. So I could see cliffs and ground, bushes and stones and sea, and all were of one pearly grey colour, or rather they were colourless; but the most colourless and greyest thing of all was Maskew's face. His hair had got awry, and his head showed much balder than when it was well trimmed; his face, too, was drawn with heavy lines, and there were rings under his eyes. Beside all that, he had got an ugly fall in trying to escape, and one cheek was muddied, and down it trickled a blood-drop where a stone had cut him. He was a sorry sight enough, and looking at him, I remembered that day in the schoolroom when this very man had struck the parson, and how our master had sat patient under it, with a blood-drop trickling down his cheek too. Maskew kept his eyes fixed for a long time on the ground, but raised them at last, and looked at me with a vacant yet pity-seeking look. Now, till that moment I had never seen a trace of Grace in his features, nor of him in hers; and yet as he gazed at me then, there was something of her present in his face, even battered as it was, so that it seemed as if she looked at me behind his eyes. And that made me the sorrier for him, and at last I felt I could not stand by and see him done to death.

When Elzevir had stuck the pin into the candle he never shut the slide again; and though no wind blew, there was a light breath moving in the morning off the sea, that got inside the lantern and set the flame askew. And so the candle guttered down one side till but little tallow was left above the pin; for though the flame grew pale and paler to the view in the growing morning light, yet it burned freely all the time. So at last there was left, as I judged, but a quarter of an hour to run before the pin should fall, and I saw that Maskew knew this as well as I, for his eyes were fixed on the lantern.

At last he spoke again, but the brave words were gone, and the thin voice was thinner. He had dropped threats, and was begging piteously for his life. 'Spare me,' he said; 'spare me, Mr Block: I have an only daughter, a young girl with none but me to guard her. Would you rob a young girl of her only help and cast her on the world? Would you have them find me dead upon the cliff and bring me back to her a bloody corpse?'

Then Elzevir answered: 'And had I not an only son, and was he not brought back to me a bloody corpse? Whose pistol was it that flashed in his face and took his life away? Do you not know? It was this very same that shall flash in yours. So make what peace you may with God, for you have little time to make it.'

With that he took the pistol from the ground where it had lain, and turning his back on Maskew, walked slowly to and fro among the bramble plumps.

Though Maskew's words about his daughter seemed but to feed Elzevir's anger, by leading him to think of David, they sank deep in my heart; and if it had seemed a fearful thing before to stand by and see a fellow creature butchered, it seemed now ten thousand times more fearful. And when I thought of Grace, and what such a deed would mean to her, my pulse beat so fierce that I must needs spring to my feet and run to reason with Elzevir, and tell him this must not be.

He was still walking among the bushes when I found him, and let me say my say till I was out of breath, and bore with me if I talked fast, and if my tongue outran my judgement.

'Thou hast a warm heart, lad,' he said, 'and 'tis for that I like thee. And if thou hast a chief place in thy heart for me, I cannot grumble if thou find a little room there even for our enemies. Would I could set thy soul at ease, and do all that thou askest. In the first flush of wrath, when he was taken plotting against our lives, it seemed a little thing enough to take his evil life. But now these morning airs have cooled me, and it goes against my will to shoot a cowering hound tied hand and foot, even though he had murdered twenty sons of mine. I have thought if there be any way to spare his life, and leave this hour's agony to read a lesson not to be unlearned until the grave. For such poltroons dread death, and in one hour they die a hundred times. But there is no way out: his life lies in the scale against the lives of all our men, yes, and thy life too. They left him in my hands well knowing I should take account of him; and am I now to play them false and turn him loose again to hang them all? It cannot be.'

Still I pleaded hard for Maskew's life, hanging on Elzevir's arm, and using every argument that I could think of to soften his purpose; but he pushed me off; and though I saw that he was loth to do it, I had a terrible conviction that he was not a man to be turned back from his resolve, and would go through with it to the end.

We came back together from the brambles to the piece of sward, and there sat Maskew where we had left him with his back against the stone. Only, while we were away he had managed to wriggle his watch out of the fob, and it lay beside him on the turf, tied to him with a black silk riband. The face of it was turned upwards, and as I passed I saw the hand pointed to five.

Sunrise was very near; for though the cliff shut out the east from us, the west over Portland was all aglow with copper-red and gold, and the candle burned low. The head of the pin was drooping, though very slightly, but as I saw it droop a month before, and I knew that the final act was not far off.

Maskew knew it too, for he made his last appeal, using such passionate words as I cannot now relate, and wriggling with his body as if to get his hands from behind his back and hold them up in supplication. He offered money: a thousand, five thousand, ten thousand pounds to be set free; he would give back the Why Not?; he would leave Moonfleet; and all the while the sweat ran down his furrowed face, and at last his voice was choked with sobs, for he was crying for his life in craven fear.

He might have spoken to a deaf man for all he moved his judge; and Elzevir's answer was to cock the pistol and prime the powder in the pan.

Then I stuck my fingers in my ears and shut my eyes, that I might neither see nor hear what followed, but in a second changed my mind and opened them again, for I had made a great resolve to stop this matter, come what might.

Maskew was making a dreadful sound between a moan and strangled cry; it almost seemed as if he thought that there were others by him beside Elzevir and me, and was shouting to them for help. The sun had risen, and his first rays blazed on a window far away in the west on top of Portland Island, and then there was a tinkle in the inside of the lantern, and the pin fell.

Elzevir looked full at Maskew, and raised his pistol; but before he had time to take aim, I dashed upon him like a wild cat, springing on his right arm, and crying to him to stop. It was an unequal struggle, a lad, though full-grown and lusty, against one of the powerfullest of men, but indignation nerved my arms, and his were weak, because he doubted of his right. So 'twas with some effort that he shook me off, and in the struggle the pistol was fired into the air.

Then I let go of him, and stumbled for a moment, tired with that bout, but pleased withal, because I saw what peace even so short a respite had brought to Maskew. For at the pistol shot 'twas as if a mask of horror had fallen from his face, and left him his old countenance again; and then I saw he turned his eyes towards the clifftop, and thought that he was looking up in thankfulness to heaven.

But now a new thing happened; for before the echoes of that pistol shot had died on the keen morning air, I thought I heard a noise of distant shouting, and looked about to see whence it could come. Elzevir looked round too, but Maskew, forgetting to upbraid me for making him miss his aim, still kept his face turned up towards the cliff. Then the voices came nearer, and there was a mingled sound as of men shouting to one another, and gathering in from different places. 'Twas from the clifftop that the voices came, and thither Elzevir and I looked up, and there too Maskew kept his eyes fixed. And in a moment there were a score of men stood on the cliff's edge high above our heads. The sky behind them was pink flushed with the keenest light of the young day, and they stood out against it sharp cut and black as the silhouette of my mother that used to hang up by the parlour chimney. They were soldiers, and I knew the tall mitre caps of the 13th, and saw the shafts of light from the sunrise come flashing round their bodies, and glance off the barrels of their matchlocks.

I knew it all now; it was the posse who had lain in ambush. Elzevir saw it too, and then all shouted at once.

'Yield at the king's command: you are our prisoners!' calls the voice of one of those black silhouettes, far up on the clifftop.

'We are lost,' cries Elzevir; 'it is the posse; but if we die, this traitor shall go before us,' and he makes towards Maskew to brain him with the pistol.

'Shoot, shoot, in the devil's name,' screams Maskew, 'or I am a dead man.'

Then there came a flash of fire along the black line of silhouettes, with a crackle like a near peal of thunder, and a fut, fut, fut, of bullets in the turf. And before Elzevir could get at him, Maskew had fallen over on the sward with a groan, and with a little red hole in the middle of his forehead.

'Run for the cliffside,' cried Elzevir to me; 'get close in, and they cannot touch thee,' and he made for the chalk wall. But I had fallen on my knees like a bullock felled by a poleaxe, and had a scorching pain in my left foot. Elzevir looked back. 'What, have they hit thee too?' he said, and ran and picked me up like a child. And then there is another flash and fut, fut, in the turf; but the shots find no billet this time, and we were lying close against the cliff, panting but safe.

10

The Escape

... How fearful
And dizzy 'tis to cast one's eyes so low!
... I'll look no more
Lest my brain turn – *Shakespeare*

The white chalk was a bulwark between us and the foe; and though one or two of them loosed off their matchlocks, trying to get at us sideways, they could not even see their quarry, and 'twas only shooting at a venture. We were safe. But for how short a time! Safe just for so long as it should please the soldiers not to come down to take us, safe with a discharged pistol in our grasp, and a shot man lying at our feet.

Elzevir was the first to speak: 'Can you stand, John? Is the bone broken?'

'I cannot stand,' I said; 'there is something gone in my leg, and I feel blood running down into my boot.'

He knelt, and rolled down the leg of my stocking; but though he only moved my foot ever so little, it caused me sharp pain, for feeling was coming back after the first numbness of the shot.

'They have broke the leg, though it bleeds little,' Elzevir said. 'We have no time to splice it here, but I will put a kerchief round, and while I wrap it, listen to how we lie, and then choose what we shall do.'

I nodded, biting my lips hard to conceal the pain he gave me, and he went on: 'We have a quarter of an hour before the posse can get down to us. But come they will, and thou canst judge what chance we have to save liberty or life with that carrion lying by us' – and he jerked his thumb at Maskew – 'though I am glad 'twas not my hand that sent him to his reckoning, and therefore do not blame thee if thou didst make me waste a charge in air. So one thing we can do is to wait here until they come, and I can account for a few of them before they shoot me down; but thou canst not fight with a broken leg, and they will take thee alive, and then there is a dance on air at Dorchester jail.'

I felt sick with pain and bitterly cast down to think that I was like to come so soon to such a vile end; so only gave a sigh, wishing heartily that Maskew were not dead, and that my leg were not broke, but that I was back again at the Why Not? or even hearing one of Dr Sherlock's sermons in my aunt's parlour.

Elzevir looked down at me when I sighed, and seeing, I suppose, that I was sorrowful, tried to put a better face on a bad business. 'Forgive me, lad,' he said, 'if I have spoke too roughly. There is yet another way that we may try; and if thou hadst but two whole legs, I would have tried it, but now 'tis little short of madness. And yet, if thou fear'st not, I will still try it. Just at the end of this flat ledge, farthest from where the bridlepath leads down, but not a hundred yards from where we stand, there is a sheep track leading up the cliff. It starts where the undercliff dies back again into the chalk face, and climbs by slants and elbow-turns up to the top. The shepherds call it the Zigzag, and even sheep lose their footing on it; and of men I never heard but one had climbed it, and that was lander Jordan, when the Excise was on his heels, half a century back. But he that tries it stakes all on head and foot, and a wounded bird like thee may not dare that flight. Yet, if thou art content to hang thy life upon a hair, I will carry thee some way; and where there is no room to carry, thou must down on hands and knees and trail thy foot.'

It was a desperate chance enough, but came as welcome as a patch of blue through lowering skies. 'Yes,' I said, 'dear Master Elzevir, let us get to it quickly; and if we fall, 'tis better far to die upon the rocks below than to wait here for them to hale us off to jail.' And with that I tried to stand, thinking I might go dot and carry even with a broken leg. But 'twas no use, and down I sank with a groan. Then Elzevir caught me up, holding me in his arms, with my head looking over his back, and made off for the Zigzag. And as we slunk along, close to the cliffside, I saw, between the brambles, Maskew lying with his face turned up to the morning sky. And there was the little red hole in the middle of his forehead, and a thread of blood that welled up from it and trickled off on to the sward.

It was a sight to stagger any man, and would have made me swoon perhaps, but that there was no time, for we were at the end of the undercliff, and Elzevir set me down for a minute, before he buckled to his task. And 'twas a task that might cow the bravest, and when I looked upon the Zigzag, it seemed better to stay where we were and fall into the hands of the posse than set foot on that awful way, and fall upon the rocks below. For the Zigzag started off as a fair enough chalk path, but in a few paces narrowed down till it was but a whiter thread against the grey-white cliff face, and afterwards turned sharply back, crossing a hundred feet direct above our heads. And then I smelt an evil stench, and looking about, saw the blown-out carcass of a rotting sheep lie close at hand.

'Faugh,' said Elzevir, ''tis a poor beast has lost his foothold.'

It was an ill omen enough, and I said as much, beseeching him to make his own way up the Zigzag and leave me where I was, for that they might have mercy on a boy.

'Tush!' he cried; 'it is thy heart that fails thee, and 'tis too late now to change counsel. We have fifteen minutes yet to win or lose with, and if we gain the clifftop in that time we shall have an hour's start, or more, for they will take all that to search the undercliff. And Maskew, too, will keep them in check a little, while they try to bring the life back to so good a man. But if we fall, why, we shall fall together, and outwit their cunning. So shut thy eyes, and keep them tight until I bid thee open them.' With that he caught me up again, and I shut my eyes firm, rebuking myself for my faint-heartedness, and not telling him how much my foot hurt me.

In a minute I knew from Elzevir's steps that he had left the turf and was upon the chalk. Now I do not believe that there were half a dozen men beside in England who would have ventured up that path, even free and untrammelled, and not a man in all the world to do it with a full-grown lad in his arms. Yet Elzevir made no bones of it, nor spoke a single word; only he went very slow, and I felt him scuffle with his foot as he set it forward, to make sure he was putting it down firm.

I said nothing, not wishing to distract him from his terrible task, and held my breath, when I could, so that I might lie quieter in his arms. Thus he went on for a time that seemed without end, and yet was really but a minute or two; and by degrees I felt the wind, that we could scarce perceive at all on the undercliff, blow fresher and cold on the cliffside. And then the path grew steeper and steeper, and Elzevir went slower and slower, till at last he spoke:

'John, I am going to stop; but open not thy eyes till I have set thee down and bid thee.'

I did as bidden, and he lowered me gently, setting me on all-fours upon the path; and speaking again:

'The path is too narrow here for me to carry thee, and thou must creep round this corner on thy hands and knees. But have a care to keep thy outer hand near to the inner, and the balance of thy body to the cliff, for there is no room to dance hornpipes here. And hold thy eyes fixed on the chalk wall, looking neither down nor seaward.'

'Twas well he told me what to do, and well I did it; for when I opened my eyes, even without moving them from the cliffside, I saw that the ledge was little more than a foot wide, and that ever so little a lean of the body would dash me on the rocks below. So I crept on, but spent much time that was so precious in travelling those ten yards to take me round the first elbow of the path; for my foot was heavy and gave me fierce pain to drag, though I tried to mask it from Elzevir. And he, forgetting what I suffered, cried out, 'Quicken thy pace, lad, if thou canst, the time is short.' Now so frail is man's temper, that though he was doing more than any ever did to save another's life, and was all I had to trust to in the world; yet because he forgot my pain and bade me quicken, my choler rose, and I nearly gave him back an angry word, but thought better of it and kept it in.

Then he told me to stop, for that the way grew wider and he would pick me up again. But here was another difficulty, for the path was still so narrow and the cliff wall so close that he could not take me up in his arms. So I lay flat on my face, and he stepped over me, setting his foot between my shoulders to do it; and then, while he knelt down upon the path, I climbed up from behind upon him, putting my arms round his neck; and so he bore me 'pickaback'. I shut my eyes firm again, and thus we moved along another spell, mounting still and feeling the wind still freshening.

At length he said that we were come to the last turn of the path, and he must set me down once more. So down upon his knees and hands he went, and I slid off behind, on to the ledge. Both were on all-fours now; Elzevir first and I following. But as I crept along, I relaxed care for a moment, and my eyes wandered from the cliffside and looked down. And far below I saw the blue sea twinkling like a dazzling mirror, and the gulls wheeling about the sheer chalk wall, and then I thought of that bloated carcass of a sheep that had fallen from this very spot perhaps, and in an instant felt a sickening qualm and swimming of the brain, and knew that I was giddy and must fall.

Then I called out to Elzevir, and he, guessing what had come over me, cries to turn upon my side, and press my belly to the cliff. And how he did it in such a narrow strait I know not; but he turned round, and lying down himself, thrust his hand firmly in my back, pressing me closer to the cliff. Yet it was none too soon, for if he had not held me tight, I should have flung myself down in sheer despair to get quit of that dreadful sickness.

'Keep thine eyes shut, John,' he said, 'and count up numbers loud to me, that I may know thou art not turning faint.' So I gave out, 'One, two, three,' and while I went on counting, heard him repeating to himself, though his words seemed thin and far off: 'We must have taken ten minutes to get here, and in five more they will be on the undercliff; and if we ever reach the top, who knows but they have left a guard! No, no, they will not leave a guard, for not a man knows of the Zigzag; and, if they knew, they would not guess that we should try it. We have but fifty yards to go to win, and now this cursed giddy fit has come upon the child, and he will fall and drag me with him; or they will see us from below, and pick us off like sitting guillemots against the cliff face.'

So he talked to himself, and all the while I would have given a world to pluck up heart and creep on farther; yet could not, for the deadly sweating fear that had hold of me. Thus I lay with my face to the cliff, and Elzevir pushing firmly in my back; and the thing that frightened me most was that there was nothing at all for the hand to take hold of, for had there been a piece of string, or even a thread of cotton, stretched along to give a semblance of support, I think I could have done it; but there was only the cliff wall, sheer and white, against that narrowest way, with never cranny to put a finger into. The wind was blowing in fresh puffs, and though I did not open my eyes, I knew that it was moving the little tufts of bent grass, and the chiding cries of the gulls seemed to invite me to be done with fear and pain and broken leg, and fling myself off on to the rocks below.

Then Elzevir spoke. 'John,' he said, 'there is no time to play the woman; another minute of this and we are lost. Pluck up thy courage, keep thy eyes to the cliff, and forward.'

Yet I could not, but answered: 'I cannot, I cannot; if I open my eyes, or move hand or foot, I shall fall on the rocks below.'

He waited a second, and then said: 'Nay, move thou must, and 'tis better to risk falling now, than fall for certain with another bullet in thee later on.' And with that he shifted his hand from my back and fixed it in my coat collar, moving backwards himself, and setting to drag me after him.

Now, I was so besotted with fright that I would not budge an inch, fearing to fall over if I opened my eyes. And Elzevir, for all he was so strong, could not pull a helpless lump backwards up that path. So he gave it up, leaving hold on me with a groan, and at that moment there rose from the undercliff, below a sound of voices and shouting.

'Zounds, they are down already!' cried Elzevir, 'and have found Maskew's body; it is all up; another minute and they will see us.'

But so strange is the force of mind on body, and the power of a greater to master a lesser fear, that when I heard those voices from below, all fright of falling left me in a moment, and I could open my eyes without a trace of giddiness. So I began to move forward again on hands and knees. And Elzevir, seeing me, thought for a moment I had gone mad, and was dragging myself over the cliff;

but then saw how it was, and moved backwards himself before me, saying in a low voice, 'Brave lad! Once creep round this turn, and I will pick thee up again. There is but fifty yards to go, and we shall foil these devils yet!'

Then we heard the voices again, but farther off, and not so loud; and knew that our pursuers had left the under-cliff and turned down on to the beach, thinking that we were hiding by the sea.

Five minutes later Elzevir stepped on to the clifftop, with me upon his back.

'We have made something of this throw,' he said, 'and are safe for another hour, though I thought thy giddy head had ruined us.'

Then he put me gently upon the springy turf, and lay down himself upon his back, stretching his arms out straight on either side, and breathing hard to recover from the task he had performed.

The day was still young, and far below us was stretched the moving floor of the Channel, with a silver-grey film of night mists not yet lifted in the offing. A hummocky up-and-down line of cliffs, all projections, dents, bays, and hollows, trended southward till it ended in the great bluff of St Alban's Head, ten miles away. The cliff face was gleaming white, the sea tawny inshore, but purest blue outside, with the straight sunpath across it, spangled and gleaming like a mackerel's back.

The relief of being once more on firm ground, and the exultation of an escape from immediate danger, removed my pain and made me forget that my leg was broken. So I lay for a moment basking in the sun; and the wind, which a few minutes before threatened to blow me from that narrow ledge, seemed now but the gentlest of breezes, fresh with the breath of the kindly sea. But this was only for a moment, for the anguish came back and grew apace, and I fell to thinking dismally of the plight we were in. How things had been against us in these last days! First there was losing the Why Not? and that was bad enough; second, there was the being known by the Excise for smugglers, and perhaps for murderers; third and last, there was the breaking of my leg, which made escape so difficult. But, most of all, there came before my eyes that grey face turned up against the morning sun, and I thought of all it meant for Grace, and would have given my own life to call back that of our worst enemy.

Then Elzevir sat up, stretching himself like one waking out of sleep, and said: 'We must be gone. They will not be back for some time yet, and, when they come, will not think to search closely for us hereabouts; but that we cannot risk, and must get clear away. This leg of thine will keep us tied for weeks, and we must find some place where we can lie hid, and tend it. Now, I know such a hiding-hole in Purbeck, which they call Joseph's Pit, and thither we must go; but it will take all the day to get there, for it is seven miles off, and I am older than I was, and thou too heavy a babe to carry over lightly.'

I did not know the pit he spoke of, but was glad to hear of some place, however far off, where I could lie still and get ease from the pain. And so he took me in his arms again and started off across the fields.

I need not tell of that weary journey, and indeed could not, if I wished; for the pain went to my head and filled me with such a drowsy anguish that I knew nothing except when some unlooked-for movement gave me a sharper twinge, and made me cry out. At first Elzevir walked briskly, but as the day wore on went slower, and was fain more than once to put me down and rest, till at last he could only carry me a hundred yards at a time. It was after noon, for the sun was past the meridian, and very hot for the time of year, when the face of the country began to change; and instead of the short sward of the open down, sprinkled with tiny white snail-shells, the ground was brashy with flat stones, and divided up into tillage fields. It was a bleak wide-bitten place enough, looking as if 'twould never pay for turning, and instead of hedges there were dreary walls built of dry stone without mortar. Behind one of these walls, broken down in places, but held together with straggling ivy, and buttressed here and there with a bramble bush, Elzevir put me down at length and said, 'I am beat, and can carry thee no farther for this present, though there is not now much farther to go. We have passed Purbeck Gates, and these walls will screen us from prying eyes if any chance comer pass along the down. And as for the soldiers, they are not like to come this way so soon, and if they come I cannot help it; for weariness and the sun's heat have made my feet like lead. A score of years ago I would have laughed at such a task, but now 'tis different, and I must take a little sleep and rest till the air is cooler. So sit thee here and lean thy shoulder up against the wall, and thus thou canst look through this broken place and watch both ways. Then, if thou see aught moving, wake me up. I wish I had a thimbleful of powder to make this whistle sound' – and he took Maskew's silver-butted pistol again from his bosom, and handled it lovingly – ''tis like my evil luck to carry firearms thirty years, and leave them at home at a pinch like this.' With that he flung himself down where there was a narrow shadow close against the bottom of the wall, and in a minute I knew from his heavy breathing that he was asleep.

The wind had freshened much, and was blowing strong from the west; and now that I was under the lee of the wall I began to perceive that drowsiness creeping upon me which overtakes a man who has been tousled for an hour or two by the wind, and gets at length into shelter. Moreover, though I was not tired by grievous toil like Elzevir, I had passed a night without sleep, and felt besides the weariness of pain to lull me to slumber. So it was, that before a quarter of an hour was past, I had much ado to keep awake, for all I knew that I was left on guard. Then I sought something to fix my thoughts, and looking on that side of the wall where the sward was, fell to counting the molehills that were cast up in numbers thereabout. And when I had exhausted them, and reckoned up thirty little heaps of dry and powdery brown earth, that lay at random on the green turf, I turned my eyes to the tillage field on the other side of the wall, and saw the inch-high blades of corn coming up between the stones. Then I fell to counting the blades, feeling glad to have discovered a reckoning that would not be exhausted at thirty, but would go on for millions, and millions, and millions; and before I had reached ten in so heroic a numeration was fast asleep.

A sharp noise woke me with a start that set the pain tingling in my leg, and though I could see nothing, I knew that a shot had been fired very near us. I was for waking Elzevir, but he was already full awake, and put a finger on his lip to show I should not speak. Then he crept a few paces down the wall to where an ivy bush overtopped it, enough for him to look through the leaves without being seen. He dropped down again with a look of relief, and said, ''Tis but a lad scaring rooks with a blunderbuss; we will not stir unless he makes this way.'

A minute later he said: 'The boy is coming straight for the wall; we shall have to show ourselves'; and while he spoke there was a rattle of falling stones, where the boy was partly climbing and partly pulling down the dry wall, and so Elzevir stood up. The boy looked frightened, and made as if he would run off, but Elzevir passed him the time of day in a civil voice, and he stopped and gave it back.

'What are you doing here, son?' Block asked.

'Scaring rooks for Farmer Topp,' was the answer.

'Have you got a charge of powder to spare?' said Elzevir, showing his pistol. 'I want to get a rabbit in the gorse for supper, and have dropped my flask. Maybe you've seen a flask in walking through the furrows?'

He whispered to me to lie still, so that it might not be perceived my leg was broken; and the boy replied:

'No, I have seen no flask; but very like have not come the same way as you, being sent out here from Lowermoigne; and as for powder, I have little left, and must save that for the rooks, or shall get a beating for my pains.'

'Come,' said Elzevir, 'give me a charge or two, and there is half a crown for thee.' And he took the coin out of his pocket and showed it.

The boy's eyes twinkled, and so would mine at so valuable a piece, and he took out from his pocket a battered cowskin flask. 'Give flask and all,' said Elzevir, 'and thou shalt have a crown,' and he showed him the larger coin.

No time was wasted in words; Elzevir had the flask in his pocket, and the boy was biting the crown.

'What shot have you?' said Elzevir.

'What! have you dropped your shot flask too?' asked the boy. And his voice had something of surprise in it.

'Nay, but my shot are over small; if thou hast a slug or two, I would take them.'

'I have a dozen goose-slugs, No. 2,' said the boy; 'but thou must pay a shilling for them. My master says I never am to use them, except I see a swan or buzzard, or something fit to cook, come over: I shall get a sound beating for my pains, and to be beat is worth a shilling.'

'If thou art beat, be beat for something more,' says Elzevir the tempter. 'Give me that firelock that thou carriest, and take a guinea.'

'Nay, I know not,' says the boy; 'there are queer tales afloat at Lowermoigne, how that a posse met the contraband this morning, and shots were fired, and a gauger got an overdose of lead – maybe of goose-slugs No. 2. The smugglers got off clear, but they say the hue and cry is up already, and that a head price will be fixed of twenty pound. So if I sell you a fowling piece, maybe I shall do wrong, and have the government upon me as well as my master.' The surprise in his voice was changed to suspicion, for while he spoke I saw that his eye had fallen on my foot, though I tried to keep it in the shadow; and that he saw the boot clotted with blood, and the kerchief tied round my leg.

''Tis for that very reason,' says Elzevir, 'that I want the firelock. These smugglers are roaming loose, and a pistol is a poor thing to stop such wicked rascals on a lone hill-side. Come, come, *thou* dost not want a piece to guard thee; they will not hurt a boy.'

He had the guinea between his finger and thumb, and the gleam of the gold was too strong to be withstood. So we gained a sorry matchlock, slugs, and powder, and the boy walked off over the furrow, whistling with his hand in his pocket, and a guinea and a crown piece in his hand.

His whistle sounded innocent enough, yet I mistrusted him, having caught his eye when he was looking at my bloody foot; and so I said as much to Elzevir, who only laughed, saying the boy was simple and harmless. But from where I sat I could peep out through the brambles in the open gap, and see without being seen – and there was my young gentleman walking carelessly enough, and whistling like any bird so long as Elzevir's head was above the wall; but when Elzevir sat down, the boy gave a careful look round, and seeing no one watching any more, dropped his whistling and made off as fast as heels would carry him. Then I knew that he had guessed who we were, and was off to warn the hue and cry; but before Elzevir was on his feet again, the boy was out of sight, over the hill brow.

'Let us move on,' said Block; ''tis but a little distance now to go, and the heat is past already. We must have slept three hours or more, for thou art but a sorry watchman, John. 'Tis when the sentry sleeps that the enemy laughs, and for thee the posse might have had us both like daylight owls.'

With that he took me on his back and made off with a lusty stride, keeping as much as possible under the brow of the hill and in the shelter of the walls. We had slept longer than we thought, for the sun was westering fast, and though the rest had refreshed me, my leg had grown stiff, and hurt the more in dangling when we started again. Elzevir was still walking strongly, in spite of the heavy burden he carried, and in less than half an hour I knew, though I had never been there before, we were in the land of the old marble quarries at the back of Anvil Point.

Although I knew little of these quarries, and certainly was in evil plight to take note of anything at that time, yet afterwards I learned much about them. Out of such excavations comes that black Purbeck marble which you see in old churches in our country, and I am told in other parts of England as well. And the way of making a marble quarry is to sink a tunnel, slanting very steeply down into the earth, like a well turned askew, till you reach fifty, seventy, or perhaps one hundred feet deep. Then from the bottom of this shaft there spread out narrow passages or tunnels, mostly six feet high, but sometimes only three or four, and in these the marble is dug. These quarries were made by men centuries ago, some say by the Romans themselves; and though some are still worked in other parts of Purbeck, those at the back of Anvil Point have been disused beyond the memory of man.

We had left the stony village fields, and the face of the country was covered once more with the closest sward, which was just putting on the brighter green of spring. This turf was not smooth, but hummocky, for under it lay heaps of worthless stone and marble drawn out of the quarries ages ago, which the green vestment had covered for the most part, though it left sometimes a little patch of broken rubble peering out at the top of a mound. There were many tumbledown walls and low gables left of the cottages of the old quarrymen; grass-covered ridges marked out the little garden-folds, and here and there still stood a forlorn gooseberry bush, or a stunted plum or apple tree with its branches all swept eastward by the up-Channel gales. As for the quarry shafts themselves, they too were covered round the tips with the green turf, and down them led a narrow flight of steep-cut steps, with a slide of soapstone at the side, on which the marble blocks were once hauled up by wooden winches. Down these steps no feet ever walked now, for not only were suffocating gases said to beset the bottom of the shafts, but men would have it that in the narrow passages below lurked evil spirits and demons. One who ought to know about such things, told me that when St Aldhelm first came to Purbeck, he bound the old pagan gods under a ban deep in these passages, but that the worst of all the crew was a certain demon called the Mandrive, who watched over the best of the black marble. And that was why such marble might only be used in churches or for graves, for if it were not for this holy purpose, the Mandrive would have power to strangle the man that hewed it.

It was by the side of one of these old shafts that Elzevir laid me down at last. The light was very low, showing all the little unevennesses of the turf; and the sward crept over the edges of the hole, and every crack and crevice in steps and slide was green with ferns. The green ferns shrouded the walls of the hole, and ruddy brown brambles overgrew the steps, till all was lost in the gloom that hung at the bottom of the pit.

Elzevir drew a deep breath or two of the cool evening air, like a man who has come through a difficult trial.

'There,' he said, 'this is Joseph's Pit, and here we must lie hid until thy foot is sound again. Once get to the bottom safe, and we can laugh at posse, and hue and cry, and at the king's crown itself. They cannot search all the quarries, and are not like to search any of them, for they are cowards at the best, and hang much on tales of the Mandrive. Ay, and such tales are true enough, for there lurk gases at the bottom of most of the shafts, like devils to strangle any that go down. And if they do come down this Joseph's Pit, we still have nineteen chances in a score they cannot thread the workings. But last, if they come down, and thread the path, there is this pistol and a rusty matchlock; and before they come to where we lie, we can hold the troop at bay and sell our lives so dear they will not care to buy them.'

We waited a few minutes, and then he took me in his arms and began to descend the steps, back first, as one goes down a hatchway. The sun was setting in a heavy bank of clouds just as we began to go down, and I could not help remembering how I had seen it set over peaceful Moonfleet only twenty-four hours ago; and how far off we were now, and how long it was likely to be before I saw that dear village and Grace again.

The stairs were still sharp cut and little worn, but Elzevir paid great care to his feet, lest he should slip on the ferns and mosses with which they were overgrown. When we reached the brambles he met them with his back, and though I heard the thorns tearing in his coat, he shoved them aside with his broad shoulders, and screened my dangling leg from getting caught. Thus he came safe without stumble to the bottom of the pit.

When we got there all was dark, but he stepped off into a narrow opening on the right hand, and walked on as if he knew the way. I could see nothing, but perceived that we were passing through endless galleries cut in the solid rock, high enough, for the most part, to allow of walking upright, but sometimes so low as to force him to bend down and carry me in a very constrained attitude. Only twice did he set me down at a turning, while he took out his tinderbox and lit a match; but at length the darkness became less dark, and I saw that we were in a large cave or room, into which the light came through some opening at the far end. At the same time I felt a colder breath and fresh salt smell in the air that told me we were very near the sea.

11

The Sea Cave

The dull loneness, the black shade,
That these hanging vaults have made:
The strange music of the waves
Beating on these hollow caves – *Wither*

He set me down in one corner, where was some loose dry silver sand upon the floor, which others had perhaps used for a resting place before. 'Thou must lie here for a month or two, lad,' he said; ''tis a mean bed, but I have known many worse, and will get straw tomorrow if I can, to better it.'

I had eaten nothing all day, nor had Elzevir, yet I felt no hunger, only a giddiness and burning thirst like that which came upon me when I was shut in the Mohune vault. So 'twas very music to me to hear a pat and splash of water dropping from the roof into a little pool upon the floor, and Elzevir made a cup out of my hat and gave a full drink of it that was icy-cool and more delicious than any smuggled wine of France.

And after that I knew little that happened for ten days or more, for fever had hold of me, and as I learned afterwards, I talked wild and could scarce be restrained from jumping up and loosing the bindings that Elzevir had put upon my leg. And all that time he nursed me as tenderly as any mother could her child, and never left the cave except when he was forced to seek food. But after the fever passed it left me very thin, as I could see from hands and arms, and weaker than a baby; and I used to lie the whole day, not thinking much, nor troubling about anything, but eating what was given me and drawing a quiet pleasure from the knowledge that strength was gradually returning. Elzevir had found a battered sea chest up on Peveril Point, and from the side of it made splints to set my leg – using his own shirt for bandages. The sand bed too was made more soft and easy with some armfuls of straw, and in one corner of the cave was a little pile of driftwood and an iron cooking pot. And all these things had Elzevir got by foraging of nights, using great care that none should see him, and taking only what would not be much missed or thought about; but soon he contrived to give Ratsey word of where we were, and after that the sexton fended for us. There were none even of the landers knew what was become of us, save only Ratsey; and he never came down the quarry, but would leave what he brought in one of the ruined cottages a half-mile from the shaft. And all the while there was strict search being made for us, and mounted excisemen scouring the country; for though at first the posse took back Maskew's dead body and said we must have fallen over the cliff, for there was nothing to be found of us, yet afterwards a farm boy brought a tale of how he had come suddenly on men lurking under a wall, and how one had a bloody foot and leg, and how the other sprung upon him and after a fierce struggle wrenched his master's rook-piece from his hands, rifled his pocket of a powder horn, and made off with them like a hare towards Corfe. And as to Maskew, some of the soldiers said that Elzevir had shot him, and others that he died by misadventure, being killed by a stray bullet of one of his own men on the hilltop; but for all that they put a head price on Elzevir of £50, and £20 for me, so we had reason to lie close. It must have been Maskew that listened that night at the door when Elzevir told me the hour at which the cargo was to be run; for the posse had been ordered to be at Hoar Head at four in the morning. So all the gang would have been taken had it not been for the Gulder making earlier, and the soldiers being delayed by tippling at the Lobster.

All this Elzevir learned from Ratsey and told me to pass the time, though in truth I had as lief not heard it, for 'tis no pleasant thing to see one's head wrote down so low as £20. And what I wanted most to know, namely how Grace fared and how she took the bad news of her father's death, I could not hear, for Elzevir said nothing, and I was shy to ask him.

Now when I came entirely to myself, and was able to take stock of things, I found that the place in which I lay was a cave some eight yards square and three in height, whose straight-cut walls showed that men had once hewed stone therefrom. On one side was that passage through which we had come in, and on the other opened a sort of door which gave on to a stone ledge eight fathoms above high-water mark. For the cave was cut out just inside that iron cliff face which lies between St Alban's Head and Swanage. But the cliffs here are different from those on the other side of the Head, being neither so high as Hoar Head nor of chalk, but standing for the most part only an hundred or an hundred and fifty feet above the sea, and showing towards it a stern face of solid rock. But though they rise not so high above the water, they go down a long way below it; so that there is fifty fathom right up to the cliff, and many a good craft out of reckoning in fog, or on a pitch-dark night, has run full against that frowning wall, and perished, ship and crew, without a soul to hear their cries. Yet, though the rock looks hard as adamant, the eternal washing of the wave has worn it out below, and even with the slightest swell there is a dull and distant booming of the surge in those cavernous deeps; and when the wind blows fresh, each roller smites the cliff like a thunderclap, till even the living rock trembles again.

It was on a ledge of that rock face that our cave opened, and sometimes on a fine day Elzevir would carry me out thither, so that I might sun myself and see all the moving Channel without myself being seen. For this ledge was carved out something like a balcony, so that when the quarry was in working they could lower the stone by pulleys to boats lying underneath, and perhaps haul up a keg or two by the way of ballast, as might be guessed by the stanchions still rusting in the rock.

Such was this gallery; and as for the inside of the cave, 'twas a great empty room, with a white floor made up of broken stone dust trodden hard of old till one would say it was plaster; and dry, without those sweaty damps so often seen in such places – save only in one corner a land-spring dropped from the roof trickling down over spiky rock icicles, and falling into a little hollow in the floor. This basin had been scooped out of set purpose, with a gutter seaward for the overflow, and round it and on the wet patch of the roof above grew a garden of ferns and other clinging plants.

The weeks moved on until we were in the middle of May, when even the nights were no longer cold, as the sun gathered power. And with the warmer days my strength too increased, and though I dared not yet stand, my leg had ceased to pain me, except for some sharp twinges now and then, which Elzevir said were caused by the bone setting. And then he would put a poultice made of grass upon the place, and once walked almost as far as Chaldron to pluck sorrel for a soothing mash.

Now though he had gone out and in so many times in safety, yet I was always ill at ease when he was away, lest he might fall into some ambush and never come back. Nor was it any thought of what would come to me if he were caught that grieved me, but only care for him; for I had come to lean in everything upon this grim and grizzled giant, and love him like a father. So when he was away I took to reading to beguile my thoughts; but found little choice of matter, having only my aunt's red prayer book that I thrust into my bosom the afternoon that I left Moonfleet, and Blackbeard's locket. For that locket hung always round my neck; and I often had the parchment out and read it; not that I did not know it now by heart, but because reading it seemed to bring Grace to my thoughts, for the last time I had read it was when I saw her in the manor woods.

Elzevir and I had often talked over what was to be done when my leg should be sound again, and resolved to take passage to St Malo in the *Bonaventure*, and there lie hid till the pursuit against us should have ceased. For though 'twas wartime, French and English were as brothers in the contraband, and the shippers would give us bit and sup, and glad to, as long as we had need of them. But of this I need not say more, because 'twas but a project, which other events came in to overturn.

Yet 'twas this very errand, namely, to fix with the *Bonaventure*'s men the time to take us over to the other side, that Elzevir had gone out, on the day of which I shall now speak. He was to go to Poole, and left our cave in the afternoon, thinking it safe to keep along the cliff edge even in the daylight, and to strike across country when dusk came on. The wind had blown fresh all the morning from south-west, and after Elzevir had left, strengthened to a gale. My leg was now so strong that I could walk across the cave with the help of a stout blackthorn that Elzevir had cut me: and so I went out that afternoon on to the ledge to watch the growing sea. There I sat down, with my back against a protecting rock, in such a place that I could see up-Channel and yet shelter from the rushing wind. The sky was overcast, and the long wall of rock showed grey with orange-brown patches and a darker line of seaweed at the base like the under strake of a boat's belly, for the tide was but beginning to make. There was a mist, half fog, half spray, scudding before the wind, and through it I could see the white-backed rollers lifting over Peveril Point; while all along the cliff-face the seabirds thronged the ledges, and sat huddled in snowy lines, knowing the mischief that was brewing in the elements.

It was a melancholy scene, and bred melancholy in my heart; and about sundown the wind southed a point or two, setting the sea more against the cliff, so that the spray began to fly even over my ledge and drove me back into the cave. The night came on much sooner than usual, and before long I was lying on my straw bed in perfect darkness. The wind had gone still more to south, and was screaming through the opening of the cave; the caverns down below bellowed and rumbled; every now and then a giant roller struck the rock such a blow as made the cave tremble, and then a second later there would fall, splattering on the ledge outside, the heavy spray that had been lifted by the impact.

I have said that I was melancholy; but worse followed, for I grew timid, and fearful of the wild night, and the loneliness, and the darkness. And all sorts of evil tales came to my mind, and I thought much of baleful heathen gods that St Aldhelm had banished to these underground cellars, and of the Mandrive who leapt on people in the dark and strangled them. And then fancy played another trick on me, and I seemed to see a man lying on the cave floor with a drawn white face upturned, and a red hole in the forehead; and at last could bear the dark no longer, but got up with my lame leg and groped round till I found a candle, for we had two or three in store. 'Twas only with much ado I got it lit and set up in the corner of the cave, and then I sat down close by trying to screen it with my coat. But do what I would the wind came gusting round the corner, blowing the flame to one side, and making the candle gutter as another candle guttered on that black day at the Why Not? And so thought whisked round till I saw Maskew's face wearing a look of evil triumph, when the pin fell at the auction, and again his face grew deadly pale, and there was the bullet mark on his brow.

Surely there were evil spirits in this place to lead my thoughts so much astray, and then there came to my mind that locket on my neck, which men had once hung round Blackbeard's to scare evil spirits from his tomb. If it could frighten them from him, might it not rout them now, and make them fly from me? And with that thought I took the parchment out, and opening it before the flickering light, although I knew all, word for word, conned it over again, and read it out aloud. It was a relief to hear a human voice, even though 'twas nothing but my own, and I took to shouting the words, having much ado even so to make them heard for the raging of the storm:

'"The days of our age are threescore years and ten; and though men be so strong that they come to fourscore years, yet is their strength then but labour and sorrow, so soon passeth it away, and we are gone."

'"And as for me, my feet are almost . . ."'

At the 'almost' I stopped, being brought up suddenly with a fierce beat of blood through my veins, and a jump fit to burst them, for I had heard a scuffling noise in the passage that led to the cave, as if someone had stumbled against a loose stone in the dark. I did not know then, but have learned since, that where there is a loud noise, such as the roaring of a cascade, the churning of a mill, or, as here, the rage and bluster of a storm – if there arise some different sound, even though it be as slight as the whistle of a bird, 'twill strike the ear clear above the general din. And so it was this night, for I caught that stumbling tread even when the gale blew loudest, and sat motionless and breathless, in my eagerness of listening, and then the gale lulled an instant, and I heard the slow beat of footsteps as of one groping his way down the passage in the dark. I knew it was not Elzevir, for first he could not be back from Poole for many hours yet, and second, he always whistled in a certain way to show 'twas he coming and gave besides a password; yet, if not Elzevir, who could it be? I blew out the light, for I did not want to guide the aim of some unknown marksman shooting at me from the dark; and then I thought of that gaunt strangler that sprang on marble workers in the gloom; yet it could not be the Mandrive, for surely he would know his own passages better than to stumble in them in the dark. It was more likely to be one of the hue and cry who had smelt us out, and hoped perhaps to be able to reconnoitre without being perceived on so awful a night. Whenever Elzevir went out foraging, he carried with him that silver-butted pistol which had once been Maskew's, but left behind the old rook-piece. We had plenty of powder and slugs now, having obtained a store of both from Ratsey, and Elzevir had bid me keep the matchlock charged, and use it or not after my own judgement, if any came to the cave; but gave as his counsel that it was better to die fighting than to swing at Dorchester, for that we should most certainly do if taken. We had agreed, moreover, on a password, which was 'Prosper the *Bonaventure*', so that I might challenge betimes any that I heard coming, and if they gave not back this countersign might know it was not Elzevir.

So now I reached out for the piece, which lay beside me on the floor, and scrambled to my feet; lifting the deckle in the darkness, and feeling with my fingers in the pan to see 'twas full of powder.

The lull in the storm still lasted, and I heard the footsteps advancing, though with uncertain slowness, and once after a heavy stumble I thought I caught a muttered oath, as if someone had struck his foot against a stone.

Then I shouted out clear in the darkness a 'Who goes there?' that rang again through the stone roofs. The footsteps stopped, but there was no answer. 'Who goes there?' I repeated. 'Answer, or I fire.'

'Prosper the *Bonaventure*,' came back out of the darkness, and I knew that I was safe. 'The devil take thee for a hot-blooded young bantam to shoot thy best friend with powder and ball, that he was fool enough to give thee'; and by this time I had guessed 'twas Master Ratsey, and recognized his voice. 'I would have let thee hear soon enough that 'twas I, if I had known I was so near thy lair; but 'tis more than a man's life is worth to creep down mole-holes in the dark, and on a night like this. And why I could not get out the gibberish about the *Bonaventure* sooner, was because I matched my shin to break a stone, and lost the wager and my breath together. And when my wind returned 'tis very like that I was trapped into an oath, which is sad enough for me, who am sexton, and so to say in small orders of the Church of England as by law established.'

By the time I had put down the gun and coaxed the candle again to light, Ratsey stepped into the cave. He wore a sou'wester, and was dripping with wet, but seemed glad to see me and shook me by the hand. He was welcome enough to me also, for he banished the dreadful loneliness, and his coming was a bit out of my old pleasant life that lay so far away, and seemed to bring me once more within reach of some that were dearest.

12

A Funeral

How he lies in his rights of a man!
Death has done all death can – *Browning*

We stood for a moment holding one another's hands; then Ratsey spoke. 'John, these two months have changed thee from boy to man. Thou wast a child when I turned that morning as we went up Hoar Head with the packhorses, and looked back on thee and Elzevir below, and Maskew lying on the ground. 'Twas a sorry business, and has broken up the finest gang that ever ran a cargo, besides driving thee and Elzevir to hide in caves and dens of the earth. Thou shouldst have come with us that morn; not have stayed behind. The work was too rough for boys: the skipper should have piped the reefing-hands.'

It was true enough, or seemed to me true then, for I felt much cast down; but only said, 'Nay, Master Ratsey, where Master Block stays, there I must stay too, and where he goes I follow.'

Then I sat down upon the bed in the corner, feeling my leg begin to ache; and the storm, which had lulled for a few minutes, came up again all the fiercer with wilder gusts and showers of spray and rain driving into the cave from seaward. So I was scarce sat down when in came a roaring blast, filling even our corner with cold, wet air, that quenched the weakling candle flame.

'God save us, what a night!' Ratsey cried.

'God save poor souls at sea,' said I.

'Amen to that,' says he, 'and would that every Amen I have said had come as truly from my heart. There will be sea enough on Moonfleet beach this night to lift a schooner to the top of it, and launch her down into the fields behind. I had as lief be in the Mohune vault as in this fearsome place, and liefer too, if half the tales men tell are true of faces that may meet one here. For God's sake let us light a fire, for I caught sight of a store of driftwood before that sickly candle went out.'

It was some time before we got a fire alight, and even after the flame had caught well hold, the rush of the wind would every now and again blow the smoke into our eyes, or send a shower of sparks dancing through the cave. But by degrees the logs began to glow clear white, and such a cheerful warmth came out, as was in itself a solace and remedy for man's afflictions.

'Ah!' said Ratsey, 'I was shrammed with wet and cold, and half dead with this baffling wind. It is a blessed thing a fire,' and he unbuttoned his pilot coat, 'and needful now, if ever. My soul is very low, lad, for this place has strange memories for me; and I recollect, forty years ago (when I was just a boy like thee), old lander Jordan's gang, and I among them, were in this very cave on such another night. I was new to the trade then, as thou might be, and could not sleep for noise of wind and sea. And in the small hours of an autumn morning, as I lay here, just where we lie now, I heard such wailing cries above the storm, ay, and such shrieks of women, as made my blood run cold and have not yet forgot them. And so I woke the gang who were all deep asleep as seasoned contrabandiers should be; but though we knew that there were fellow creatures fighting for their lives in the seething flood beneath us, we could not stir hand or foot to save them, for nothing could be seen for rain and spray, and 'twas not till next morning that we learned the *Florida* had foundered just below with every soul on board. Ay, 'tis a queer life, and you and Block are in a queer strait now, and that is what I came to tell you. See here.' And he took out of his pocket an oblong strip of printed paper:

G.R.

Whitehall, 15 May 1758

Whereas it hath been humbly represented to the King that on Friday, the night of the 16th of April last, Thomas Maskew, a Justice of the Peace, was most inhumanly

164

murdered at Hoar Head, a lone place in the Parish of Chaldron, in the County of Dorset, by one ELZEVIR BLOCK and one JOHN TRENCHARD, both of the Parish of Moonfleet, in the aforesaid County: His Majesty, for the better discovering and bringing to Justice these Persons, is pleased to promise His Most Gracious PARDON to any of the Persons concerned therein, except the Persons who actually committed the said Murder; and, as a further Encouragement, a REWARD OF FIFTY POUNDS to any Person who shall furnish such INFORMATION as shall lead to the APPREHENSION of the said ELZEVIR BLOCK, and a REWARD of TWENTY POUNDS to any Person who shall furnish such INFORMATION as shall lead to the APPREHENSION of the said JOHN TRENCHARD. Such INFORMATION to be given to ME, or to the GOVERNOR of HIS MAJESTY'S GAOL in Dorchester.

HOLDERNESSE.

'There – that's the bill,' he said; 'and a vastly fine piece it is, and yet I wish that 'twas played with other actors. Now, in Moonfleet there is none that know your hiding place, and not a man, nor woman either, that would tell if they knew it ten times over. But fifty pounds for Elzevir, and twenty pounds for an empty pumpkin-top like thine, is a fair round sum, and there are vagabonds about this countryside scurvy enough to try to earn it. And some of these have set the excisemen on *my* track, with tales of how it is I that know where you lie hid, and bring you meat and drink. So it is that I cannot stir abroad now, no, not even to the church o' Sundays, without having some rogue lurking at my heels to watch my movements. And that is why I chose such a night to come hither, knowing these knaves like dry skins, but never thinking that the wind would blow like this. I am come to tell Block that 'tis not safe for me to be so much in Purbeck, and that I dare no longer bring food or what not, or these manhounds will scent you out. Your leg is sound again, and 'tis best to be flitting while you may, and there's the *Éperon d'Or*, and Chauvelais to give you welcome on the other side.'

I told him how Elzevir was gone this very night to Poole to settle with the *Bonaventure*, when she should come to take us off; and at that Ratsey seemed pleased. There were many things I wished to learn of him, and especially how Grace did, but felt a shyness, and durst not ask him. And he said no more for a minute, seeming low-hearted and crouching over the fire. So we sat huddled in the corner by the glowing logs, the red light flickering on the cave roof, and showing the lines on Ratsey's face; while the steam rose from his drying clothes. The gale blew as fiercely as ever, but the tide had fallen, and there was not so much spray coming into the cave. Then Ratsey spoke again –

'My heart is very heavy, John, tonight, to think how all the good old times are gone, and how that Master Block can never again go back to Moonfleet. It was as fine a lander's crew as ever stood together, not even excepting Captain Jordan's, and now must all be broken up; for this mess of Maskew's has made the place too hot to hold us, and 'twill be many a long day before another cargo's run on Moonfleet beach. But how to get the liquor out of Mohune's vault I know not; and that reminds me, I have something in my pouches for Elzevir an' thee'; and with that he drew forth either lapel a great wicker-bound flask. He put one to his lips, tilting it and drinking long and deep, and then passed it to me, with a sigh of satisfaction. 'Ah, that has the right smack. Here, take it, child, and warm thy heart; 'tis the true milk of Ararat, and the last thou'lt taste this side the Channel.'

Then I drank too, but lightly, for the good liquor was no stranger to me, though it was only so few months ago that I had tasted it for the first time in the Why Not? and in a minute it tingled in my fingertips. Soon a grateful sense of warmth and comfort stole over me, and our state seemed not so desperate, nor even the night so wild. Ratsey, too, wore a more cheerful air, and the lines in his face were not so deeply marked; the golden, sparkling influence of the flask had loosed his tongue, and he was talking now of what I most wanted to hear.

'Yes, yes, it is a sad break-up, and what will happen to the old Why Not? I cannot tell. None have passed the threshold since you left, only the duchy men came and sealed the doors, making it felony to force them. And even these lawyer chaps know not where the right stands, for Maskew never paid a rent and died before he took possession; and Master Block's term is long expired, and now he is in hiding and an outlaw.

'But I am sorriest for Maskew's girl, who grows thin and pale as any lily. For when the soldiers brought the body back, the men stood at their doors and cursed the clay, and some of the fishwives spat at it; and old Mother Veitch, who kept house for him, swore he had never paid her a penny of wages, and that she was afear'd to stop under the same roof with such an evil corpse. So out she goes from the manor house, leaving that poor child alone in it with her dead father; and there were not wanting some to say it was all a judgement; and called to mind how Elzevir had been once left alone with his dead son at the Why Not? But in the village there was not a man that doubted that 'twas Block had sent Maskew to his account, nor did I doubt it either, till a tale got abroad that he was killed by a stray shot fired by the posse from the cliff. And when they took the hue-and-cry papers to the manor house for his lass, as next of kin, to sign the requisition, she would not set her name to it, saying that Block had never lifted his hand against her father when they met at Moonfleet or on the road, and that she never would believe he was the man to let his anger sleep so long and then attack an enemy in cold blood. And as for thee, she knew thee for a trusty lad, who would not do such things himself, nor yet stand by whilst others did them.'

Now what Ratsey said was sweeter than any music in my ears, and I felt myself a better man, as anyone must of whom a true woman speaks well, and that I must live uprightly to deserve such praise. Then I resolved that come what might I would make my way once more to Moonfleet, before we fled from England, and see Grace; so that I might tell her all that happened about her father's death, saving only that Elzevir had meant himself to put Maskew away; for it was no use to tell her this when she had said that he could never think to do such a thing, and besides, for all I knew, he never did mean to shoot, but only to frighten him. Though I thus resolved, I said nothing of it to Master Ratsey, but only nodded, and he went on –

'Well, seeing there was no one save this poor girl to look to putting Maskew under ground, I must needs take it in hand myself; roughing together a sound coffin and digging as fair a grave for him as could be made for any lord, except that lords have always vaults to sleep in. Then I got Mother Nutting's fish cart to carry the body down, for there was not a man in Moonfleet would lay hand to the coffin to bear it; and off we started down the street, I leading the wall-eyed pony, and the coffin following on the trolley. There was no mourner to see him home except his daughter, and she without a bit of black upon her, for she had no time to get her crapes; and yet she needed none, having grief writ plain enough upon her face.

'When we got to the churchyard, a crowd was gathered there, men and women and children, not only from Moonfleet but from Ringstave and Monkbury. They were not come to mourn, but to make gibes to show how much they hated him, and many of the children had old pots and pans for rough music. Parson Glennie was waiting in the church, and there he waited, for the cart could not pass the gate, and we had no bearers to lift the coffin. Then I looked round to see if there was any that would help to lift, but when I tried to meet a man's eye he looked away, and all I could see was the bitter scowling faces of the women. And all the while the girl stood by the trolley looking on the ground. She had a little kerchief over her head that let the hair fall about her shoulders, and her face was very white, with eyes red and swollen through weeping. But when she knew that all that crowd was there to mock her father, and that there was not a man would raise hand to lift him, she laid her head upon the coffin, hiding her face in her hands, and sobbed bitterly.'

Ratsey stopped for a moment and drank again deep at the flask; and as for me, I still said nothing, feeling a great lump in my throat; and reflecting how hatred and passion have power to turn men to brutes.

'I am a rough man,' Ratsey resumed, 'but tender-like withal, and when I saw her weep, I ran off to the church to tell the parson how it was, and beg him to come out and try if we two could lift the coffin. So out he came just as he was, with surplice on his back and book in hand. But when the men knew what he was come for, and looked upon that tall, fair girl bowed down over her father's coffin, their hearts were moved, and first Sam Tewkesbury stepped out with a sheepish air, and then Garrett, and then four others. So now we had six fine bearers, and 'twas only women that could still look hard and scowling, and even they said no word, and not a boy beat on his pan.

'Then Mr Glennie, seeing he was not wanted for bearer, changed to parson, and strikes up with "I am the resurrection and the life". 'Tis a great text, John, and though I've heard it scores and scores of times, it never sounded sweeter than on that day. For 'twas a fine afternoon, and what with there being no wind, but the sun bright and the sea still and blue, there was a calm on everything that seemed to say "Rest in peace, rest in peace". And was not the spring with us, and the whole land preaching of resurrection, the birds singing, trees and flowers waking from their winter sleep, and cowslips yellow on the very graves? Then surely 'tis a fond thing to push our enmities beyond the grave, and perhaps even *he* was not so bad as we held him, but might have tricked himself into thinking he did right to hunt down the contraband. I know not how it was, but something like this came into my mind, and did perhaps to others, for we

got him under without a sign or word from any that stood there. There was not one sound heard inside the church or out, except Mr Glennie's reading and my amens, and now and then a sob from the poor child. But when 'twas all over, and the coffin safe lowered, up she walks to Sam Tewkesbury saying, through her tears, "I thank you, sir, for your kindness," and holds out her hand. So he took it, looking askew, and afterwards the five other bearers; and then she walked away by herself, and no one moved till she had left the churchyard gate, letting her pass out like a queen.'

'And so she is a queen,' I said, not being able to keep from speaking, for very pride to hear how she had borne herself, and because she had always shown kindness to me. 'So she is, and fairer than any queen to boot.'

Ratsey gave me a questioning look, and I could see a little smile upon his face in the firelight. 'Ay, she is fair enough,' said he, as though reflecting to himself, 'but white and thin. Mayhap she would make a match for thee – if ye were man and woman, and not boy and girl; if she were not rich, and thou not poor and an outlaw; and – if she would have thee.'

It vexed me to hear his banter, and to think how I had let my secret out, so I did not answer, and we sat by the embers for a while without speaking, while the wind still blew through the cave like a funnel.

Ratsey spoke first. 'John, pass me the flask; I can hear voices mounting the cliff of those poor souls of the *Florida*.'

With that he took another heavy pull, and flung a log on the fire, till sparks flew about as in a smithy, and the flame that had slumbered woke again and leapt out white, blue, and green from the salt wood. Now, as the light danced and flickered I saw a piece of parchment lying at Ratsey's feet: and this was none other than the writing out of Blackbeard's locket, which I had been reading when I first heard footsteps in the passage, and had dropped in my alarm of hostile visitors. Ratsey saw it too, and stretched out his hand to pick it up. I would have concealed it if I could, because I had never told him how I had rifled Blackbeard's coffin, and did not want to be questioned as to how I had come by the writing. But to try to stop him getting hold of it would only have spurred his curiosity, and so I said nothing when he took it in his hands.

'What is this, son?' asked he.

'It is only Scripture verses,' I answered, 'which I got some time ago. 'Tis said they are a spell against spirits of evil, and I was reading them to keep off the loneliness of this place, when you came in and made me drop them.'

I was afraid lest he should ask whence I had got them, but he did not, thinking perhaps that my aunt had given them to me. The heat of the flames had curled the parchment a little, and he spread it out on his knee, conning it in the firelight.

''Tis well written,' he said, 'and good verses enough, but he who put them together for a spell knew little how to keep off evil spirits, for this would not keep a flea from a black cat. I could do ten times better myself, being not without some little understanding of such things,' and he nodded seriously; 'and though I never yet met any from the other world, they would not take me unprepared if they should come. For I have spent half my life in graveyard or church, and 'twould be as foolish to move about such places and have no words to meet an evil visitor withal, as to bear money on a lonely road without a pistol. So one day, after Parson Glennie had preached from Habakkuk, how that "the vision is for an appointed time, but at the end it shall speak and not lie: though it tarry, wait for it, because it will surely come, it will not tarry," I talked with him on these matters, and got from him three or four rousing texts such as spectres fear more than a burned child does the fire. I will learn them all to thee some day, but for the moment take this Latin which I got by heart: "*Abite a me in ignem eternum qui paratus est diabolo at angelis ejus.*" Englished it means: "Depart from me into eternal fire prepared for the devil and his angels," but hath at least double that power in Latin. So get that after me by heart, and use it freely if thou art led to think that there are evil presences near, and in such lonely places as this cave.'

I humoured him by doing as he desired; and that the rather because I hoped his thoughts would thus be turned away from the writing; but as soon as I had the spell by rote he turned back to the parchment, saying, 'He was but a poor divine who wrote this, for beside choosing ill-fitting verses, he cannot even give right numbers to them. For see here, "The days of our age are threescore years and ten; and though men be so strong that they come to fourscore years, yet is their strength then but labour and sorrow, so soon passeth it away, and we are gone," and he writes "Psalm 90, 21". Now I have said that psalm with Parson verse and verse about for every sleeper we have laid to rest in churchyard mould for thirty years; and know it hath not twenty verses in it, all told, and this same verse is the clerk's verse and cometh tenth, and yet he calls it twenty-first. I wish I had here a Common Prayer, and I would prove my words.'

He stopped and flung me back the parchment scornfully; but I folded it and slipped it in my pocket, brooding all the while over a strange thought that his last words had brought to me. Nor did I tell him that I had by me my aunt's prayer book, wishing to examine for myself more closely whether he was right, after he should have gone.

'I must be away,' he said at last, 'though loth to leave this good fire and liquor. I would fain wait till Elzevir was back, and fainer till this gale was spent, but it may not be; the nights are short, and I must be out of Purbeck before sunrise. So tell Block what I say, that he and thou must flit; and pass the flask, for I have fifteen miles to walk against the wind, and must keep off these midnight chills.'

He drank again, and then rose to his feet, shaking himself like a dog; and walking briskly across the cave twice or thrice to make sure, as I thought, that the Ararat milk had not confused his steps. Then he shook my hand warmly, and disappeared in the deep shadow of the passage mouth.

The wind was blowing more fitfully than before, and there was some sign of a lull between the gusts. I stood at the opening of the passage, and listened till the echo of Ratsey's footsteps died away, and then returning to the corner, flung more wood on the fire, and lit the candle. After that I took out again the parchment, and also my aunt's red prayer book, and sat down to study them. First I looked out in the book that text about the 'days of our life', and found that it was indeed in the ninetieth psalm, but the tenth verse, just as Ratsey said, and not the twenty-first as it was writ on the parchment. And then I took the second text, and here again the psalm was given correct, but the verse was two, and not six, as my scribe had it. It was just the same with the other three – the number of the psalm was right but the verse wrong. So here was a discovery, for all was painfully written smooth and clean without a blot, and yet in every verse an error. But if the second number did not stand for the verse, what else should it mean? I had scarce formed the question to myself before I had the answer, and knew that it must be the number of the word chosen in each text to make a secret meaning. I was in as great a fever and excitement now as when I found the locket in the Mohune vault, and could scarce count with trembling fingers as far as twenty-one, in the first verse, for hurry and amaze. It was 'fourscore' that the number fell on in the first text, 'feet' in the second, 'deep' in the third, 'well' in the fourth, 'north' in the fifth.

Fourscore – feet – deep – well – north.

There was the cipher read, and what an easy trick! And yet I had not lighted on it all this while, nor ever should have, but for Sexton Ratsey and his burial verse. It was a cunning plan of Blackbeard; but other folk were quite as cunning as he, and here was all his treasure at our feet. I chuckled over that to myself, rubbing my hands, and read it through again:

Fourscore – feet – deep – well – north.

'Twas all so simple, and the word in the fourth verse 'well' and not 'vale' or 'pool' as I had stuck at so often in trying to unriddle it. How was it I had not guessed as much before? And here was something to tell Elzevir when he came back, that the clue was found to the cipher, and the secret out. I would not reveal it all at once, but tease him by making him guess, and at last tell him everything, and we would set to work at once to make ourselves rich men. And then I thought once more of Grace, and how the laugh would be on my side now, for all Master Ratsey's banter about her being rich and me being poor!

Fourscore – feet – deep – well – north.

I read it again, and somehow it was this time a little less clear, and I fell to thinking what it was exactly that I should tell Elzevir, and how we were to get to work to find the treasure. 'Twas hid in a *well* – that was plain enough, but in what well? – and what did 'north' mean? Was it the *north well*, or to *north of the well* – or, was it fourscore feet *north* of the *deep well*? I stared at the verses as if the ink would change colour and show some other sense, and then a veil seemed drawn across the writing, and the meaning to slip away, and be as far as ever from my grasp. *Fourscore – feet – deep – well – north*: and by degrees exulting gladness gave way to bewilderment and disquiet of spirit, and in the gusts of wind I heard Blackbeard himself laughing and mocking me for thinking I had found his treasure. Still I read and re-read it, juggling with the words and turning them about to squeeze new meaning from them.

'Fourscore feet deep *in the north well* – 'fourscore feet deep in the well *to north*' – 'fourscore feet *north of the deep well* – so the words went round and round in my head, till I was tired and giddy, and fell unawares asleep.

It was daylight when I awoke, and the wind had fallen, though I could still hear the thunder of the swell against the rock face down below. The fire was yet burning, and by it sat Elzevir, cooking something in the pot. He looked fresh and keen, like a man risen from a long night's sleep, rather than one who had spent the hours of darkness in struggling against a gale, and must afterwards remain watching because, forsooth, the sentinel sleeps.

He spoke as soon as he saw that I was awake, laughing and saying: 'How goes the night, Watchman? This is the second time that I have caught thee napping, and didst sleep so sound it might have taken a cold pistol's lips against thy forehead to awake thee.'

I was too full of my story even to beg his pardon, but began at once to tell him what had happened; and how, by following the hint that Ratsey dropped, I had made out, as I thought, a secret meaning in these verses. Elzevir heard me patiently, and with more show of interest towards the end; and then took the parchment in his hands, reading it carefully, and checking the errors of numbering by the help of the red prayer book.

'I believe thou art right,' he said at length; 'for why should the figures all be false if there is no hidden trickery in it? If't had been one or two were wrong, I would have said some priest had copied them in error; for priests are thriftless folk, and had as lief set a thing down wrong as right; but with all wrong there is no room for chance. So if he means it, let us see what 'tis he means. First he says 'tis in a well. But what well? And the depth he gives of fourscore feet is over-deep for any well near Moonfleet.'

I was for saying it must be the well at the manor house, but before the words left my mouth, remembered there was no well at the manor at all, for the house was watered by a runnel brook that broke out from the woods above, and jumping down from stone to stone ran through the manor gardens, and emptied itself into the Fleet below.

'And now I come to think on it,' Elzevir went on, ''tis more likely that the well he speaks of was not in these parts at all. For see here, this Blackbeard was a spendthrift, squandering all he had, and would most surely have squandered the jewel too, could he have laid his hands on it. And yet 'tis said he did not, therefore I think he must have stowed it safe in some place where afterwards he could not get at it. For if't had been near Moonfleet, he would have had it up a hundred times. But thou hast often talked of Blackbeard and his end with Parson Glennie; so speak up, lad, and let us hear all that thou know'st of these tales. Maybe 'twill help us to come to some judgement.'

So I told him all that Mr Glennie had told me, how that Colonel John Mohune, whom men called Blackbeard, was a wastrel from his youth, and squandered all his substance in riotous living. Thus being at his last turn, he changed from royalist to rebel, and was set to guard the king in the castle of Carisbrooke. But there he stooped to a bribe, and took from his royal prisoner a splendid diamond of the crown to let him go; then, with the jewel in his pocket, turned traitor again, and showed a file of soldiers into the room where the king was stuck between the window bars, escaping. But no one trusted Blackbeard after that, and so he lost his post, and came back in his age, a broken man, to Moonfleet. There he rusted out his life, but when he neared his end was filled with fear, and sent for a clergyman to give him consolation. And 'twas at the parson's instance that he made a will, and bequeathed the diamond, which was the only thing he had left, to the Mohune almshouses at Moonfleet. These were the very houses that he had robbed and let go to ruin, and they never benefited by his testament, for when it was opened there was the bequest plain enough, but not a word to say where was the jewel. Some said that it was all a mockery, and that Blackbeard never had the jewel; others that the jewel was in his hand when he died, but carried off by some that stood by. But most thought, and handed down the tale, that being taken suddenly, he died before he could reveal the safe place of the jewel; and that in his last throes he struggled hard to speak as if he had some secret to unburden.

All this I told Elzevir, and he listened close as though some of it was new to him. When I was speaking of Blackbeard being at Carisbrooke, he made a little quick move as though to speak, but did not, waiting till I had finished the tale. Then he broke out with: 'John, the diamond is yet at Carisbrooke. I wonder I had not thought of Carisbrooke before you spoke; and there he can get fourscore feet, and twice and thrice fourscore, if he list, and none to stop him. 'Tis Carisbrooke. I have heard of that well from childhood, and once saw it when a boy. It is dug in the castle keep, and goes down fifty fathoms or more into the bowels of the chalk below. It is so deep no man can draw the buckets on a winch, but they must have an ass inside a treadwheel to hoist them up. Now, why this Colonel John Mohune, whom we call Blackbeard, should have chosen a well at all to hide his jewel in, I cannot say; but given he chose a well, 'twas odds he would choose Carisbrooke. 'Tis a known place, and I have heard that people come as far as from London to see the castle and this well.'

He spoke quick and with more fire than I had known him use before, and I felt he was right. It seemed indeed natural enough that if Blackbeard was to hide the diamond in a well, it would be in the well of that very castle where he had earned it so evilly.

'When he says the "well north",' continued Elzevir, ''tis clear he means to take a compass and mark north by needle, and at eighty feet in the well side below that point will lie the treasure. I fixed yesterday with the *Bonaventure*'s men that they should lie underneath this ledge tomorrow sennight, if the sea be smooth, and take us off on the spring tide. At midnight is their hour, and I said eight days on, to give thy leg a week wherewith to strengthen. I thought to make for St Malo, and leave thee at the *Éperon d'Or* with old Chauvelais, where thou couldst learn to patter French until these evil times have blown by. But now, if thou art set to hunt this treasure up, and hast a mind to run thy head into a noose; why, I am not so old but that I too can play the fool, and we will let St Malo be, and make for Carisbrooke. I know the castle; it is not two miles distant from Newport, and at Newport we can lie at the Bugle, which is an inn addicted to the contraband. The king's writ runs but lamely in the Channel Isles and Wight, and if we wear some other kit than this, maybe we shall find Newport as safe as St Malo.'

This was just what I wanted, and so we settled there and then that we would get the *Bonaventure* to land us in the Isle of Wight instead of at St Malo. Since man first walked upon this earth, a tale of buried treasure must have had a master power to stir his blood, and mine was hotly stirred. Even Elzevir, though he did not show it, was moved, I thought, at heart; and we chafed in our cave prison, and those eight days went wearily enough. Yet 'twas not time lost, for every day my leg grew stronger; and like a wolf which I saw once in a cage at Dorchester Fair, I spent hours in marching round the cave to kill the time and put more vigour in my steps. Ratsey did not visit us again, but in spite of what he said, met Elzevir more than once, and got money for him from Dorchester and many other things he needed. It was after meeting Ratsey that Elzevir came back one night, bringing a long whip in one hand, and in the other a bundle which held clothes to mask us in the next scene. There was a carter's smock for him, white and quilted over with needlework, such as carters wear on the Down farms, and for me a smaller one, and hats and leather leggings all to match. We tried them on, and were for all the world carter and carter's boy; and I laughed long to see Elzevir stand there and practise how to crack his whip and cry 'Who-ho' as carters do to horses. And for all he was so grave, there was a smile on his face too, and he showed me how to twist a wisp of straw out of the bed to bind above my ankles at the bottom of the leggings. He had cut off his beard, and yet lost nothing of his looks; for his jaw and deep chin showed firm and powerful. And as for me, we made a broth of young walnut leaves and twigs, and tanned my hands and face with it a ruddy brown, so that I looked a different lad.

13
An Interview

No human creature stirred to go or come,
No face looked forth from shut or open casement,
No chimney smoked, there was no sign of home
From parapet to basement – *Hood*

A nd so the days went on, until there came to be but
two nights more before we were to leave our cave.
Now I have said that the delay chafed us, because we were
impatient to get at the treasure; but there was something
else that vexed me and made me more unquiet with every
day that passed. And this was that I had resolved to see
Grace before I left these parts, and yet knew not how to
tell it to Elzevir. But on this evening, seeing the time was
grown so short, I knew that I must speak or drop my
purpose, and so spoke.

We were sitting like the seabirds on the ledge outside
our cave, looking towards St Alban's Head and watching
the last glow of sunset. The evening vapours began to
sweep down-Channel, and Elzevir shrugged his shoulders.

'The night turns chill,' he said, and got up to go back to the cave. So then I thought my time was come, and following him inside said:

'Dear Master Elzevir, you have watched over me all this while and tended me kinder than any father could his son; and 'tis to you I owe my life, and that my leg is strong again. Yet I am restless this night, and beg that you will give me leave to climb the shaft and walk abroad. It is two months and more that I have been in the cave and seen nothing but stone walls, and I would gladly tread once more upon the Down.'

'Say not that I have saved thy life,' Elzevir broke in; ''twas I who brought thy life in danger; and but for me thou mightst even now be lying snug abed at Moonfleet, instead of hiding in the chambers of these rocks. So speak not of that, but if thou hast a mind to air thyself an hour, I see little harm in it. These wayward fancies fall on men as they get better of sickness; and I must go tonight to that ruined house of which I spoke to thee, to fetch a pocket compass Master Ratsey was to put there. So thou canst come with me and smell the night air on the down.'

He had agreed more readily than I looked for, and so I pushed the matter, saying:

'Nay, master, grant me leave to go yet a little farther afield. You know that I was born in Moonfleet, and have been bred there all my life, and love the trees and stream and very stones of it. And I have set my heart on seeing it once more before we leave these parts for good and all. So give me leave to walk along the down and look on Moonfleet but this once, and in this ploughboy guise I shall be safe enough, and will come back to you tomorrow night.'

He looked at me a moment without speaking; and all the while I felt he saw me through and through, and yet he was not angry. But I turned red, and cast my eyes upon the ground, and then he spoke:

'Lad, I have known men risk their lives for many things: for gold, and love, and hate; but never one would play with death that he might see a tree or stream or stones. And when men say they love a place or town, thou mayst be sure 'tis not the place they love but some that live there; or that they loved some in the past, and so would see the spot again to kindle memory withal. Thus when thou speakest of Moonfleet, I may guess that thou hast someone there to see – or hope to see. It cannot be thine aunt, for there is no love lost between ye; and besides, no man ever perilled his life to bid adieu to an aunt. So have no secrets from me, John, but tell me straight, and I will judge whether this second treasure that thou seekest is true gold enough to fling thy life into the scale against it.'

Then I told him all, keeping nothing back, but trying to make him see that there was little danger in my visiting Moonfleet, for none would know me in a carter's dress, and that my knowledge of the place would let me use a hedge or wall or wood for cover; and finally, if I were seen, my leg was now sound, and there were few could beat me in a running match upon the down. So I talked on, not so much in the hope of convincing him as to keep saying something; for I durst not look up, and feared to hear an angry word from him when I should stop. But at last I had spoken all I could, and ceased because I had no more. Yet he did not break out as I had thought, but there was silence; and after a moment I looked up, and saw by his face that his thoughts were wandering. When he spoke there was no anger in his voice, but only something sad.

'Thou art a foolish lad,' he said. 'Yet I was young once myself, and my ways have been too dark to make me wish to darken others, or try to chill young blood. Now thine own life has got a shadow on't already that I have helped to cast, so take the brightness of it while thou mayst, and get thee gone. But for this girl, I know her for a comely lass and good-hearted, and have wondered often how she came to have *him* for her father. I am glad now I have not his blood on my hands; and never would have gone to take it then, for all the evil he had brought on me, but that the lives of every mother's son hung on his life. So make thy mind at ease, and get thee gone and see these streams and trees and stones thou talkest of. Yet if thou'rt shot upon the Down, or taken off to jail, blame thine own folly and not me. And I will walk with thee to Purbeck Gates tonight, and then come back and wait. But if thou art not here again by midnight tomorrow, I shall believe that thou art taken in some snare, and come out to seek thee.'

I took his hand, and thanked him with what words I could that he had let me go, and then got on the smock, putting some bread and meat in my pockets, as I was likely to find little to eat on my journey. It was dark before we left the cave, for there is little dusk with us, and the division between day and night sharper than in more northern parts. Elzevir took me by the hand and led me through the darkness of the workings, telling me where I should stoop, and when the way was uneven. Thus we came to the bottom of the shaft, and looking up through ferns and brambles, I could see the deep blue of the sky overhead, and a great star gazing down full at us. We climbed the steps with the soapstone slide at one side, and then walked on briskly over the springy turf through the hillocks of the covered quarry heaps and the ruins of the deserted cottages.

There was a heavy dew which got through my boots before we had gone half a mile, and though there was no moon, the sky was very clear, and I could see the veil of gossamers spread silvery white over the grass. Neither of us spoke, partly because it was safer not to speak, for the voice carries far in a still night on the Downs; and partly, I think, because the beauty of the starry heaven had taken hold upon us both, filling our hearts with thoughts too big for words. We soon reached that ruined cottage of which Elzevir had spoken, and in what had once been an oven, found the compass safe enough as Ratsey had promised. Then on again over the solitary hills, not speaking ourselves, and neither seeing light in window nor hearing dog stir, until we reached that strange defile which men call the Gates of Purbeck. Here is a natural road nicking the highest summit of the hill, with walls as sharp as if the hand of man had cut them, through which have walked for ages all the few travellers in this lonely place, shepherds and sailors, soldiers and excisemen. And although, as I suppose, no carts have been through it for centuries, there are ruts in the chalk floor as wide and deep as if the carts of giants used it in past times.

So here Elzevir stopped, and drawing from his bosom that silver-butted pistol of which I have spoken, thrust it in my hand. 'Here, take it, child,' he said, 'but use it not till thou art closely pressed, and then if thou *must* shoot, shoot low – it flings.' I took it and gripped his hand, and so we parted, he going back to Purbeck, and I making along the top of the ridge at the back of Hoar Head. It must have been near three when I reached a great grass-grown mound called Culliford Tree, that marks the resting place of some old warrior of the past. The top is planted with a clump of trees that cut the skyline, and there I sat awhile to rest. But not for long, for looking back towards Purbeck, I could see the faint hint of dawn low on the sea line behind St Alban's Head, and so pressed forward knowing I had a full ten miles to cover yet.

Thus I travelled on, and soon came to the first sign of man, namely a flock of lambs being fed with turnips on a summer fallow. The sun was well up now, and flushed all with a rosy glow, showing the sheep and the roots they eat white against the brown earth. Still I saw no shepherd, nor even dog, and about seven o'clock stood safe on Weatherbeech Hill that looks down over Moonfleet.

There at my feet lay the manor woods and the old house, and lower down the white road and the straggling cottages, and farther still the Why Not? and the glassy Fleet, and beyond that the open sea. I cannot say how sad, yet sweet, the sight was: it seemed like the mirage of the desert, of which I had been told – so beautiful, but never to be reached again by me. The air was still, and the blue smoke of the morning wood fires rose straight up, but none from the Why Not? or manor house. The sun was already very hot, and I dropped at once from the hilltop, digging my heels into the brown-burned turf, and keeping as much as might be among the furze champs. So I was soon in the wood, and made straight for the little dell and lay down there, burying myself in the wild rhubarb and burdocks, yet so that I could see the doorway of the manor house over the lip of the hill.

Then I reflected what I was to do, or how I should get to speak with Grace: and thought I would first wait an hour or two, and see whether she came out, and afterwards, if she did not, would go down boldly and knock at the door. This seemed not very dangerous, for it was likely, from what Ratsey had said, that there was no one with her in the house, and if there was it would be but an old woman, to whom I could pass as a stranger in my disguise, and ask my way to some house in the village. So I lay still and munched a piece of bread, and heard the clock in the church tower strike eight and afterwards nine, but saw no one move in the house. The wood was all alive with singing birds, and with the calling of cuckoo and wood pigeon. There were deep patches of green shade and lighter patches of yellow sunlight, in which the iris leaves gleamed with a sheeny white, and a shimmering blue sea of ground ivy spread all through the wood. It struck ten, and as the heat increased the birds sang less and the droning of the bees grew more distinct, and at last I got up, shook myself, smoothed my smock, and making a turn, came out on the road that led to the house.

Though my disguise was good, I fear I made but an indifferent bad ploughboy when walking, and found a difficulty in dealing with my hands, not knowing how ploughboys are wont to carry them. So I came round in front of the house, and gave a rat-tat on the door, while my pulse beat as loud inside of me as ever did the knocker without. The sound ran round the building, and backwards among the walks, and all was silent as before. I waited a minute, and was for knocking again, thinking there might be no one in the house, and then heard a light footstep coming along the corridor, yet durst not look through the window to see who it was in passing, as I might have done, but kept myself close to the door.

The bolts were being drawn, and a girl's voice asked, 'Who is there?' I gave a jump to hear that voice, knowing it well for Grace's, and had a mind to shout out my name. But then I remembered there might be some in the house with her besides, and that I must remain disguised. Moreover, laughing is so mixed with crying in our world, and trifling things with serious, that even in this pass I believe I was secretly pleased to have to play a trick on her, and test whether she would find me out in this dress or not. So I spoke out in our round Dorset speech, such as they talk it out in the vale, saying, 'A poor boy who is out of his way.'

Then she opened one leaf of the door, and asked me whither I would go, looking at me as one might at a stranger and not knowing who it was.

I answered that I was a farm lad who had walked from Purbeck, and sought an inn called the Why Not? kept by one Master Block. When she heard that, she gave a little start, and looked me over again, yet could make nothing of it, but said:

'Good lad, if you will step on to this terrace I can show you the Why Not? inn, but 'tis shut these two months or more, and Master Block away.'

With that she turned towards the terrace, I following, but when we were outside of earshot from the door, I spoke in my own voice, quick but low:

'Grace, it is I, John Trenchard, who am come to say goodbye before I leave these parts, and have much to tell that you would wish to hear. Are there any beside in the house with you?'

Now many girls who had suffered as she had, and were thus surprised, would have screamed, or perhaps swooned, but she did neither, only flushing a little and saying, also quick and low, 'Let us go back to the house; I am alone.'

So we went back, and after the door was bolted, took both hands and stood up face to face in the passage looking into one another's eyes. I was tired with a long walk and sleepless night, and so full of joy to see her again that my head swam and all seemed a sweet dream. Then she squeezed my hands, and I knew 'twas real, and was for kissing her for very love; but she guessed what I would be at, perhaps, and cast my hands loose, drawing back a little, as if to see me better, and saying, 'John, you have grown a man in these two months.' So I did not kiss her.

But if it was true that I was grown a man, it was truer still that she was grown a woman, and as tall as I. And these recent sufferings had taken from her something of light and frolic girlhood, and left her with a manner more staid and sober. She was dressed in black, with longer skirts, and her hair caught up behind; and perhaps it was the mourning frock that made her look pale and thin, as Ratsey said. So while I looked at her, she looked at me, and could not choose but smile to see my carter's smock; and as for my brown face and hands, thought I had been hiding in some country underneath the sun, until I told her of the walnut juice.

Then before we fell to talking, she said it was better we should sit in the garden, for that a woman might come in to help her with the house, and anyway it was safer, so that I might get out at the back in case of need. So she led the way down the corridor and through the living part of the house, and we passed several rooms, and one little parlour lined with shelves and musty books. The blinds were pulled, but let enough light in to show a high-backed horsehair chair that stood at the table. In front of it lay an open volume, and a pair of horn-rimmed spectacles, that I had often seen on Maskew's nose; so I knew it was his study, and that nothing had been moved since last he sat there. Even now I trembled to think in whose house I was, and half expected the old attorney to step in and hale me off to jail; till I remembered how all my trouble had come about, and how I last had seen him with his face turned up against the morning sun.

Thus we came to the garden, where I had never been before. It was a great square, shut in with a brick wall of twelve or fifteen feet, big enough to suit a palace, but then ill kept and sorely overgrown. I could spend long in speaking of that plot; how the flowers and fruit trees, pot-herbs, spice, and simples ran all wild and intermixed. The pink brick walls caught every ray of sun that fell, and that morning there was a hushed, close heat in it, and a warm breath rose from the strawberry beds, for they were then in full bearing. I was glad enough to get out of the sun when Grace led the way into a walk of medlar trees and quinces, where the boughs interlaced and formed an alley to a brick summer house. This summer house stands in the angle of the south wall, and by it two fig trees, whose tops you can see from the outside. They are well known for the biggest and the earliest bearing of all that part, and Grace showed me how, if danger threatened, I might climb up their boughs and scale the wall.

We sat in the summer house, and I told her all that had happened at her father's death, only concealing that Elzevir had meant to do the deed himself; because it was no use to tell her that, and besides, for all I knew, he never did mean to shoot, but only to frighten.

She wept again while I spoke, but afterwards dried her tears, and must needs look at my leg to see the bullet wound, and if it was all soundly healed.

Then I told her of the secret sense that Master Ratsey's words put into the texts written on the parchment. I had showed her the locket before, but we had it out again now; and she read and read again the writing, while I pointed out how the words fell, and told her I was going away to get the diamond and come back the richest man in all the countryside.

Then she said, 'Ah, John! Set not your heart too much upon this diamond. If what they say is true, 'twas evilly come by, and will bring evil with it. Even this wicked man durst not spend it for himself, but meant to give it to the poor; so, if indeed you ever find it, keep it not for yourself, but set his soul at rest by doing with it what he meant to do, or it will bring a curse upon you.'

I only smiled at what she said, taking it to be a girlish fancy, and did not tell her why I wanted so much to be rich – namely, to marry her one day. Then, having talked long about my own concerns as selfishly as a man always does, I thought to ask after herself, and what she was going to do. She told me that a month past lawyers had come to Moonfleet, and pressed her to leave the place, and they would give her in charge to a lady in London, because, said they, her father had died without a will, and so she must be made a ward of Chancery. But she had begged them to let her be, for she could never live anywhere else than in Moonfleet, and that the air and commodity of the place suited her well. So they went off, saying that they must take direction of the Court to know whether she might stay here or not, and here she yet was. This made me sad, for all I knew of Chancery was that whatever it put hand on fell to ruin, as witness the Chancery Mills at Cerne, or the Chancery Wharf at Wareham; and certainly it would take little enough to ruin the manor house, for it was three parts in decay already.

Thus we talked, and after that she put on a calico bonnet and picked me a dish of strawberries, staying to pull the finest, although the sun was beating down from mid-heaven, and brought me bread and meat from the house. Then she rolled up a shawl to make me a pillow, and bade me lie down on the seat that ran round the summer house and get to sleep, for I had told her that I had walked all night, and must be back again at the cave come midnight. She went back to the house, and that was the most sweet and peaceful sleep that ever I knew, for I was very tired, and had this thought to soothe me as I fell asleep – that I had seen Grace, and that she was so kind to me.

She was sitting beside me when I awoke and knitting a piece of work. The heat of the day was somewhat less, and she told me that it was past five o'clock by the sundial; so I knew that I must go. She made me take a packet of victuals and a bottle of milk, and as she put it into my pocket the bottle struck on the butt of Maskew's pistol, which I had in my bosom. 'What have you there?' she said; but I did not tell her, fearing to call up bitter memories.

We stood hand in hand again, as we had done in the morning, and she said: 'John, you will wander on the sea, and may perhaps put into Moonfleet. Though you have not been here of late, I have kept a candle burning at the window every night, as in the past. So, if you come to beach on any night you will see that light, and know Grace remembers you. And if you see it not, then know that I am dead or gone, for I will think of you every night till you come back again.' I had nothing to say, for my heart was too full with her sweet words and with the sorrow of parting, but only drew her close to me and kissed her; and this time she did not step back, but kissed me again.

Then I climbed up the fig tree, thinking it safer so to get out over the wall than to go back to the front of the house, and as I sat on the wall ready to drop the other side, turned to her and said goodbye.

'Goodbye,' cried she; 'and have a care how you touch the treasure; it was evilly come by, and will bring a curse with it.'

'Goodbye, goodbye,' I said, and dropped on to the soft leafy bottom of the wood.

14

The Well House

For those thou mayest not look upon
Are gathering fast round the yawning stone – *Scott*

It wanted yet half an hour of midnight when I found myself at the shaft of the marble quarry, and before I had well set foot on the steps to descend, heard Elzevir's voice challenging out of the darkness below. I gave back 'Prosper the *Bonaventure*' and so came home again to sleep the last time in our cave.

The next night was well suited to flight. There was a spring tide with full moon, and a light breeze setting off the land which left the water smooth under the cliff. We saw the *Bonaventure* cruising in the Channel before sundown, and after the darkness fell she lay close in and took us off in her boat. There were several men on board of her that I knew, and they greeted us kindly, and made much of us. I was indeed glad to be among them again, and yet felt a pang at leaving our dear Dorset coast, and the old cave that had been hospital and home to me for two months.

The wind set us up-Channel, and by daybreak they put us ashore at Cowes, so we walked to Newport and came there before many were stirring. Such as we saw in the street paid no heed to us but took us doubtless for some carter and his boy who had brought corn in from the country for the Southampton packet, and were about early to lead the team home again. 'Tis a little place enough this Newport, and we soon found the Bugle; but Elzevir made so good a carter that the landlord did not know him, though he had his acquaintance before. So they fenced a little with one another.

'Have you bed and victuals for a plain country man and his boy?' says Elzevir.

'Nay, that I have not,' says the landlord, looking him up and down, and not liking to take in strangers who might use their eyes inside, and perhaps get on the trail of the contraband. ''Tis near the Summer Statute and the place overfull already. I cannot move my gentlemen, and would bid you try the Wheatsheaf, which is a good house, and not so full as this.'

'Ay, 'tis a busy time, and 'tis these fairs that make things *prosper*,' and Elzevir marked the last word a little as he said it.

The man looked harder at him, and asked, 'Prosper what?' as if he were hard of hearing.

'Prosper the *Bonaventure*,' was the answer, and then the landlord caught Elzevir by the hand, shaking it hard and saying, 'Why, you are Master Block, and I expecting you this morn, and never knew you.' He laughed as he stared at us again, and Elzevir smiled too. Then the landlord led us in. 'And this is?' he said, looking at me.

'This is a well-licked whelp,' replied Elzevir, 'who got a bullet in the leg two months ago in that touch under Hoar Head; and is worth more than he looks, for they have put twenty golden guineas on his head – so have a care of such a precious top-knot.'

So long as we stopped at the Bugle we had the best of lodging and the choicest meat and drink, and all the while the landlord treated Elzevir as though he were a prince. And so he was indeed a prince among the contrabandiers, and held, as I found out long afterwards, for captain of all landers between Start and Solent. At first the landlord would take no money of us, saying that he was in our debt, and had received many a good turn from Master Block in the past, but Elzevir had got gold from Dorchester before we left the cave and forced him to take payment. I was glad enough to lie between clean sweet sheets at night instead of on a heap of sand, and sit once more knife and fork in hand before a well-filled trencher. 'Twas thought best I should show myself as little as possible, so I was content to pass my time in a room at the back of the house whilst Elzevir went abroad to make enquiries how we could find entrance to the castle at Carisbrooke. Nor did the time hang heavy on my hands, for I found some old books in the Bugle, and among them several to my taste, especially a *History of Corfe Castle*, which set forth how there was a secret passage from the ruins to some of the old marble quarries, and perhaps to that very one that sheltered us.

Elzevir was out most of the day, so that I saw him only at breakfast and supper. He had been several times to Carisbrooke, and told me that the castle was used as a jail for persons taken in the wars, and was now full of French prisoners. He had met several of the turnkeys or jailers, drinking with them in the inns there, and making out that he was himself a carter, who waited at Newport till a wind-bound ship should bring grindstones from Lyme Regis. Thus he was able at last to enter the castle and to see well house and well, and spent some days in trying to devise a plan whereby we might get at the well without making the man who had charge of it privy to our full design; but in this did not succeed.

There is a slip of garden at the back of the Bugle, which runs down to a little stream, and one evening when I was taking the air there after dark, Elzevir returned and said the time was come for us to put Blackbeard's cipher to the proof.

'I have tried every way,' he said, 'to see if we could work this secretly; but 'tis not to be done without the privity of the man who keeps the well, and even with his help it is not easy. He is a man I do not trust, but have been forced to tell him there is treasure hidden in the well, yet without saying where it lies or how to get it. He promises to let us search the well, taking one-third the value of all we find, for his share; for I said not that thou and I were one at heart, but only that there was a boy who had the key, and claimed an equal third with both of us. Tomorrow we must be up betimes, and at the castle gates by six o'clock for him to let us in. And thou shalt not be carter any more, but mason's boy, and I a mason, for I have got coats in the house, brushes and trowels and lime bucket, and we are going to Carisbrooke to plaster up a weak patch in this same well side.'

Elzevir had thought carefully over this plan, and when we left the Bugle next morning we were better masons in our splashed clothes than ever we had been farm servants. I carried a bucket and a brush, and Elzevir a plasterer's hammer and a coil of stout twine over his arm. It was a wet morning, and had been raining all night. The sky was stagnant, and one-coloured without wind, and the heavy drops fell straight down out of a grey veil that covered everything. The air struck cold when we first came out, but trudging over the heavy road soon made us remember that it was July, and we were very hot and soaking wet when we stood at the gateway of Carisbrooke Castle. Here are two flanking towers and a stout gatehouse reached by a stone bridge crossing the moat; and when I saw it I remembered that 'twas here Colonel Mohune had earned the wages of his unrighteousness, and thought how many times he must have passed these gates. Elzevir knocked as one that had a right, and we were evidently expected, for a wicket in the heavy door was opened at once. The man who let us in was tall and stout, but had a puffy face, and too much flesh on him to be very strong, though he was not, I think, more than thirty years of age. He gave Elzevir a smile, and passed the time of day civilly enough, nodding also to me; but I did not like his oily black hair, and a shifty eye that turned away uneasily when one met it.

'Good morning, Master Well-wright,' he said to Elzevir. 'You have brought ugly weather with you, and are drowning wet; will you take a sup of ale before you get to work?'

Elzevir thanked him kindly but would not drink, so the man led on and we followed him. We crossed a bailey or outer court where the rain had made the gravel very miry, and came on the other side to a door which led by steps into a large hall. This building had once been a banquet room, I think, for there was an inscription over it very plain in lead: *He led me into his banquet hall, and his banner over me was love.*

I had time to read this while the turnkey unlocked the door with one of a heavy bunch of keys that he carried at his girdle. But when we entered, what a disappointment! – for there were no banquets now, no banners, no love, but the whole place gutted and turned into a barrack for

French prisoners. The air was very close, as where men had slept all night, and a thick steam on the windows. Most of the prisoners were still asleep, and lay stretched out on straw palliasses round the walls, but some were sitting up and making models of ships out of fish bones, or building up crucifixes inside bottles, as sailors love to do in their spare time. They paid little heed to us as we passed, though the sleepy guards, who were lounging on their matchlocks, nodded to our conductor, and thus we went right through that evil-smelling whitewashed room. We left it at the other end, went down three steps into the open air again, crossed another small court, and so came to a square building of stone with a high roof like the large dovecots that you may see in old stackyards.

Here our guide took another key, and, while the door was being opened, Elzevir whispered to me, 'It is the well house,' and my pulse beat quick to think we were so near our goal.

The building was open to the roof, and the first thing to be seen in it was that treadwheel of which Elzevir had spoken. It was a great open wheel of wood, ten or twelve feet across, and very like a millwheel, only the space between the rims was boarded flat, but had treads nailed on it to give foothold to a donkey. The patient beast was lying loose stabled on some straw in a corner of the room, and, as soon as we came in, stood up and stretched himself, knowing that the day's work was to begin. 'He was here long before my time,' the turnkey said, 'and knows the place so well that he goes into the wheel and sets to work by himself.' At the side of the wheel was the well mouth, a dark, round opening with a low parapet round it, rising two feet from the floor.

We were so near our goal. Yet, were we near it at all? How did we know Mohune had meant to tell the place of hiding for the diamond in those words? They might have meant a dozen things beside. And if it was of the diamond they spoke, then how did we know the well was this one? There were a hundred wells beside. These thoughts came to me, making hope less sure; and perhaps it was the steamy overcast morning and the rain, or a scant breakfast, that beat my spirit down – for I have known men's mood change much with weather and with food; but sure it was that now we stood so near to put it to the touch, I liked our business less and less.

As soon as we were entered the turnkey locked the door from the inside, and when he let the key drop to its place, and it jangled with the others on his belt, it seemed to me he had us as his prisoners in a trap. I tried to catch his eye to see if it looked bad or good, but could not, for he kept his shifty face turned always somewhere else; and then it came to my mind that if the treasure was really fraught with evil, this coarse dark-haired man, who could not look one straight, was to become a minister of ruin to bring the curse home to us.

But if I was weak and timid Elzevir had no misgivings. He had taken the coil of twine off his arm and was undoing it. 'We will let an end of this down the well,' he said, 'and I have made a knot in it at eighty feet. This lad thinks the treasure is in the well wall, eighty feet below us, so when the knot is on well lip we shall know we have the right depth.' I tried again to see what look the turnkey wore when he heard where the treasure was, but could not, and so fell to examining the well.

A spindle ran from the axle of the wheel across the well, and on the spindle was a drum to take the rope. There was some clutch or fastening which could be fixed or loosed at will to make the drum turn with the treadwheel, or let it run free, and a footbrake to lower the bucket fast or slow, or stop it altogether.

'I will get into the bucket,' Elzevir said, turning to me, 'and this good man will lower me gently by the brake until I reach the string end down below. Then I will shout, and so fix you the wheel and give me time to search.'

This was not what I looked for, having thought that it was I should go; and though I liked going down the well little enough, yet somehow now I felt I would rather do that than have Master Elzevir down the hole, and me left locked alone with this villainous fellow up above.

So I said, 'No, master, that cannot be; 'tis my place to go, being smaller and a lighter weight than thou; and thou shalt stop here and help this gentleman to lower me down.'

Elzevir spoke a few words to try to change my purpose, but soon gave in, knowing it was certainly the better plan, and having only thought to go himself because he doubted if I had the heart to do it. But the turnkey showed much ill humour at the change, and strove to let the plan stand as it was, and for Elzevir to go down the well. Things that were settled, he said, should remain settled; he was not one for changes; it was a man's task this and no child's play; a boy would not have his senses about him, and might overlook the place. I fixed my eyes on Elzevir to let him know what I thought, and Master Turnkey's words fell lightly on his ears as water on a duck's back. Then this ill-eyed man tried to work upon my fears; saying that the well is deep and the bucket small, I shall get giddy and be overbalanced. I do not say that these forebodings were without effect on me, but I had made up my mind that, bad as it might be to go down, it was yet worse to have Master Elzevir prisoned in the well, and I remain above. Thus the turnkey perceived at last that he was speaking to deaf ears, and turned to the business.

Yet there was one fear that still held me, for thinking of what I had heard of the quarry shafts in Purbeck, how men had gone down to explore, and there been taken with a sudden giddiness, and never lived to tell what they had seen; and so I said to Master Elzevir, 'Art sure the well is clean, and that no deadly gases lurk below?'

'Thou mayst be sure I knew the well was sweet before I let thee talk of going down,' he answered. 'For yesterday we lowered a candle to the water, and the flame burned bright and steady; and where the candle lives, there man lives too. But thou art right: these gases change from day to day, and we will try the thing again. So bring the candle, Master Jailer.'

The jailer brought a candle fixed on a wooden triangle, which he was wont to show strangers who came to see the well, and lowered it on a string. It was not till then I knew what a task I had before me, for looking over the parapet, and taking care not to lose my balance, because the parapet was low, and the floor round it green and slippery with water splashings, I watched the candle sink into that cavernous depth, and from a bright flame turn into a little twinkling star, and then to a mere point of light. At last it rested on the water, and there was a shimmer where the wood frame had set ripples moving. We watched it twinkle for a little while, and the jailer raised the candle from the water, and dropped down a stone from some he kept there for that purpose. This stone struck the wall halfway down, and went from side to side, crashing and whirring till it met the water with a booming plunge; and there rose a groan and moan from the eddies, like those dreadful sounds of the surge that I heard on lonely nights in the sea caverns underneath our hiding place in Purbeck. The jailer looked at me then for the first time, and his eyes had an ugly meaning, as if he said, 'There – that is how you will sound when you fall from your perch.' But it was no use to frighten, for I had made up my mind.

They pulled the candle up forthwith and put it in my hand, and I flung the plasterer's hammer into the bucket, where it hung above the well, and then got in myself. The turnkey stood at the brake wheel, and Elzevir leant over the parapet to steady the rope. 'Art sure that thou canst do it, lad?' he said, speaking low, and put his hand kindly on my shoulder. 'Are head and heart sure? Thou art my diamond, and I would rather lose all other diamonds in the world than aught should come to thee. So, if thou doubtest, let me go, or let not any go at all.'

'Never doubt, master,' I said, touched by tenderness, and wrung his hand. 'My head is sure; I have no broken leg to turn it silly now' – for I guessed he was thinking of Hoar Head and how I had gone giddy on the Zigzag.

15

The Well

The grave doth gape and doting death is near

— Shakespeare

The bucket was large, for all that the turnkey had tried to frighten me into thinking it small, and I could crouch in it low enough to feel safe of not falling out. Moreover, such a venture was not entirely new to me, for I had once been over Gad Cliff in a basket, to get two peregrines' eggs; yet none the less I felt ill at ease and fearful, when the bucket began to sink into that dreadful depth, and the air to grow chilly as I went down. They lowered me gently enough, so that I was able to take stock of the way the wall was made, and found that for the most part it was cut through solid chalk; but here and there, where the chalk failed or was broken away, they had lined the walls with brick, patching them now on this side, now on that, and now all round. By degrees the light, which was dim even overground that rainy day, died out in the well, till all was black as night but for my candle, and far overhead I could see the well mouth, white and round like a lustreless full moon.

I kept an eye all the time on Elzevir's cord that hung down the well side, and when I saw it was coming to a finish, shouted to them to stop, and they brought the bucket up near level with the end of it, so I knew I was about eighty feet deep. Then I raised myself, standing up in the bucket and holding by the rope, and began to look round, knowing not all the while what I looked for, but thinking to see a hole in the wall, or perhaps the diamond itself shining out of a cranny. But I could perceive nothing; and what made it more difficult was that the walls here were lined completely with small flat bricks, and looked much the same all round. I examined these bricks as closely as I might, and took course by course, looking first at the north side where the plumbline hung, and afterwards turning round in the bucket till I was afraid of getting giddy; but to little purpose. They could see my candle moving round and round from the well top, and knew no doubt what I was at, but Master Turnkey grew impatient, and shouted down, 'What are you doing? Have you found nothing? Can you see no treasure?'

'No,' I called back, 'I can see nothing,' and then, 'Are you sure, Master Block, that you have measured the plummet true to eighty feet?'

I heard them talking together, but could not make out what they said, for the bim-bom and echo in the well, till

Elzevir shouted again, 'They say this floor has been raised; you must try lower.'

Then the bucket began to move lower, slowly, and I crouched down in it again, not wishing to look too much into the unfathomable, dark abyss below. And all the while there rose groanings and moanings from eddies in the bottom of the well, as if the spirits that kept watch over the jewel were yammering together that one should be so near it; and clear above them all I heard Grace's voice, sweet and grave, 'Have a care, have a care how you touch the treasure; it was evilly come by, and will bring a curse with it.'

But I had set foot on this way now, and must go through with it, so when the bucket stopped some six feet lower down, I fell again to diligently examining the walls. They were still built of the shallow bricks, and scanning them course by course as before, I could at first see nothing, but as I moved my eyes downward they were brought up by a mark scratched on a brick, close to the hanging plummet line.

Now, however lightly a man may glance through a book, yet if his own name, or even only one like it, should be printed on the page, his eyes will instantly be stopped by it; so too, if his name be mentioned by others in their speech, though it should be whispered never so low, his ears will catch it. Thus it was with this mark, for though it was very slight, so that I think not one in a thousand would ever have noticed it at all, yet it stopped my eyes and brought up my thoughts suddenly, because I knew by instinct that it had something to do with me and what I sought.

The sides of this well are not moist, green, or clammy, like the sides of some others where damp and noxious exhalations abound, but dry and clean; for it is said that there are below hidden entrances and exits for the water, which keep it always moving. So these bricks were also dry and clean, and this mark as sharp as if made yesterday, though the issue showed that 'twas put there a very long time ago. Now the mark was not deeply or regularly graven, but roughly scratched, as I have known boys score their names, or alphabet letters, or a date, on the alabaster figures that lie in Moonfleet church. And here, too, was scored a letter of the alphabet, a plain 'Y', and would have passed for nothing more perhaps to any not born in Moonfleet; but to me it was the cross pall, or black 'Y' of the Mohunes, under whose shadow we were all brought up. So as soon as I saw that, I knew I was near what I sought, and that Colonel John Mohune had put this sign there a century ago, either by his own hands or by those of a servant; and then I thought of Mr Glennie's story, that the Colonel's conscience was always unquiet, because of a servant whom he had put away, and now I seemed to understand something more of it.

My heart throbbed fiercely, as many another's heart has throbbed when he has come near the fulfilment of a great desire, whether lawful or guilty, and I tried to get at the brick. But though by holding on to the rope with my left hand, I could reach over far enough to touch the brick with my right, 'twas as much as I could do, and so I shouted up the well that they must bring me nearer in to the side. They understood what I would be at, and slipped a noose over the well rope and so drew it in to the side, and made it fast till I should give the word to loose again. Thus I was brought close to the well wall, and the marked brick near about the level of my face when I stood up in the bucket. There was nothing to show that this brick had been tampered with, nor did it sound hollow when tapped, though when I came to look closely at the joints, it seemed as though there was more cement than usual about the edges. But I never doubted that what we sought was to be found behind it, and so got to work at once, fixing the wooden frame of the candle in the fastening of the chain, and chipping out the mortar setting with the plasterer's hammer.

When they saw above that first I was to be pulled in to the side, and afterwards fell to work on the wall of the well, they guessed, no doubt, how matters were, and I had scarce begun chipping when I heard the turnkey's voice again, sharp and greedy, 'What are you doing? Have you found nothing?' It chafed me that this grasping fellow should be always shouting to me while Elzevir was content to stay quiet, so I cried back that I had found nothing, and that he should know what I was doing in good time.

Soon I had the mortar out of the joints, and the brick loose enough to prise it forward, by putting the edge of the hammer in the crack. I lifted it clean out and put it in the bucket, to see later on, in case of need, if there was a hollow for anything to be hidden in; but never had occasion to look at it again, for there, behind the brick, was a little hole in the wall, and in the hole what I sought. I had my fingers in the wall too quick for words, and brought out a little parchment bag, for all the world like those dried fish eggs cast up on the beach that children call shepherds' purses. Now, shepherds' purses are crisp, and crackle to the touch, and sometimes I have known a pebble get inside one and rattle like a pea in a drum; and this little bag that I pulled out was dry too, and crackling, and had something of the size of a small pebble that rattled in the inside of it. Only I knew well that this was no pebble, and set to work to get it out. But though the little bag was parched and dry, 'twas not so easily torn, and at last I struck off the corner of it with the sharp edge of my hammer against the bucket. Then I shook it carefully, and out into my hand there dropped a pure crystal as big as a walnut. I had never in my life seen a diamond, either large or small – yet even if I had not known that Blackbeard had buried a diamond, and if we had not come hither of set purpose to find it, I should not have doubted that what I had in my hand was a diamond, and this of matchless size and brilliance. It was cut into many facets, and though there was little or no light in the well save my candle, there seemed to be in this stone the light of a thousand fires that flashed out, sparkling red and blue and green, as I turned it between my fingers. At first I could think of nothing else, neither how it got there, nor how I had come to find it, but only of it, the diamond, and that with such a prize Elzevir and I could live happily ever afterwards, and that I should be a rich man and able to go back to Moonfleet. So I crouched down in the bottom of the bucket, being filled entirely with such thoughts, and turned it over and over again, wondering continually more and more to see the fiery light fly out of it. I was, as it were, dazed by its brilliance, and by the possibilities of wealth that it contained, and had, perhaps, a desire to keep it to myself as long as might be; so that I thought nothing of the two who were waiting for me at the well mouth, till I was suddenly called back by the harsh voice of the turnkey, crying as before –

'What are you doing? Have you found nothing?'

'Yes,' I shouted back, 'I have found the treasure; you can pull me up.' The words were scarcely out of my mouth before the bucket began to move, and I went up a great deal faster than I had gone down. Yet in that short journey other thoughts came to my mind, and I heard Grace's voice again, sweet and grave, 'Have a care, have a care how you touch the treasure; it was evilly come by, and will bring a curse with it.' At the same time I remembered how

I had been led to the discovery of this jewel – first, by Mr Glennie's stories, second, by my finding the locket, and third, by Ratsey giving me the hint that the writing was a cipher, and so had come to the hiding place without a swerve or stumble; and it seemed to me that I could not have reached it so straight without a leading hand, but whether good or evil, who should say?

As I neared the top I heard the turnkey urging the donkey to trot faster in the wheel, so that the bucket might rise the quicker, but just before my head was level with the ground he set the brake on and fixed me where I was. I was glad to see the light again, and Elzevir's face looking kindly on me, but vexed to be brought up thus suddenly just when I was expecting to set foot on *terra firma*.

The turnkey had stopped me through his covetous eagerness, so that he might get sooner at the jewel, and now he craned over the low parapet and reached out his hand to me, crying – 'Where is the treasure? Where is the treasure? Give me the treasure!'

I held the diamond between finger and thumb of my right hand, and waved it for Elzevir to see. By stretching out my arm I could have placed it in the turnkey's hand, and was just going to do so, when I caught his eyes for the second time that day, and something in them made me stop. There was a look in his face that brought back to me the memory of an autumn evening, when I sat in my aunt's parlour reading the book called the *Arabian Nights*;

and how, in the story of the *Wonderful Lamp*, Aladdin's wicked uncle stands at the top of the stairs when the boy is coming up out of the underground cavern, and will not let him out, unless he first gives up the treasure. But Aladdin refused to give up his lamp until he should stand safe on the ground again, because he guessed that if he did, his uncle would shut him up in the cavern and leave him to die there; and the look in the turnkey's eyes made me refuse to hand him the jewel till I was safe out of the well, for a horrible fear seized me that, as soon as he had taken it from me, he meant to let me fall down and drown below.

So when he reached down his hand and said, 'Give me the treasure,' I answered, 'Pull me up then; I cannot show it you in the bucket.'

'Nay, lad,' he said, cozening me, ''tis safer to give it me now, and have both hands free to help you getting out; these stones are wet and greasy, and you may chance to slip, and having no hand to save you, fall back in the well.'

But I was not to be cheated, and said again sturdily, 'No, you must pull me up first.'

Then he took to scowling, and cried in an angry tone, 'Give me the treasure, I say, or it will be the worse for you'; but Elzevir would not let him speak to me that way, and broke in roughly, 'Let the boy up, he is sure-footed and will not slip. 'Tis his treasure, and he shall do with it as he likes: only that thou shalt have a third of it when we have sold it.'

Then he: "'Tis not his treasure – no, nor yours either, but mine, for it is in my well, and I have let you get it. Yet I will give you a half-share in it; but as for this boy, what has he to do with it? We will give him a golden guinea, and he will be richly paid for his pains.'

'Tush,' cries Elzevir, 'let us have no more fooling; this boy shall have his share, or I will know the reason why.'

'Ay, you shall know the reason, fair enough,' answers the turnkey, 'and 'tis because your name is Block, and there is a price of £50 upon your head, and £20 upon this boy's. You thought to outwit me, and are yourself outwitted; and here I have you in a trap, and neither leaves this room, except with hands tied, and bound for the gallows, unless I first have the jewel safe in my purse.'

On that I whipped the diamond back quick into the little parchment bag, and thrust both down snug into my breeches pocket, meaning to have a fight for it, anyway, before I let it go. And looking up again, I saw the turnkey's hand on the butt of his pistol, and cried, 'Beware, beware! He draws on you.' But before the words were out of my mouth, the turnkey had his weapon up and levelled full at Elzevir. 'Surrender,' he cries, 'or I shoot you dead, and the £50 is mine,' and never giving time for answer, fires. Elzevir stood on the other side of the well mouth, and it seemed the other could not miss him at such a distance; but as I blinked my eyes at the flash, I felt the bullet strike the iron chain to which I was holding, and saw that Elzevir was safe.

The turnkey saw it too, and flinging away his pistol, sprang round the well and was at Elzevir's throat before he knew whether he was hit or not. I have said that the turnkey was a tall, strong man, and twenty years the younger of the two; so doubtless when he made for Elzevir, he thought he would easily have him broken down and handcuffed, and then turn to me. But he reckoned without his host, for though Elzevir was the shorter and older man, he was wonderfully strong, and seasoned as a salted thong. Then they hugged one another and began a terrible struggle: for Elzevir knew that he was wrestling for life, and I daresay the turnkey guessed that the stakes were much the same for him too.

As soon as I saw what they were at, and that the bucket was safe fixed, I laid hold of the well chain, and climbing up by it swung myself on to the top of the parapet, being eager to help Elzevir, and get the turnkey gagged and bound while we made our escape. But before I was well on the firm ground again, I saw that little help of mine was needed, for the turnkey was flagging, and there was a look of anguish and desperate surprise upon his face, to find that the man he had thought to master so lightly was strong as a giant. They were swaying to and fro, and the jailer's grip was slackening, for his muscles were overwrought and tired; but Elzevir held him firm as a vice, and I saw from his eyes and the bearing of his body that he was gathering himself up to give his enemy a fall.

Now I guessed that the fall he would use would be the Compton Toss, for though I had never seen him give it, yet he was well known for a wrestler in his younger days, and the Compton Toss for his most certain fall. I shall not explain the method of it, but those who have seen it used will know that 'tis a deadly fall, and he who lets himself get thrown that way even upon grass, is seldom fit to wrestle another bout the same day. Still, 'tis a difficult fall to use, and perhaps Elzevir would never have been able to give it, had not the other at that moment taken one hand off the waist, and tried to make a clutch with it at the throat. But the only way of avoiding that fall, and indeed most others, is to keep both hands firm between hip and shoulder blade, and the moment Elzevir felt one hand off his back, he had the jailer off his feet and gave him Compton's Toss. I do not know whether Elzevir had been so taxed by the fierce struggle that he could not put his fullest force into the throw, or whether the other, being a very strong and heavy man, needed more to fling him; but so it was, that instead of the turnkey going down straight as he should, with the back of his head on the floor (for that is the real damage of the toss), he must needs stagger backwards a pace or two, trying to regain his footing before he went over.

It was those few staggering paces that ruined him, for with the last he came upon the stones close to the well mouth, that had been made wet and slippery by continual spilling there of water. Then up flew his heels, and he fell backwards with all his weight.

As soon as I saw how near the well mouth he was got, I shouted out and ran to save him; but Elzevir saw it quicker than I, and springing forward seized him by the belt just when he turned over. The parapet wall was very low, and caught the turnkey behind the knee as he staggered, tripping him over into the well mouth. He gave a bitter cry, and there was a wrench on his face when he knew where he was come, and 'twas then Elzevir caught him by the belt. For a moment I thought he was saved, seeing Elzevir setting his body low back with heels pressed firm against the parapet wall to stand the strain. Then the belt gave way at the fastening, and Elzevir fell sprawling on the floor. But the other went backwards down the well.

I got to the parapet just as he fell head first into that black abyss. There was a second of silence, then a dreadful noise like a coconut being broken on a pavement – for we once had coconuts in plenty at Moonfleet, when the *Bataviaman* came on the beach, then a deep echoing blow, where he rebounded and struck the wall again, and last of all, the thud and thundering splash, when he reached the water at the bottom. I held my breath for sheer horror, and listened to see if he would cry, though I knew at heart he would never cry again, after that first sickening smash; but there was no sound or voice, except the moaning voices of the water eddies that I had heard before.

Elzevir slung himself into the bucket. 'You can handle the brake,' he said to me; 'let me down quick into the well.' I took the brake lever, lowering him as quickly as I durst, till I heard the bucket touch water at the bottom, and then stood by and listened. All was still, and yet I started once, and could not help looking round over my shoulder, for it seemed as if I was not alone in the well house; and though I could see no one, yet I had a fancy of a tall black-bearded man, with coppery face, chasing another round and round the well mouth. Both vanished from my fancy just as the pursuer had his hand on the pursued; but Mr Glennie's story came back again to my mind, how that Colonel Mohune's conscience was always unquiet because of a servant he had put away, and I guessed now that the turnkey was not the first man these walls had seen go headlong down the well.

Elzevir had been in the well so long that I began to fear something had happened to him, when he shouted to me to bring him up. So I fixed the clutch, and set the donkey going in the treadwheel; and the patient drudge started on his round, recking nothing whether it was a bucket of water he brought up, or a live man, or a dead man, while I looked over the parapet, and waited with a cramping suspense to see whether Elzevir would be alone, or have something with him. But when the bucket came in sight there was only Elzevir in it, so I knew the turnkey had never come to the top of the water again, and, indeed, there was but little chance he should after that first knock. Elzevir said nothing to me, till I spoke: 'Let us fling the jewel down the well after him, Master Block; it was evilly come by, and will bring a curse with it.'

He hesitated for a moment while I half hoped yet half feared he was going to do as I asked, but then said:

'No, no; thou art not fit to keep so precious a thing. Give it me. It is thy treasure, and I will never touch penny of it; but fling it down the well thou shalt not; for this man has lost his life for it, and we have risked ours for it – ay, and may lose them for it too, perhaps.'

So I gave him the jewel.

16

The Jewel

All that glisters is not gold – *Shakespeare*

There was the turnkey's belt lying on the floor, with the keys and manacles fixed to it, just as it had failed and come off him at the fatal moment. Elzevir picked it up, tried the keys till he found the right one, and unlocked the door of the well house.

'There are other locks to open before we get out,' I said.

'Ay,' he answered, 'but it is more than our life is worth to be seen with these keys, so send them down the well, after their master.'

I took them back and flung them, belt and keys and handcuffs, clanking down against the sides into the blackness and the hidden water at the bottom. Then we took pail and hammer, brush and ropes, and turned our backs upon that hateful place. There was the little court to cross before we came to the doors of the banquet hall. They were locked, but we knocked until a guard opened them. He knew us for the plasterer-men, who had passed an hour before, and only asked, 'Where is Ephraim?' meaning the turnkey. 'He is stopping behind in the well house,' Elzevir said, and so we passed on through the hall, where the prisoners were making what breakfast they might of odds and ends, with a savoury smell of cooking and a great patter of French.

At the outer gate was another guard to be passed, but they opened for us without question, cursing Ephraim under their breath, that he did not take the pains to let his own men out. Then the wicket of the great gates swung to behind us, and we went into the open again. As soon as we were out of sight we quickened our pace, and the weather having much bettered, and a fresh breeze springing up, we came back to the Bugle about ten in the forenoon.

I believe that neither of us spoke a word during that walk, and though Elzevir had not yet seen the diamond, he never even took the pains to draw it out of the little parchment bag, in which it still lay hid in his pocket. Yet if I did not speak I thought, and my thoughts were sad enough. For here were we a second time, flying for our lives, and if we had not the full guilt of blood upon our hands, yet blood was surely there. So this flight was very bitter to me, because the scene of death of which I had been witness this morning seemed to take me farther still away from all my old happy life, and to stand like another dreadful obstacle between Grace and me. In the family Bible lying on the table in my aunt's best parlour was a picture of Cain, which I had often looked at with fear on wet Sunday afternoons. It showed

Cain striding along in the midst of a boundless desert, with his sons and their wives striding behind him, and their little children carried slung on poles. There was a quick, swinging motion in the bodies of all, as though they must needs always stride as fast as they might, and never rest, and their faces were set hard, and thin with eternal wandering and disquiet. But the thinnest and most restless-looking and hardest face was Cain's, and on the middle of his forehead there was a dark spot, which God had set to show that none might touch him, because he was the first murderer, and cursed forever. This had always been to me a dreadful picture, though I could not choose but look at it, and was sorry indeed for Cain, for all he was so wicked, because it seemed so hard to have to wander up and down the world all his life long, and never be able to come to moorings. And yet this very thing had come upon me now, for here we were, with the blood of two men on our hands, wanderers on the face of the earth, who durst never go home; and if the mark of Cain was not on my forehead already, I felt it might come out there at any minute.

When we reached the Bugle I went upstairs and flung myself upon the bed to try to rest a little and think, but Elzevir shut himself in with the landlord, and I could hear them talking earnestly in the room under me. After a while he came up and said that he had considered with the landlord how we could best get away, telling him that we must be off at once, but letting him suppose that we were eager to leave the place because some of the Excise had got wind of our whereabouts. He had said nothing to our host about the turnkey, wishing as few persons as possible to know of that matter, but doubted not that we should by all means hasten our departure from the island, for that as soon as the turnkey was missed enquiry would certainly be made for the plasterers with whom he was last seen.

Yet in this thing at least Fortune favoured us, for there was now lying at Cowes, and ready to sail that night, a Dutch couper that had run a cargo of Hollands on the other side of the island, and was going back to Scheveningen freighted with wool. Our landlord knew the Dutch captain well, having often done business for him, and so could give us letters of recommendation which would ensure us a passage to the Low Countries. Thus in the afternoon we were on the road, making our way from Newport to Cowes in a new disguise, for we had changed our clothes again, and now wore the common sailor dress of blue.

The clouds had returned after the rain, and the afternoon was wet, and worse than the morning, so I shall not say anything of another weary and silent walk. We arrived on Cowes quay by eight in the evening, and found the couper ready to make sail, and waiting only for the tide to set out. Her name was the *Gouden Droom*, and she was a little larger than the *Bonaventure*, but had a smaller crew, and was not near so well found. Elzevir exchanged a few words with the captain, and gave him the landlord's letter, and after that they let us come on board, but said nothing to us. We judged that we were best out of the way, so went below; and finding her laden deep, and even the cabin full of bales of wool, flung ourselves on them to rest. I was so tired and heavy with sleep that my eyes closed almost before I was lain down, and never opened till the next morning was well advanced.

I shall not say anything about our voyage, nor how we came safe to Scheveningen, because it has little to do with this story. Elzevir had settled that we should go to Holland, not only because the couper was waiting to sail thither, for we might doubtless have found other boats before long to take us elsewhere – but also because he had learned at Newport that the Hague was the first market in the world for diamonds. This he told me after we were safe housed in a little tavern in the town, which was frequented by seamen, but those of the better class, such as mates and skippers of small vessels. Here we lay for several days while Elzevir made such enquiry as he could without waking suspicion as to who were the best dealers in precious stones, and the most able to pay a good price for a valuable jewel. It was lucky, too, for us that Elzevir could speak the Dutch language – not well indeed, but enough to make himself understood, and to understand others. When I asked where he had learned it, he told me that he came of Dutch blood on his mother's side, and so got his name of Elzevir; and that he could once speak in

Dutch as readily as in English, only that his mother dying when he was yet a boy he lost something of the facility.

As the days passed, the memory of that dreadful morning at Carisbrooke became dimmer to me, and my mind more cheerful or composed. I got the diamond back from Elzevir, and had it out many times, both by day and by night, and every time it seemed more brilliant and wonderful than the last. Often of nights, after all the house was gone to rest, I would lock the door of the room, and sit with a candle burning on the table, and turn the diamond over in my hands. It was, as I have said, as big as a pigeon's egg or walnut, delicately cut and faceted all over, perfect and flawless, without speck or stain, and yet, for all it was so clear and colourless, there flew out from the depth of it such flashes and sparkles of red, blue, and green, as made one wonder whence these tints could come. Thus while I sat and watched it I would tell Elzevir stories from the *Arabian Nights*, of wondrous jewels, though I believe there never was a stone that the eagles brought up from the Valley of Diamonds, no, nor any in the Caliph's crown itself, that could excel this gem of ours.

You may be sure that at such times we talked much of the value that was to be put upon the stone, and what was likely to be got for it, but never could settle, not having any experience of such things. Only, I was sure that it must be worth thousands of pounds, and so sat and rubbed my hands, saying that though life was like a game of hazard, and our throws had hitherto been bad enough, yet we had made something of this last. But all the while a strange change was coming over us both, and our parts seemed turned about. For whereas a few days before it was I who wished to fling the diamond away, feeling overwrought and heavy-hearted in that awful well house, and Elzevir who held me from it; now it was he that seemed to set little store by it, and I to whom it was all in all. He seldom cared to look much at the jewel, and one night when I was praising it to him, spoke out:

'Set not thy heart too much upon this stone. It is thine, and thine to deal with. Never a penny will I touch that we may get for it. Yet, were I thou, and reached great wealth with it, and so came back one day to Moonfleet, I would not spend it all on my own ends, but put aside a part to build the poor-houses again, as men say Blackbeard meant to do with it.'

I did not know what made him speak like this, and was not willing, even in fancy, to agree to what he counselled; for with that gem before me, lustrous, and all the brighter for lying on a rough deal table, I could only think of the wealth it was to bring to us, and how I would most certainly go back one day to Moonfleet and marry Grace. So I never answered Elzevir, but took the diamond and slipped it back in the silver locket, which still hung round my neck, for that was the safest place for it that we could think of.

We spent some days in wandering round the town making enquiries, and learned that most of the diamond buyers lived near one another in a certain little street, whose name I have forgotten, but that the richest and best known of them was one Krispijn Aldobrand. He was a Jew by birth, but had lived all his life in the Hague, and besides having bought and sold some of the finest stones, was said to ask few questions, and to trouble little whence stones came, so they were but good. Thus, after much thought and many changes of purpose, we chose this Aldobrand, and settled we would put the matter to the touch with him.

We took an evening in late summer for our venture, and came to Aldobrand's house about an hour before sundown. I remember the place well, though I have not seen it for so long, and am certainly never like to see it again. It was a low house of two storeys standing back a little from the street, with some wooden palings and a grass plot before it, and a stone-flagged path leading up to the door. The front of it was whitewashed, with green shutters, and had a shiny-leaved magnolia trained round about the windows. These jewellers had no shops, though sometimes they set a single necklace or bracelet in a bottom window, but put up notices proclaiming their trade. Thus there was over Aldobrand's door a board stuck out to say that he bought and sold jewels, and would lend money on diamonds or other valuables.

A sturdy serving man opened the door, and when he heard our business was to sell a jewel, left us in a stone-floored hall or lobby, while he went upstairs to ask whether his master would see us. A few minutes later the stairs creaked, and Aldobrand himself came down. He was a little wizened man with yellow skin and deep wrinkles, not less than seventy years old; and I saw he wore shoes of polished leather, silver-buckled, and tilted-heeled to add to his stature. He began speaking to us from the landing, not coming down into the hall, but leaning over the handrail:

'Well, my sons, what would you with me? I hear you have a jewel to sell, but you must know I do not purchase sailors' flotsam. So if 'tis a moonstone or catseye, or some pinhead diamonds, keep them to make brooches for your sweethearts, for Aldobrand buys no toys like that.'

He had a thin and squeaky voice, and spoke to us in our own tongue, guessing no doubt that we were English from our faces. 'Twas true he handled the language badly enough, yet I was glad he used it, for so I could follow all that was said.

'No toys like that,' he said again, repeating his last words, and Elzevir answered: 'May it please your worship, we are sailors from oversea, and this boy has a diamond that he would sell.'

I had the gem in my hand all ready, and when the old man squeaked peevishly, 'Out with it then, let's see, let's see,' I reached it out to him. He stretched down over the banisters, and took it; holding out his palm hollowed, as if 'twas some little paltry stone that might otherwise fall and be lost. It nettled me to have him thus underrate our treasure, even though he had never seen it, and so I plumped it down into his hand as if it were as big as a pumpkin. Now the hall was a dim place, being lit only by a half-circle of glass over the door, and so I could not see very well; yet in reaching down he brought his head near mine, and I could swear his face changed when he felt the size of the stone in his hand, and turned from impatience and contempt to wonder and delight. He took the jewel quickly from his palm, and held it up between finger and thumb, and when he spoke again, his voice was changed as well as his face, and had lost most of the sharp impatience.

'There is not light enough to see in this dark place – follow me,' and he turned back and went upstairs rapidly, holding the stone in his hand; and we close at his heels, being anxious not to lose sight of him now that he had our diamond, for all he was so rich and well known a man.

Thus we came to another landing, and there he flung open the door of a room which looked out west, and had the light of the setting sun streaming in full flood through the window. The change from the dimness of the stairs to this level red blaze was so quick that for a minute I could make out nothing, but turning my back to the window saw presently that the room was panelled all through with painted wood, with a bed let into the wall on one side, and shelves round the others, on which were many small coffers and strongboxes of iron. The jeweller was sitting at a table with his face to the sun, holding the diamond up against the light, and gazing into it closely, so that I could see every working of his face. The hard and cunning look had come back to it, and he turned suddenly upon me and asked quite sharply, 'What is your name, boy? Whence do you come?'

Now I was not used to walk under false names, and he took me unawares, so I must needs blurt out, 'My name is John Trenchard, sir, and I come from Moonfleet, in Dorset.'

A second later I could have bitten off my tongue for having said as much, and saw Elzevir frowning at me to make me hold my peace. But 'twas too late then, for the merchant was writing down my answer in a parchment ledger. And though it would seem to most but a little thing that he should thus take down my name and birthplace, and only vexed us at the time, because we would not have it known at all whence we came; yet in the overrulings of Providence it was ordered that this note in Mr Aldobrand's book should hereafter change the issue of my life.

'From Moonfleet, in Dorset,' he repeated to himself, as he finished writing my answer. 'And how did John Trenchard come by this?' and he tapped the diamond as it lay on the table before him.

Then Elzevir broke in quickly, fearing no doubt lest I should be betrayed into saying more: 'Nay, sir, we are not come to play at questions and answers, but to know whether your worship will buy this diamond, and at what price. We have no time to tell long histories, and so must only say that we are English sailors, and that the stone is fairly come by.' And he let his fingers play with the diamond on the table, as if he feared it might slip away from him.

'Softly, softly,' said the old man; 'all stones are fairly come by; but had you told me whence you got this, I might have spared myself some tedious tests, which now I must crave pardon for making.'

He opened a cupboard in the panelling, and took out from it a little pair of scales, some crystals, a blackstone, and a bottle full of a green liquid. Then he sat down again, drew the diamond gently from Elzevir's fingers, which were loth to part with it, and began using his scales; balancing the diamond carefully, now against a crystal, now against some small brass weights. I stood with my back to the sunset, watching the red light fall upon this old man as he weighed the diamond, rubbed it on the blackstone, or let fall on it a drop of the liquor, and so could see the wonder and emotion fade away from his face, and only hard craftiness left in it.

I watched him meddling till I could bear to watch no longer, feeling a fierce feverish suspense as to what he might say, and my pulse beating so quick that I could scarce stand still. For was not the decisive moment very nigh when we should know, from these parched-up lips, the value of the jewel, and whether it was worth risking life for, whether the fabric of our hopes was built on sure foundation or on slippery sand? So I turned my back on the diamond merchant, and looked out of the window, waiting all the while to catch the slightest word that might come from his lips.

I have found then and at other times that in such moments, though the mind be occupied entirely by one overwhelming thought, yet the eyes take in, as it were unwittingly, all that lies before them, so that we can afterwards recall a face or landscape of which at the time we took no note. Thus it was with me that night, for though I was thinking of nothing but the jewel, yet I noted everything that could be seen through the window, and the recollection was of use to me later on. The window was made in the French style, reaching down to the floor, and opening like a door with two leaves. It led on to a little balcony, and now stood open (for the day was still very hot), and on the wall below was trained a pear tree, which half embowered the balcony with its green leaves. The window could be well protected in case of need, having latticed wooden blinds inside, and heavy shutters shod with iron on the outer wall, and there were besides strong bolts and sockets from which ran certain wires whose use I did not know. Below the balcony was a square garden plot, shut in with a brick wall, and kept very neat and trim. There were hollyhocks round the walls, and many-coloured poppies, with many other shrubs and flowers. My eyes fell on one especially, a tall red-blossomed rushy kind of flower, that I had never seen before; and that seemed indeed to be something out of the common, for it stood in the middle of a little earth plot, and had the whole bed nearly to itself.

I was looking at this flower, not thinking of it, but wondering all the while whether Mr Aldobrand would say the diamond was worth ten thousand pounds, or fifty, or a hundred thousand, when I heard him speaking, and turned round quick. 'My sons, and you especially, son John,' he said, and turned to me: 'this stone that you have brought me is no stone at all, but glass – or rather paste, for so we call it. Not but what it is good paste, and perhaps the best that I have seen, and so I had to try it to make sure. But against high chymic tests no sham can stand; and first it is too light in weight, and second, when rubbed on this basanus or black-stone, traces no line of white, as any diamond must. But, third and last, I have tried it with the hermeneutic proof, and dipped it in this most costly lembic; and the liquor remains pure green and clear, not turbid orange, a diamond leaves it.'

As he spoke the room spun round, and I felt the sickness and heart-sinking that comes with the sudden destruction of long-cherished hope. So it was all a sham, a bit of glass, for which we had risked our lives. Blackbeard had only mocked us even in his death, and from rich men we were become the poorest outcasts. And all the other bright fancies that had been built on this worthless thing fell down at once, like a house of cards. There was no money now with which to go back rich to Moonfleet, no money to cloak past offences, no money to marry Grace; and with that I gave a sigh, and my knees failing should have fallen had not Elzevir held me.

'Nay, son John,' squeaked the old man, seeing I was so put about, 'take it not hardly, for though this is but paste, I say not it is worthless. It is as fine work as ever I have seen, and I will offer you ten silver crowns for it; which is a goodly sum for a sailor lad to have in hand, and more than all the other buyers in this town would bid you for it.'

'Tush, tush,' cried Elzevir, and I could hear the bitterness and disappointment in his voice, however much he tried to hide it; 'we are not come to beg for silver crowns, so keep them in your purse. And the devil take this shining sham; we are well quit of it; there is a curse upon the thing!' And with that he caught up the stone and flung it away out of the window in his anger.

This brought the diamond buyer to his feet in a moment. 'You fool, you cursed fool!' he shrieked. 'Are you come here to beard me? And when I say the thing is worth ten silver crowns, do you fling it to the winds?'

I had sprung forward with a half-thought of catching Elzevir's arm; but it was too late – the stone flew up in the air, caught the low rays of the setting sun for a moment, and then fell among the flowers. I could not see it as it fell, yet followed with my eyes the line in which it should have fallen, and thought I saw a glimmer where it touched the earth. It was only a flash or sparkle for an instant, just at the stem of that same rushy red-flowered plant, and then nothing more to be seen; but as I faced round I saw the little man's eyes turned that way too, and perhaps he saw the flash as well as I.

'There's for your ten crowns!' said Elzevir. 'Let us be going, lad.' And he took me by the arm and marched me out of the room and down the stairs.

'Go, and a blight on you!' says Mr Aldobrand, his voice being not so high as when he cried out last, but in his usual squeak; and then he repeated, 'A blight on you,' just for a parting shot as we went through the door.

We passed two more waiting men on the stairs, but they said nothing to us, and so we came to the street.

We walked along together for some time without a word, and then Elzevir said, 'Cheer up, lad, cheer up. Thou saidst thyself thou fearedst there was a curse on the thing, so now it is gone, maybe we are well quit of it.'

Yet I could not say anything, being too much disappointed to find the diamond was a sham, and bitterly cast down at the loss of all our hopes. It was all very well to think there was a curse upon the stone so long as we had it, and to feign that we were ready to part with it; but now it was gone I knew that at heart I never wished to part with it at all, and would have risked any curse to have it back again. There was supper waiting for us when we got back, but I had no stomach for victuals and sat moodily while Elzevir ate, and he not much. But when I sat and brooded over what had happened, a new thought came to my mind and I jumped up and cried, 'Elzevir, we are fools! The stone is no sham; 'tis a real diamond!'

He put down his knife and fork, and looked at me, not saying anything, but waiting for me to say more, and yet did not show so much surprise as I expected. Then I reminded him how the old merchant's face was full of wonder and delight when first he saw the stone, which showed he thought it was real then, and how afterwards, though he schooled his voice to bring out long words to deceive us, he was ready enough to spring to his feet and shriek out loud when Elzevir threw the stone into the garden. I spoke fast, and in talking to him convinced myself, so when I stopped for want of breath I was quite sure that the stone was indeed a diamond, and that Aldobrand had duped us.

Still Elzevir showed little eagerness, and only said –

''Tis like enough that what you say is true, but what would you have us do? The stone is flung away.'

'Yes,' I answered; 'but I saw where it fell, and know the very place; let us go back now at once and get it.'

'Do you not think that Aldobrand saw the place too?' asked Elzevir; and then I remembered how, when I turned back to the room after seeing the stone fall, I caught the eyes of the old merchant looking the same way; and how he spoke more quietly after that, and not with the bitter cry he used when Elzevir tossed the jewel out of the window.

'I do not know,' I said doubtfully; 'let us go back and see. It fell just by the stem of a red flower that I marked well. What!' I added, seeing him still hesitate and draw back, 'Do you doubt? Shall we not go and get it?'

Still he did not answer for a minute, and then spoke slowly, as if weighing his words. 'I cannot tell. I think that all you say is true, and that this stone is real. Nay, I was half of that mind when I threw it away, and yet I would not say we are not best without it. 'Twas you who first spoke of a curse upon the jewel, and I laughed at that as being a childish tale. But now I cannot tell; for ever since we first scented this treasure luck has run against us, John; yes, run against us very strong; and here we are, flying from home, called outlaws, and with blood upon our hands. Not that blood frightens me, for I have stood face to face with men in fair fight, and never felt a death blow given so weigh on my soul; but these two men came to a tricksy kind of end, and yet I could not help it. 'Tis true that all my life I've served the contraband, but no man ever knew me do a foul action; and now I do not like that men should call me felon, and like it less that they should call thee felon too. Perhaps there may be after all some curse that hangs about this stone, and leads to ruin those that handle it. I cannot say, for I am not a Parson Glennie in these things; but Blackbeard in an evil mood may have tied the treasure up to be a curse to any that use it for themselves. What do we want with this thing at all? I have got money to be touched at need; we may lie quiet this side the Channel, where thou shalt learn an honest trade, and when the mischief has blown over we will go back to Moonfleet. So let the jewel be, John; shall we not let the jewel be?'

He spoke earnestly, and most earnestly at the end, taking me by the hand and looking me full in the face. But I could not look him back again, and turned my eyes away, for I was wilful, and would not bring myself to let the diamond go. Yet all the while I thought that what he said was true, and I remembered that sermon that Mr Glennie preached, saying that life was like a 'Y', and that to each comes a time when two ways part, and where he must choose whether he will take the broad and sloping road or the steep and narrow path. So now I guessed that long ago I had chosen the broad road, and now was but walking farther down it in seeking after this evil treasure, and still I could not bear to give all up, and persuaded myself that it was a child's folly to madly fling away so fine a stone. So instead of listening to good advice from one so much older than me, I set to work to talk him over, and persuaded him that if we got the diamond again, and ever could sell it, we would give the money to build up the Mohune almshouses, knowing well in my heart that I never meant to do any such thing. Thus at the last Elzevir, who was the stubbornest of men, and never yielded, was overborne by his great love to me, and yielded here.

It was ten o'clock before we set out together, to go again to Aldobrand's, meaning to climb the garden wall and get the stone. I walked quickly enough, and talked all the time to silence my own misgivings, but Elzevir hung back a little and said nothing, for it was sorely against his judgement that he came at all. But as we neared the place I ceased my chatter, and so we went on in silence, each busy with his own thoughts, We did not come in front of Aldobrand's house, but turned out of the main street down a side lane which we guessed would skirt the garden wall. There were few people moving even in the streets, and in this little lane there was not a soul to meet as we crept along in the shadow of the high walls. We were not mistaken, for soon we came to what we judged was the outside of Aldobrand's garden.

Here we paused for a minute, and I believe Elzevir was for making a last remonstrance, but I gave him no chance, for I had found a place where some bricks were loosened in the wall face, and set myself to climb. It was easy enough to scale for us, and in a minute we both dropped down in a bed of soft mould on the other side. We pushed through some gooseberry bushes that caught the clothes, and distinguishing the outline of the house, made that way, till in a few steps we stood on the pelouse or turf, which I had seen from the balcony three hours before. I knew the twirl of the walks, and the pattern of the beds; the rank of hollyhocks that stood up all along the wall, and the poppies breathing out a faint sickly odour in the night. An utter silence held all the garden, and, the night being very clear, there was still enough light to show the colours of the flowers when one looked close at them, though the green of the leaves was turned to grey.

We kept in the shadow of the wall, and looked expectantly at the house. But no murmur came from it, it might have been a house of the dead for any noise the living made there; nor was there light in any window, except in one behind the balcony, to which our eyes were turned first. In that room there was someone not yet gone to rest, for we could see a lattice of light where a lamp shone through the open work of the wooden blinds.

'He is up still,' I whispered, 'and the outside shutters are not closed.' Elzevir nodded, and then I made straight for the bed where the red flower grew. I had no need of any light to see the bells of that great rushy thing, for it was different from any of the rest, and besides that was planted by itself.

I pointed it out to Elzevir. 'The stone lies by the stalk of that flower,' I said, 'on the side nearest to the house'; and then I stayed him with my hand upon his arm, that he should stand where he was at the bed's edge, while I stepped on and got the stone.

My feet sank in the soft earth as I passed through the fringe of poppies circling the outside of the bed, and so I stood beside the tall rushy flower. The scarlet of its bells was almost black, but there was no mistaking it, and I stooped to pick the diamond up. Was it possible? Was there nothing for my outstretched hand to finger, except the soft rich loam, and on the darkness of the ground no guiding sparkle? I knelt down to make more sure, and looked all round the plant, and still found nothing, though it was light enough to see a pebble, much more to catch the gleam and flash of the great diamond I knew so well.

It was not there, and yet I knew that I had seen it fall beyond all room for doubt.

'It is gone, Elzevir; it is gone!' I cried out in my anguish, but only heard a 'Hush!' from him to bid me not to speak so loud. Then I fell on my knees again, and sifted the mould through my fingers, to make sure the stone had not sunk in and been overlooked.

But it was all to no purpose, and at last I stepped back to where Elzevir was, and begged him to light a piece of match in the shelter of the hollyhocks; and I would screen it with my hands, so that the light should fall upon the ground, and not be seen from the house, and so search round the flower. He did as I asked, not because he thought that I should find anything, but rather to humour me; and, as he put the lighted match into my hands, said, speaking low, 'Let the stone be, lad, let it be; for either thou didst fail to mark the place right, or others have been here before thee. 'Tis ruled we should not touch the stone again, and so 'tis best; let be, let be; let us get home.'

He put his hand upon my shoulder gently, and spoke with such an earnestness and pleading in his voice that one would have thought it was a woman rather than a great rough giant; and yet I would not hear, and broke away, sheltering the match in my hollowed hands, and making back to the red flower. But this time, just as I stepped upon the mould, coming to the bed from the house side, the light fell on the ground, and there I saw something that brought me up short.

It was but a dint or impress on the soft brown loam, and yet, before my eyes were well upon it, I knew it for the print of a sharp heel – a sharp deep heel, having just in front of it the outline of a little foot. There is a story every boy was given to read when I was young, of Crusoe wrecked upon a desert isle, who, walking one day on the shore, was staggered by a single footprint in the sand, because he learned thus that there were savages in that sad place, where he thought he stood alone. Yet I believe even that footprint in the sand was never greater blow to him than was this impress in the garden mould to me, for I remembered well the little shoes of polished leather, with their silver buckles and high-tilted heels.

He *had* been here before us. I found another footprint, and another leading towards the middle of the bed; and then I flung the match away, trampling the fire out in the soil. It was no use searching farther now, for I knew well there was no diamond here for us.

I stepped back to the lawn, and caught Elzevir by the arm. 'Aldobrand has been here before us, and stole away the jewel,' I whispered sharp; and looking wildly round in the still night, saw the lattice of lamplight shining through the wooden blinds of the balcony window.

'Well, there's an end of it!' said he. 'And we are saved further question. 'Tis gone, so let us cry good riddance to it and be off.' So he turned to go back, and there was one more chance for me to choose the better way and go with him; but still I could not give the jewel up, and must go farther on the other path which led to ruin for us both. For I had my eyes fixed on the light coming through the blinds of that window, and saw how thick and strong the boughs of the pear tree were trained against the wall about the balcony.

'Elzevir,' I said, swallowing the bitter disappointment which rose in my throat, 'I cannot go till I have seen what is doing in that room above. I will climb to the balcony and look in through the chinks. Perhaps he is not there, perhaps he has left our diamond there and we may get it back again.' So I went straight to the house, not giving him time to raise a word to stop me, for there was something in me driving me on, and I was not to be stopped by anyone from that purpose.

There was no need to fear any seeing us, for all the windows except that one, were tight shuttered, and though our footsteps on the soft lawn woke no sound, I knew that Elzevir was following me. It was no easy task to climb the pear tree, for all that the boughs looked so strong, for they lay close against the wall, and gave little hold for hand or foot. Twice, or more, an unripe pear was broken off, and fell rustling down through the leaves to earth, and I paused and waited to hear if anyone was disturbed in the room above; but all was deathly still, and at last I got my hand upon the parapet, and so came safe to the balcony.

I was panting from the hard climb, yet did not wait to get my breath, but made straight for the window to see what was going on inside. The outer shutters were still flung back, as they had been in the afternoon, and there was no difficulty in looking in, for I found an opening in the lattice blind just level with my eyes, and could see all the room inside. It was well lit, as for a marriage feast, and I think there were a score of candles or more burning in holders on the table, or in sconces on the wall. At the table, on the farther side of it from me, and facing the window, sat Aldobrand, just as he sat when he told us the stone was a sham. His face was turned towards the window, and as I looked full at him it seemed impossible but that he should know that I was there.

In front of him, on the table, lay the diamond – our diamond, my diamond; for I knew it was a diamond now, and not false. It was not alone, but had a dozen more cut gems laid beside it on the table, each a little apart from the other; yet there was no mistaking mine, which was thrice as big as any of the rest. And if it surpassed them in size, how much more did it excel in fierceness and sparkle! All the candles in the room were mirrored in it, and as the splendour flashed from every line and facet that I knew so well, it seemed to call to me, 'Am I not queen of all diamonds of the world? Am I not your diamond? Will you not take me to yourself again? Will you save me from this sorry trickster?'

I had my eyes fixed, but still knew that Elzevir was beside me. He would not let me risk myself in any hazard alone without he stood by me himself to help in case of need; and yet his faithfulness but galled me now, and I asked myself with a sneer, Am I never to stir hand or foot without this man to dog me? The merchant sat still for a minute as though thinking, and then he took one of the diamonds that lay on the table, and then another, and set them close beside the great stone, pitting them, as it were, with it. Yet how could any match with that? For it outshone them all as the sun outshines the stars in heaven.

Then the old man took the stone and weighed it in the scales which stood on the table before him, balancing it carefully, and a dozen times, against some little weights of brass; and then he wrote with pen and ink in a sheepskin book, and afterwards on a sheet of paper as though casting up numbers. What would I not have given to see the figures that he wrote? For was he not casting up the value of the jewel, and summing out the profits he would make? After that he took the stone between finger and thumb, holding it up before his eyes, and placing it now this way, now that, so that the light might best fall on it. I could have cursed him for the wondering love of that fair jewel that overspread his face; and cursed him ten times more for the smile upon his lips, because I guessed he laughed to think how he had duped two simple sailors that very afternoon.

There was the diamond in his hands – our diamond, my diamond – in his hands, and I but two yards from my own; only a flimsy veil of wood and glass to keep me from the treasure he had basely stolen from us. Then I felt Elzevir's hand upon my shoulder. 'Let us be going,' he said; 'a minute more and he may come to put these shutters to, and find us here. Let us be going. Diamonds are not for simple folk like us; this is an evil stone, and brings a curse with it. Let us be going, John.'

But I shook off the kind hand roughly, forgetting how he had saved my life, and nursed me for many weary weeks and stood by me through bad and worse; for just now the man at the table rose and took out a little iron box from a cupboard at the back of the room. I knew that he was going to lock my treasure into it, and that I should see it no more. But the great jewel lying lonely on the table flashed and sparkled in the light of twenty candles, and called to me, 'Am I not queen of all diamonds of the world? Am I not your diamond? Save me from the hands of this scurvy robber.'

Then I hurled myself forward with all my weight full on the joining of the window frames, and in a second crashed through the glass, and through the wooden blind into the room behind.

The noise of splintered wood and glass had not died away before there was a sound as of bells ringing all over

the house, and the wires I had seen in the afternoon dangled loose in front of my face. But I cared neither for bells nor wires, for there lay the great jewel flashing before me. The merchant had turned sharp round at the crash, and darted for the diamond, crying 'Thieves! Thieves! Thieves!' He was nearer to it than I, and as I dashed forward our hands met across the table, with his underneath upon the stone. But I gripped him by the wrist, and though he struggled, he was but a weak old man, and in a few seconds I had it twisted from his grasp. In a few seconds – but before they were past the diamond was well in my hand – the door burst open, and in rushed six sturdy serving men with staves and bludgeons.

Elzevir had given a little groan when he saw me force the window, but followed me into the room and was now at my side. 'Thieves! Thieves! Thieves!' screamed the merchant, falling back exhausted in his chair and pointing to us, and then the knaves fell on too quick for us to make for the window. Two set on me and four on Elzevir; and one man, even a giant, cannot fight with four – above all when they carry staves.

Never had I seen Master Block overborne or worsted by any odds; and Fortune was kind to me, at least in this, that she let me not see the issue then, for a staff caught me so round a knock on the head as made the diamond drop out of my hand, and laid me swooning on the floor.

17

At Ymeguen

As if a thief should steal a tainted vest,
Some dead man's spoil, and sicken of his pest – *Hood*

'TIS bitterer to me than wormwood the memory of what followed, and I shall tell the story in the fewest words I may. We were cast into prison, and lay there for months in a stone cell with little light, and only foul straw to lie on. At first we were cut and bruised from that tussle and cudgelling in Aldobrand's house, and it was long before we were recovered of our wounds, for we had nothing but bread and water to live on, and that so bad as barely to hold body and soul together. Afterwards the heavy fetters that were put about our ankles set up sores and galled us so that we scarce could move for pain. And if the iron galled my flesh, my spirit chafed ten times more within those damp and dismal walls; yet all that time Elzevir never breathed a word of reproach, though it was my wilfulness had led us into so terrible a strait.

At last came our jailer, one morning, and said that we must be brought up that day before the *Geregt*, which is their Court of Assize, to be tried for our crime. So we were marched off to the courthouse, in spite of sores and heavy irons, and were glad enough to see the daylight once more, and drink the open air, even though it should be to our death that we were walking; for the jailer said they were like to hang us for what we had done. In the courthouse our business was soon over, because there were many to speak against us, but none to plead our cause; and all being done in the Dutch language I understood nothing of it, except what Elzevir told me afterwards.

There was Mr Aldobrand in his black gown and buckled shoes with tip-tilted heels, standing at a table and giving evidence: how that one afternoon in August came two evil-looking English sailors to his house under pretence of selling a diamond, which turned out to be but a lump of glass: and that having taken observation of all his dwelling, and more particularly the approaches to his business room, they went their ways. But later in the same day, or rather night, as he sat matching together certain diamonds for a coronet ordered by the most illustrious the Holy Roman Emperor, these same ill-favoured English sailors burst suddenly through shutters and window, and made forcible entry into his business room. There they furiously attacked him, wrenched the diamond from his hand, and beat him within an ace of his life. But by the good Providence of God, and his own foresight, the window was fitted with a certain alarm, which rang bells in other parts of the house. Thus his trusty servants were summoned, and after being themselves attacked and nearly overborne, succeeded at last in mastering these scurvy ruffians and handing them over to the law, from which Mr Aldobrand claimed sovereign justice.

Thus much Elzevir explained to me afterwards, but at that time when that pretender spoke of the diamond as being his own, Elzevir cut in and said in open court that 'twas a lie, and that this precious stone was none other than the one that we had offered in the afternoon, when Aldobrand had said 'twas glass. Then the diamond merchant laughed, and took from his purse our great diamond, which seemed to fill the place with light and dazzled half the court. He turned it over in his hand, poising it in his palm like a great flourishing lamp of light, and asked if 'twas likely that two common sailormen should hawk a stone like that. Nay more, that the court might know what daring rogues they had to deal with, he pulled out from his pocket the quittance given him by Shalamof the Jew of Petersburg, for this same jewel, and showed it to the judge. Whether 'twas a forged quittance or one for some other stone we knew not, but Elzevir spoke again, saying that the stone was ours and we had found it in England. When Mr Aldobrand laughed again, and held the jewel up once more: were such pebbles, he asked, found on the shore by every squalid fisherman? And the great diamond flashed as he put it back into his purse, and cried to me, 'Am I not queen of all the diamonds of the world? Must I house with this base rascal?' but I was powerless now to help.

After Aldobrand, the serving men gave witness, telling how they had trapped us in the act, red-handed: and as for this jewel, they had seen their master handle it any time in these six months past.

But Elzevir was galled to the quick with all their falsehoods, and burst out again, that they were liars and the jewel ours; till a jailer who stood by struck him on the mouth and cut his lip, to silence him.

The process was soon finished, and the judge in his red robes stood up and sentenced us to the galleys for life; bidding us admire the mercy of the law to outlanders, for had we been but Dutchmen, we should sure have hanged.

Then they took and marched us out of court, as well as we could walk for fetters, and Elzevir with a bleeding mouth. But as we passed the place where Aldobrand sat, hc bows to me and says in English, 'Your servant, Mr Trenchard. I wish you a good day, Sir John Trenchard of Moonfleet, in Dorset.' The jailer paused a moment, hearing Aldobrand speak to us though not understanding what he said, so I had time to answer him:

'Good day, Sir Aldobrand, Liar, and Thief; and may the diamond bring you evil in this present life, and damnation in that which is to come.'

So we parted from him, and at that same time departed from our liberty and from all joys of life.

We were fettered together with other prisoners in droves of six, our wrists manacled to a long bar, but I was put into a different gang from Elzevir. Thus we marched a ten days' journey into the country to a place called Ymeguen, where a royal fortress was building. That was a weary march for me, for 'twas January, with wet and miry roads, and I had little enough clothes upon my back to keep off rain and cold. On either side rode guards on horseback, with loaded flintlocks across the saddlebow, and long whips in their hands with which they let fly at any laggard; though 'twas hard enough for men to walk where the mud was over the horses' fetlocks. I had no chance to speak to Elzevir all the journey, and indeed spoke nothing at all, for those to whom I was chained were brute beasts rather than men, and spoke only in Dutch to boot.

There was but little of the building of the fortress begun when we reached Ymeguen, and the task that we were set to was the digging of the trenches and other earthworks. I believe that there were five hundred men employed in this way, and all of them condemned like us to galley work for life. We were divided into squads of twenty-five, but Elzevir was drafted to another squad and a different part of the workings, so I saw him no more except at odd times, now and again, when our gangs met, and we could exchange a word or two in passing.

Thus I had no solace of any company but my own, and was driven to thinking, and to occupy my mind with the recollection of the past. And at first the life of my boyhood, now lost forever, was constantly present even in my dreams, and I would wake up thinking that I was at school again under Mr Glennie, or talking in the summer house with Grace, or climbing Weatherbeech Hill with the salt Channel breeze singing through the trees. But alas! these things faded when I opened my eyes, and knew the foul-smelling wood hut and floor of fetid straw where fifty of us lay in fetters every night. I say I dreamed these things at first, but by degrees remembrance grew blunted and the images less clear, and even these sweet, sad visions of the night came to me less often. Thus life became a weary round, in which month followed month, season followed season, year followed year, and brought always the same eternal profitless work. And yet the work was merciful, for it dulled the biting edge of thought, and the unchanging evenness of life gave wings to time.

In all the years the locusts ate for me at Ymeguen, there is but one thing I need speak of here. I had been there a week when I was loosed one morning from my irons, and taken from work into a little hut apart, where there stood a half-dozen of the guard, and in the midst a stout wooden chair with clamps and bands. A fire burned on the floor, and there was a fume and smoke that filled the air with a smell of burned meat. My heart misgave me when I saw that chair and fire, and smelt that sickly smell, for I guessed this was a torture room, and these the torturers waiting. They forced me into the chair and bound me there with lashings and a cramp about the head; and then one took a red iron from the fire upon the floor, and tried it a little way from his hand to prove the heat. I had screwed up my heart to bear the pain as best I might, but when I saw that iron sighed for sheer relief, because I knew it for only a branding tool, and not the torture. And so they branded me on the left cheek, setting the iron between the nose and cheekbone, where 'twas plainest to be seen. I took the pain and scorching light enough, seeing that I had looked for much worse, and should not have made mention of the thing here at all, were it not for the branding mark they used. Now this mark was a 'Y', being the first letter of Ymeguen, and set on all the prisoners that worked there, as I found afterwards; but to me 'twas much more than a mere letter, and nothing less than the black 'Y' itself, or cross pall of the Mohunes. Thus as a sheep is marked, with his owner's keel, and can be claimed wherever he may be, so here was I branded with the keel of the Mohunes and marked for theirs in life or death, whithersoever I should wander. 'Twas three months after that, and the mark healed and well set, that I saw Elzevir again; and as we passed each other in the trench and called a greeting, I saw that he too bore the cross pall full on his left cheek.

Thus years went on and I was grown from boy to man, and that no weak one either: for though they gave us but scant food and bad, the air was fresh and strong, because Ymeguen was meant for palace as well as fortress, and they chose a healthful site. And by degrees the moats were dug, and ramparts built, and stone by stone the castle rose till 'twas near the finish, and so our labour was not wanted. Every day squads of our fellow prisoners marched away, and my gang was left till nearly last, being engaged in making good a culvert that heavy rains had broken down.

It was in the tenth year of our captivity, and in the twenty-sixth of my age, that one morning instead of the guard marching us to work, they handed us over to a party of mounted soldiers, from whose matchlocks and long whips I knew that we were going to leave Ymeguen. Before we left, another gang joined us, and how my heart went out when I saw Elzevir among them! It was two years or more since we had met even to pass a greeting, for I worked outside the fortress and he on the great tower inside, and I took note his hair was whiter and a sadder look upon his face. And as for the cross pall on his cheek, I never thought of it at all, for we were all so well used to the mark, that if one bore it not stamped upon his face we should have stared at him as on a man born with but one eye. But though his look was sad, yet Elzevir had a kind smile and hearty greeting for me as he passed, and on the march, when they served out our food, we got a chance to speak a word or two together. Yet how could we find room for much gladness, for even the pleasure of meeting was marred because we were forced thus to take note, as it were, of each other's misery, and to know that the one had nothing for his old age but to break in prison, and the other nothing but the prison to eat away the strength of his prime.

Before long, all knew whither we were bound, for it leaked out we were to march to the Hague and thence to Scheveningen, to take ship to the settlements of Java, where they use transported felons on the sugar farms. Was this the end of young hopes and lofty aims – to live and die a slave in the Dutch plantations? Hopes of Grace, hopes of seeing Moonfleet again, were dead long long ago; and now was there to be no hope of liberty, or even wholesome air, this side the grave, but only burning sun and steaming swamps, and the crack of the slave driver's whip till the end came? Could it be so? Could it be so? And yet what help was there, or what release? Had I not watched ten years for any gleam or loophole of relief, and never found it? If we were shut in cells or dungeons in the deepest rock we might have schemed escape, but here in the open, fettered up in droves, what could we do? They were bitter thoughts enough that filled my heart as I trudged along the rough roads, fettered by my wrist to the long bar; and seeing Elzevir's white hair and bowed shoulders trudging in front of me, remembered when that head had scarce a grizzle on it, and the back was straight as the massive stubborn pillars in old Moonfleet church. What was it had brought us to this pitch? And then I called to mind a July evening, years ago, the twilight summer house and a sweet grave voice that said, 'Have a care how you touch the treasure; it was evilly come by, and will bring a curse with it.' Ay, 'twas the diamond had done it all, and brought a blight upon my life, since that first night I spent in Moonfleet vault; and I cursed the stone, and Blackbeard and his lost Mohunes, and trudged on bearing their cognizance branded on my face.

We marched back to the Hague, and through that very street where Aldobrand dwelt, only the house was shut, and the board that bore his name taken away; so it seemed that he had left the place or else was dead. Thus we reached the quays at last, and though I knew that I was leaving Europe and leaving all hope behind, yet 'twas a delight to smell the sea again and fill my nostrils with the keen salt air.

18

In the Bay

Let broad leagues dissever
Him from yonder foam,
O God! to think man ever
Comes too near his home – *Hood*

The ship that was to carry us swung at the buoy a quarter of a mile off shore, and there were rowboats waiting to take us to her. She was a brig of some 120 tons burthen, and as we came under the stern I saw her name was the *Aurungzebe*.

'Twas with regret unspeakable I took my last look at Europe; and casting my eyes round saw the smoke of the town dark against the darkening sky; yet knew that neither smoke nor sky was half as black as was the prospect of my life.

They sent us down to the orlop or lowest deck, a foul place where was no air nor light, and shut the hatches down on top of us. There were thirty of us all told, hustled and driven like pigs into this deck, which was to be our pigsty for six months or more. Here was just light enough, when they had the hatches off, to show us what sort of place it was, namely, as foul as it smelt, with never table, seat, nor anything, but roughest planks and balks; and there they changed our bonds, taking away the bar, and putting a tight bracelet round one wrist, with a padlocked chain running through a loop on it. Thus we were still ironed, six together, but had a greater freedom and more scope to move. And more than this, the man who shifted the chains, whether through caprice, or perhaps because he really wished to show us what pity he might, padlocked me on to the same chain with Elzevir, saying, we were English swine and might sink or swim together. Then the hatches were put on, and there they left us in the dark to think or sleep or curse the time away. The weariness of Ymeguen was bad indeed, and yet it was a heaven to this night of hell, where all we had to look for was twice a day the moving of the hatches, and half an hour's glimmer of a ship's lantern, while they served us out the broken victuals that the Dutch crew would not eat.

I shall say nothing of the foulness of this place, because 'twas too foul to be written on paper; and if 'twas foul at starting, 'twas ten times worse when we reached open sea, for of all the prisoners only Elzevir and I were sailors, and the rest took the motion unkindly.

From the first we made bad weather of it, for though we were below and could see nothing, yet 'twas easy enough to tell there was a heavy head sea running, almost as soon as we were well out of harbour. Although Elzevir and I had not had any chance of talking freely for so long, and were now able to speak as we liked, being linked so close together, we said but little. And this, not because we did not value very greatly one another's company, but because we had nothing to talk of except memories of the past, and those were too bitter, and came too readily to our minds, to need any to summon them. There was, too, the banishment from Europe, from all and everything we loved, and the awful certainty of slavery that lay continuously on us like a weight of lead. Thus we said little.

We had been out a week, I think – for time is difficult enough to measure where there is neither clock nor sun nor stars – when the weather, which had moderated a little, began to grow much worse. The ship plunged and laboured heavily, and this added much to our discomfort; because there was nothing to hold on by, and unless we lay flat on the filthy deck, we ran a risk of being flung to the side whenever there came a more violent lurch or roll. Though we were so deep down, yet the roaring of wind and wave was loud enough to reach us, and there was such a noise when the ship went about, such grinding of ropes, with creaking and groaning of timbers, as would make a landsman fear the brig was going to pieces. And this some of our fellow prisoners feared indeed, and fell to crying, or kneeling chained together as they were upon the sloping deck, while they tried to remember long-forgotten prayers. For my own part, I wondered why these poor wretches should pray to be delivered from the sea, when all that was before them was lifelong slavery; but I was perhaps able to look more calmly on the matter myself as having been at sea, and not thinking that the vessel was going to founder because of the noise. Yet the storm rose till 'twas very plain that we were in a raging sea, and the streams which began to trickle through the joinings of the hatch showed that water had got below.

'I have known better ships go under for less than this,' Elzevir said to me; 'and if our skipper hath not a tight craft, and stout hands to work her, there will soon be two score slaves the less to cut the canes in Java. I cannot guess where we are now – maybe off Ushant, maybe not so far, for this sea is too short for the Bay; but the saints send us sea room, for we have been wearing these three hours.'

'Twas true enough that we had gone to wearing, as one might tell from the heavier roll or wallowing when we went round, instead of the plunging of a tack; but there was no chance of getting at our whereabouts. The only thing we had to reckon time withal, was the taking off of the hatch twice a day for food; and even this poor clock kept not the hour too well, for often there were such gaps and intervals as made our bellies pine, and at this present we had waited so long that I craved even that filthy broken meat they fed us with.

So we were glad enough to hear a noise at the hatch just as Elzevir had done speaking, and the cover was flung off, letting in a splash of salt water and a little dim and dusky light. But instead of the guard with their muskets and lanterns and the tubs of broken victuals, there was only one man, and that the jailer who had padlocked us into gangs at the beginning of the voyage.

He bent down for a moment over the hatch, holding on to the combing to steady himself in the seaway, and flung a key on a chain down into the orlop, right among us. 'Take it,' he shouted in Dutch, 'and make the most of it. God helps the brave, and the devil takes the hindmost.'

That said, he stayed not one moment, but turned about quick and was gone. For an instant none knew what this play portended, and there was the key lying on the deck, and the hatch left open. Then Elzevir saw what it all meant, and seized the key. 'John,' cries he, speaking to me in English, 'the ship is foundering, and they are giving us a chance to save our lives, and not drown like rats in a trap.' With that he tried the key on the padlock which held our chain, and it fitted so well that in a trice our gang was free. Off fell the chain clanking on the floor, and nothing left of our bonds but an iron bracelet clamped round the left wrist. You may be sure the others were quick enough to make use of the key when they knew what 'twas, but we waited not to see more, but made for the ladder.

Now Elzevir and I, being used to the sea, were first through the hatchway above, and oh, the strength and sweet coolness of the sea air, instead of the warm, fetid reek of the orlop below! There was a good deal of water sousing about on the main deck, but nothing to show the ship was sinking, yet none of the crew was to be seen. We stayed there not a second, but moved to the companion as fast as we could for the heavy pitching of the ship, and so came on deck.

The dusk of a winter's evening was setting in, yet with ample light to see near at hand, and the first thing I perceived was that the deck was empty. There was not a living soul but us upon it. The brig was broached to, with her bows against the heaviest sea I ever saw, and the waves swept her fore and aft; so we made for the tail of the deck-house, and there took stock. But before we got there I knew why 'twas the crew were gone, and why they let us loose, for Elzevir pointed to something whither we were drifting, and shouted in my ear so that I heard it above all the raging of the tempest – 'We are on a lee shore.'

We were lying head to sea, and never a bit of canvas left except one storm staysail. There were tattered ribands fluttering on the yards to show where the sails had been blown away, and every now and then the staysail would flap like a gun going off, to show it wanted to follow them. But for all we lay head to sea, we were moving backwards, and each great wave as it passed carried us on stern first with a leap and swirling lift. 'Twas over the stern that Elzevir pointed, in the course that we were going, and there was such a mist, what with the wind and rain and spindrift, that one could see but a little way. And yet

I saw too far, for in the mist to which we were making a sternboard, I saw a white line like a fringe or valance to the sea; and then I looked to starboard, and there was the same white fringe, and then to larboard, and the white fringe was there too. Only those who know the sea know how terrible were Elzevir's words uttered in such a place. A moment before I was exalted with the keen salt wind, and with a hope and freedom that had been strangers for long; but now 'twas all dashed, and death, that is so far off to the young, had moved nearer by fifty years – was moving a year nearer every minute.

'We are on a lee shore,' Elzevir shouted; and I looked and knew what the white fringe was, and that we should be in the breakers in half an hour. What a whirl of wind and wave and sea, what a whirl of thought and wild conjecture! What was that land to which we were drifting? Was it cliff, with deep water and iron face, where a good ship is shattered at a blow, and death comes like a thunderclap? Or was it shelving sand, where there is stranding, and the pound, pound, pound of the waves for howls, before she goes to pieces and all is over?

We were in a bay, for there was the long white crescent of surf reaching far away on either side, till it was lost in the dusk, and the brig helpless in the midst of it. Elzevir had hold of my arm, and gripped it hard as he looked to larboard. I followed his eyes, and where one horn of the white crescent faded into the mist, caught a dark shadow in the air, and knew it was high land looming behind. And then the murk and driving rain lifted ever so little, and as it were only for that purpose; and we saw a misty bluff slope down into the sea, like the long head of a basking alligator poised upon the water, and stared into each other's eyes, and cried together, 'The Snout!'

It had vanished almost before it was seen, and yet we knew there was no mistake; it was the Snout that was there looming behind the moving rack, and we were in Moonfleet Bay. Oh, what a rush of thought then came, dazing me with its sweet bitterness, to think that after all these weary years of prison and exile we had come back to Moonfleet! We were so near to all we loved, so near – only a mile of broken water – and yet so far, for death lay between, and we had come back to Moonfleet to die. There was a change came over Elzevir's features when he saw the Snout; his face had lost its sadness and wore a look of sober happiness. He put his mouth close to my ear and said: 'There is some strange leading hand has brought us home at last, and I had rather drown on Moonfleet beach than live in prison any more, and drown we must within an hour. Yet we will play the man, and make a fight for life.' And then, as if gathering together all his force: 'We have weathered bad times together, and who knows but we shall weather this?'

The other prisoners were on deck now, and had found their way aft. They were wild with fear, being landsmen and never having seen an angry sea, and indeed that sea might have frighted sailors too. So they stumbled along drenched with the waves, and clustered round Elzevir, for they looked on him as a leader, because he knew the ways of the sea and was the only one left calm in this dreadful strait.

It was plain that when the Dutch crew found they were embayed, and that the ship must drift into the breakers, they had taken to the boats, for gig and jollyboat were gone and only the pinnace left amidships. 'Twas too heavy a boat perhaps for them to have got out in such a fearful sea; but there it lay, and it was to that the prisoners turned their eyes. Some had hold of Elzevir's arms, some fell upon the deck and caught him by the knees, beseeching him to show them how to get the pinnace out.

Then he spoke out, shouting to make them hear: 'Friends, any man that takes to boat is lost. I know this bay and know this beach, and was indeed born hereabouts, but never knew a boat come to land in such a sea, save bottom uppermost. So if you want my counsel, there you have it, namely, to stick by the ship. In half an hour we shall be in the breakers; and I will put the helm up and try to head the brig bows on to the beach; so every man will have a chance to fight for his own life, and God have mercy on those that drown.'

I knew what he said was the truth, and there was nothing for it but to stick to the ship, though that was small chance enough; but those poor, fear-demented souls would have nothing of his advice now 'twas given, and must needs go for the boat. Then some came up from below who had been in the spirit room and were full of drink and drink courage, and heartened on the rest, saying they would have the pinnace out, and every soul should be saved. Indeed, Fate seemed to point them that road, for a heavier sea than any came on board, and cleared away a great piece of larboard bulwarks that had been working loose, and made, as it were, a clear launching way for the boat. Again did Elzevir try to prevail with them to stand by the ship, but they turned away and all made for the pinnace. It lay amidships and was a heavy boat enough, but with so many hands to help they got it to the broken bulwarks. Then Elzevir, seeing they would have it out at any price, showed them how to take advantage of the sea, and shifted the helm a little till the *Aurungzebe* fell off to larboard, and put the gap in the bulwarks on the lee. So in a few minutes there it lay at a rope's-end on the sheltered side, deep laden with thirty men, who were ill found with oars, and much worse found with skill to use them. There were one or two, before they left, shouted to Elzevir and me to try to make us follow them; partly, I think, because they really liked Elzevir, and partly that they might have a sailor in the boat to direct them; but the others cast off and left us with a curse, saying that we might go and drown for obstinate Englishmen.

So we two were left alone on the brig, which kept drifting backwards slowly; but the pinnace was soon lost to sight, though we saw that they were rowing wild as soon as she passed out of the shelter of the ship, and that they had much ado to keep her head to the sea.

Then Elzevir went to the kicking wheel, and beckoned me to help him, and between us we put the helm hard up. I saw then that he had given up all hope of the wind shifting, and was trying to run her dead for the beach.

She was broached-to with her bows in the wind, but gradually paid off as the staysail filled, and so she headed straight for shore. The November night had fallen, and it was very dark, only the white fringe of the breakers could be seen, and grew plainer as we drew closer to it. The wind was blowing fiercer than ever, and the waves broke more fiercely nearer the shore. They had lost their dirty yellow colour when the light died, and were rolling after us like great black mountains, with a combing white top that seemed as if they must overwhelm us every minute. Twice they pooped us, and we were up to our waists in icy water, but still held to the wheel for our lives.

The white line was nearer to us now, and above all the rage of wind and sea I could hear the awful roar of the undertow sucking back the pebbles on the beach. The last time I could remember hearing that roar was when I lay, as a boy, one summer's night 'twixt sleep and waking, in the little whitewashed bedroom at my aunt's; and I wondered now if any sat before their inland hearths this night, and hearing that far distant roar, would throw another log on the fire, and thank God they were not fighting for their lives in Moonfleet Bay. I could picture all that was going on this night on the beach – how Ratsey and the landers would have sighted the *Aurungzebe*, perhaps at noon, perhaps before, and knew she was embayed, and nothing could save her but the wind drawing to east. But the wind would hold pinned in the south, and they would see sail after sail blown off her, and watch her wear and wear, and every time come nearer in; and the talk would run through the street that there was a ship could not weather the South, and must come ashore by sundown. Then half the village would be gathered on the beach, with the men ready to risk their lives for ours, and in no wise wishing for the ship to be wrecked; yet anxious not to lose their chance of booty, if Providence should rule that wrecked she must be. And I knew Ratsey would be there, and Damen, Tewkesbury, and Laver, and like enough Parson Glennie, and perhaps – and at that perhaps, my thoughts came back to where we were, for I heard Elzevir speaking to me:

'Look,' he said, 'there's a light!'

'Twas but the faintest twinkle, or not even that; only something that told there was a light behind drift and darkness. It grew clearer as we looked at it, and again was lost in the mirk, and then Elzevir said, 'Maskew's Match!'

It was a long-forgotten name that came to me from so far off, down such long alleys of the memory, that I had, as it were, to grope and grapple with it to know what it should mean. Then it all came back, and I was a boy again on the trawler, creeping shorewards in the light breeze of an August night, and watching that friendly twinkle from the manor woods above the village. Had she not promised she would keep that lamp alight to guide all sailors every night till I came back again; was she not waiting still for me, was I not coming back to her now? But what a coming back! No more a boy, not on an August night, but broken, branded convict in the November gale! 'Twas well, indeed, there was between us that white fringe of death, that she might never see what I had fallen to.

'Twas likely Elzevir had something of the same thoughts, for he spoke again, forgetting perhaps that I was man now, and no longer boy, and using a name he had not used for years. 'Johnnie,' he said, 'I am cold and sore downhearted. In ten minutes we shall be in the surf. Go down to the spirit locker, drink thyself, and bring me up a bottle here. We shall both need a young man's strength, and I have not got it any more.'

I did as he bid me, and found the locker though the cabin was all awash, and having drunk myself, took him the bottle back. 'Twas good Hollands enough, being from the captain's own store, but nothing to the old Ararat milk of the Why Not? Elzevir took a pull at it, and then flung the bottle away. ''Tis sound liquor,' he laughed, ' "and good for autumn chills", as Ratsey would have said.'

We were very near the white fringe now, and the waves followed us higher and more curling. Then there was a sickly wan glow that spread itself through the watery air in front of us, and I knew that they were burning a blue light on the beach. They would all be there waiting for us, though we could not see them, and they did not know that there were only two men that they were signalling to, and those two Moonfleet born. They burn that light in Moonfleet Bay just where a little streak of clay crops out beneath the pebbles, and if a vessel can make that spot she gets a softer bottom. So we put the wheel over a bit, and set her straight for the flare.

There was a deafening noise as we came near the shore, the shrieking of the wind in the rigging, the crash of the combing seas, and over all the awful grinding roar of the undertow sucking down the pebbles.

'It is coming now,' Elzevir said; and I could see dim figures moving in the misty glare from the blue light; and then, just as the *Aurungzebe* was making fair for the signal, a monstrous combing sea pooped her and washed us both from the wheel, forward in a swirling flood. We grasped at anything we could, and so brought up bruised and half-drowned in the forechains; but as the wheel ran free, another sea struck her and slewed her round. There was a second while the water seemed over, under, and on every side, and then the *Aurungzebe* went broadside on Moonfleet beach, with a noise like thunder and a blow that stunned us.

I have seen ships come ashore in that same place before and since, and bump on and off with every wave, till the stout balks could stand the pounding no more and parted. But 'twas not so with our poor brig, for after that first fearful shock she never moved again, being flung so firm upon the beach by one great swamping wave that never another had power to uproot her. Only she careened over beachwards, turning herself away from the seas, as a child bows his head to escape a cruel master's ferule, and then her masts broke off, first the fore and then the main, with a splitting crash that made itself heard above all.

We were on the lee side underneath the shelter of the deckhouse clinging to the shrouds, now up to our knees in water as the wave came on, now left high and dry when it went back. The blue light was still burning, but the ship was beached a little to the right of it, and the dim group of fishermen had moved up along the beach till they were opposite us. Thus we were but a hundred feet distant from them, but 'twas the interval of death and life, for between us and the shore was a maddened race of seething water, white foaming waves that leapt up from all sides against our broken bulwarks, or sucked back the pebbles with a grinding roar till they left the beach nearly dry.

We stood there for a minute hanging on, and waiting for resolution to come back to us after the shock of grounding. On the weather side the seas struck and curled over the brig with a noise like thunder, and the force of countless tons. They came over the top of the deckhouse in a cataract of solid water, and there was a crash, crash, crash of rending wood, as plank after plank gave way before that stern assault. We could feel the deckhouse itself quiver, and shake again as we stood with our backs against it, and at last it moved so much that we knew it must soon be washed over on us.

The moment had come. 'We must go after the next big wave runs back,' Elzevir shouted. 'Jump when I give the word, and get as far up the pebbles as you can before the next comes in: they will throw us a rope's-end to catch; so now goodbye, John, and God save us both!'

I wrung his hand, and took off my convict clothes, keeping my boots on to meet the pebbles, and was so cold that I almost longed for the surf. Then we stood waiting side by side till a great wave came in, turning the space 'twixt ship and shore into a boiling cauldron: a minute later 'twas all sucked back again with a roar, and we jumped.

I fell on hands and feet where the water was a yard deep under the ship, but got my footing and floundered through the slop, in a desperate struggle to climb as high as might be on the beach before the next wave came in. I saw the string of men lashed together and reaching down as far as man might, to save any that came through the surf, and heard them shout to cheer us, and marked a coil of rope flung out. Elzevir was by my side and saw it too, and we both kept our feet and plunged forward through the quivering slack water; but then there came an awful thunder behind, the crash of the sea over the wreck, and we knew that another mountain wave was on our heels. It came in with a swishing roar, a rush and rise of furious water that swept us like corks up the beach, till we were within touch of the rope's-end, and the men shouted again to hearten us as they flung it out. Elzevir seized it with his left hand and reached out his right to me. Our fingers touched, and in that very moment the wave fell instantly, with an awful suck, and I was swept down the beach again. Yet the undertow took me not back to sea, for amid the floating wreckage floated the shattered maintop, and in the truck of that great spar I caught, and so was left with it upon the beach thirty paces from the men and Elzevir. Then he left his own assured salvation, namely the rope, and strode down again into the very jaws of death to catch me by the hand and set me on my feet. Sight and breath were failing me; I was numb with cold and half dead from the buffeting of the sea; yet his giant strength was powerful to save me then, as it had saved me before. So when we heard once more the warning crash and thunder of the returning wave we were but a fathom distant from the rope. 'Take heart, lad,' he cried; ''tis now or never,' and as the water reached our breasts gave me a fierce shove forward with his hands. There was a roar of water in my ears, with a great shouting of the men upon the beach, and then I caught the rope.

19

On the Beach

Toll for the brave,
The grave that are no more;
All sunk beneath the wave
Fast by their native shore – *Cowper*

The night was cold, and I had nothing on me save breeches and boots, and those drenched with the sea, and had been wrestling with the surf so long that there was little left in me. Yet once I clutched the rope I clung to it for very life, and in a minute found myself in the midst of the beachmen. I heard them shout again, and felt strong hands seize me, but could not see their faces for a mist that swam before my eyes, and could not speak because my throat and tongue were cracked with the salt water, and the voice would not come. There was a crowd about me of men and some women, and I spread out my hands, blindly, to catch hold of them, but my knees failed and let me down upon the beach. And after that I remember only having coats flung over me, and being carried off out of the wind, and laid in warmest blankets before a fire. I was numb with the cold, my hair was matted with the salt, and my flesh white and shrivelled, but they forced liquor into my mouth, and so I lay in drowsy content till utter weariness bound me in sleep.

It was a deep and dreamless sleep for hours, and when it left me, gently and as it were inch by inch, I found I was still lying wrapped in blankets by the fire. Oh, what a vast and infinite peace was that, to lie there half asleep, yet wake enough to know that I had slipped my prison and the pains of death, and was a free man here in my native place! At last I shifted myself a little, growing more awake; and opening my eyes saw I was not alone, for two men sat at a table by me with glasses and a bottle before them.

'He is coming to,' said one, 'and may live yet to tell us who he is, and from what port his craft sailed.'

'There has been many a craft,' the other said, 'has sailed for many a port, and made this beach her last; and many an honest man has landed on it, and never one alive in such a sea. Nor would this one be living either, if it had not been for that other brave heart to stand by and save him. Brave heart, brave heart,' he said over to himself. 'Here, pass me the bottle or I shall get the vapours. 'Tis good against these early chills, and I have not been in this place for ten years past, since poor Elzevir was cut adrift.'

I could not see the speaker's face from where I lay upon the floor, yet seemed to know his voice; and so was fumbling in my weakened mind to put a name to it, when he spoke of Elzevir, and sent my thoughts flying elsewhere.

'Elzevir,' I said, 'where is Elzevir?' and sat up to look round, expecting to see him lying near me, and remembering the wreck more clearly now, and how he had saved me with that last shove forward on the beach. But he was not to be seen, and so I guessed that his great strength had brought him round quicker than had my youth, and that he was gone back to the beach.

'Hush,' said one of the men at the table, 'lie down and get to sleep again'; and then he added, speaking to his comrade: 'His brain is wandering yet: do you see how he has caught up my words about Elzevir?'

'No,' I struck in, 'my head is clear enough; I am speaking of Elzevir Block. I pray you tell me where he is. Is he well again?' They got up and stared at one another and at me, when I named Elzevir Block, and then I knew the one that spoke for Master Ratsey, only greyer than he was.

'Who are you,' he cried, 'who talk of Elzevir Block?'

'Do you not know me, Master Ratsey?' and I looked full in his face. 'I am John Trenchard, who left you so long ago. I pray you tell me where is Master Block?'

Master Ratsey looked as if he had seen a ghost, and was struck dumb at first: but then ran up and shook me by the hand so warmly that I fell back again on my pillow, while he poured out questions in a flood – how had I fared, where had I been, whence had I come? – until I stopped him, saying: 'Softly, kind friend, and I will answer; only tell me first, where is Master Elzevir?'

'Nay, that I cannot say,' he answered, 'for never a soul has set eyes on Elzevir since that summer morning we put thee and him ashore at Newport.'

'Oh, fool me not!' I cried out, chafing at his excuses; 'I am not wandering now. 'Twas Elzevir that saved me in the surf last night. 'Twas he that landed with me.'

There was a look of sad amaze that came on Ratsey's face when I said that; a look that woke in me an awful surmise. 'What!' cried he, 'Was that Master Elzevir that dragged thee through the surf?'

'Ay, 'twas he landed with me, 'twas he landed with me,' I said; trying, as it were, to make true by repeating that which I feared was not the truth. There was a minute's silence, and then Ratsey spoke very softly: 'There was none landed with you; there was no soul saved from that ship alive save you.'

His words fell, one by one, upon my ear as if they were drops of molten lead. 'It is not true,' I cried; 'he pulled me up the beach himself, and it was he that pushed me forward to the rope.'

'Ay, he saved thee, and then the undertow got hold of him and swept him down under the curl. I could not see his face, but might have known there never was a man, save Elzevir, could fight the surf on Moonfleet beach like that. Yet had we known 'twas he, we could have done no more, for many risked their lives last night to save you both. We could have done no more.'

Then I gave a great groan for utter anguish, to think that he had given up the safety he had won for himself, and laid down his life, there on the beach, for me; to think that he had died on the threshold of his home; that I should never get a kind look from him again, nor ever hear his kindly voice.

It is wearisome to others to talk of deep grief, and beside that no words, even of the wisest man, can ever set it forth, nor even if we were able could our memory bear to tell it. So I shall not speak more of that terrible blow, only to say that sorrow, so far from casting my body down, as one might have expected, gave it strength, and I rose up from the mattress where I had been lying. They tried to stop me, and even to hold me back, but for all I was so weak, I pushed them aside and must needs fling a blanket round me and away back to the beach.

The morning was breaking as I left the Why Not? for 'twas in no other place but that I lay, and the wind, though still high, had abated. There were light clouds crossing the heaven very swiftly, and between them patches of clear sky where the stars were growing paler before the dawn. The stars were growing paler; but there was another star, that shone out from the manor woods above the village, although I could not see the house, and told me Grace, like the wise virgins, kept her lamp alight all night.

Yet even that light shone without lustre for me then, for my heart was too full to think of anything but of him who had laid down his life for mine, and of the strong kind heart that was stilled forever.

'Twas well I knew the way, so sure of old, from Why Not? to beach; for I took no heed to path or feet, but plunged along in the morning dusk, blind with sorrow and weariness of spirit. There was a fire of driftwood burning at the back of the beach, and round it crouched a group of men in reefing jackets and sou'westers waiting for morning to save what they might from the wreck; but I gave them a wide berth and so passed in the darkness without a word, and came to the top of the beach. There was light enough to make out what was doing. The sea was running very high, but with the falling wind the waves came in more leisurely and with less of broken water, curling over in a tawny sweep and regular thunderous beat all along the bay for miles. There was no sign left of the hull of the *Aurungzebe*, but the beach was strewn with so much wreckage as one would have thought could never come from so small a ship. There were barrels and kegs, gratings and hatch covers, booms and pieces of masts and trucks; and beside all that, the heaving water inshore was covered with a floating mask of broken matchwood, and the waves, as they curled over, carried up and dashed down on the pebble planks and beams beyond number. There were a dozen or more of men on the seaward side of the beach, with oilskins to keep the wet out, prowling up and down the pebbles to see what they could lay their hands on; and now and then they would run down almost into the white fringe, risking their lives to save a keg as they had risked them to save their fellows last night – as they had risked their lives to save ours, as Elzevir had risked his life to save mine, and lost it there in the white fringe.

I sat down at the top of the beach, with elbows on knees, head between hands, and face set out to sea, not knowing well why I was there or what I sought, but only thinking that Elzevir was floating somewhere in that floating skin of wreckwood, and that I must be at hand to meet him when he came ashore. He would surely come in time, for I had seen others come ashore that way. For when the *Bataviaman* went on the beach, I stood as near her as our rescuers had stood to us last night, and there were some aboard who took the fatal leap from off her bows and tried to battle through the surf. I was so near them I could mark their features and read the wild hope in their faces at the first, and then the undertow took hold of them, and never one that saved his life that day. And yet all came to beach at last, and I knew them by their dead faces for the men I had seen hoping against hope 'twixt ship and shore; some naked and some clothed, some bruised and sorely beaten by the pebbles and the sea, and some sound and untouched – all came to beach at last.

So I sat and waited for him to come; and none of the beach-walkers said anything to me, the Moonfleet men thinking I came from Ringstave, and the Langton men that I belonged to Moonfleet; and both that I had marked some cask at sea for my own and was waiting till it should come in. Only after a while Master Ratsey joined me, and sitting down by me, begged me to eat bread and meat that he had brought. Now I had little heart to eat, but took what he gave me to save myself from his importunities, and having once tasted was led by nature to eat all, and was much benefited thereby. Yet I could not talk with Ratsey, nor answer any of his questions, though another time I should have put a thousand to him myself; and he seeing 'twas no good sat by me in silence, using a spyglass now and again to make out the things floating at sea. As the day grew the men left the fire at the back of the beach, and came down to the seafront where the waves were continually casting up fresh spoil. And there all worked with a will, not each one for his own hand, but all to make a common hoard which should be divided afterwards.

Among the flotsam moving outside the breakers I could see more than one dark ball, like black buoys, bobbing up and down, and lifting as the wave came by: and knew them for the heads of drowned men. Yet though I took Ratsey's glass and scanned all carefully enough, I could make nothing of them, but saw the pinnace floating bottom-up, and farther out another boat deserted and down to her gunwale in the water. 'Twas midday before the first body was cast up, when the sky was breaking a little, and a thin and watery sun trying to get through, and afterwards three other bodies followed. They were part of the pinnace's crew, for all had the iron ring on the left wrist, as Ratsey told me, who went down to see them, though he said nothing of the branded 'Y', and they were taken up and put under some sheeting at the back of the beach, there to lie till a grave should be made ready for them.

Then I felt something that told me he was coming and saw a body rolled over in the surf, and knew it for the one I sought. 'Twas nearest me he was flung up, and I ran down the beach, caring nothing for the white foam, nor for the undertow, and laid hold of him: for had he not left the rescue line last night, and run down into the surf to save my worthless life? Ratsey was at my side, and so between us we drew him up out of the running foam, and then I wrung the water from his hair, and wiped his face and, kneeling down there, kissed him.

When they saw that we had got a body, others of the men came up, and stared to see me handle him so tenderly. But when they knew, at last, I was a stranger and had the iron ring upon my wrist, and a 'Y' burned upon my cheek, they stared the more; until the tale went round that I was he who had come through the surf last night alive, and this poor body was my friend who had laid down his life for me. Then I saw Ratsey speak with one and another of the group, and knew that he was telling them our names; and some that I had known came up and shook me by the hand, not saying anything because they saw my heart was full; and some bent down and looked in Elzevir's face, and touched his hands as if to greet him. Sea and stones had been merciful with him, and he showed neither bruise nor wound, but his face wore a look of great peace, and his eyes and mouth were shut. Even I, who knew where 'twas, could scarcely see the 'Y' mark on his cheek, for the paleness of death had taken out the colour of the scar, and left his face as smooth and mellow-white as the alabaster figures in Moonfleet church. His body was naked from the waist up, as he had stripped for jumping from the brig, and we could see the great broad chest and swelling muscles that had pulled him out of many a desperate pass, and only failed him, for the first and last time so few hours ago.

They stood for a little while looking in silence at the old lander who had run his last cargo on Moonfleet beach, and then they laid his arms down by his side, and slung him in a sail, and carried him away. I walked beside, and as we came down across the sea meadows, the sun broke out and we met little groups of schoolchildren making their way down to the beach to see what was doing with the wreck. They stood aside to let us go by, the boys pulling their caps and the girls dropping a curtsy, when they knew that it was a poor drowned body passing; and as I saw the children I thought I saw myself among them, and I was no more a man, but just come out from Mr Glennie's teaching in the old almshouse hall.

Thus we came to the Why Not? and there set him down. The inn had not been let, as I learned afterwards, since Maskew died; and they had put a fire in it last night for the first time, knowing that the brig would be wrecked, and thinking that some might come off with their lives and require tending. The door stood open, and they carried him into the parlour, where the fire was still burning, and laid him down on the trestle table, covering his face and body with the sail. This done they all stood round a little while, awkwardly enough, as not knowing what to do; and then slipped away one by one, because grief is a thing that only women know how to handle, and they wanted to be back on the beach to get what might be from the wreck. Last of all went Master Ratsey, saying he saw that I would as lief be alone, and that he would come back before dark.

So I was left alone with my dead friend, and with a host of bitterest thoughts. The room had not been cleaned; there were spiderwebs on the beams, and the dust stood so thick on the windowpanes as to shut out half the light. The dust was on everything: on chairs and tables, save on the trestle table where he lay. 'Twas on this very trestle they had laid out David's body; 'twas in this very room that this still form, who would never more know either joy or sorrow, had bowed down and wept over his son. The room was just as we had left it an April evening years ago, and on the dresser lay the great backgammon board, so dusty that one could not read the lettering on it: 'Life is like a game of hazard; the skilful player will make something of the worst of throws'; but what unskilful players we had been, how bad our throws, how little we had made of them!

'Twas with thoughts like this that I was busy while the short afternoon was spent, and the story went up and down the village, how that Elzevir Block and John Trenchard, who left so long ago, were come back to Moonfleet, and that the old lander was drowned saving the young man's life. The dusk was creeping up as I turned back the sail from off his face and took another look at my lost friend, my only friend; for who was there now to care a jot for me? I might go and drown myself on Moonfleet beach, for anyone that would grieve over me. What did it profit me to have broken bonds and to be free again? What use was freedom to me now? Where was I to go, what was I to do? My friend was gone.

So I went back and sat with my head in my hands looking into the fire, when I heard someone step into the room, but did not turn, thinking it was Master Ratsey come back and treading lightly so as not to disturb me. Then I felt a light touch on my shoulder, and looking up saw standing by me a tall and stately woman, girl no longer, but woman in the full strength and beauty of youth. I knew her in a moment, for she had altered little, except her oval face had something more of dignity, and the tawny hair that used to fly about her back was now gathered up. She was looking down at me, and let her hand rest on my shoulder. 'John,' she said, 'have you forgotten me? May I not share your sorrow? Did you not think to tell me you were come? Did you not see the light, did you not know there was a friend that waited for you?'

I said nothing, not being able to speak, but marvelling how she had come just in the point of time to prove me wrong to think I had no friend; and she went on:

'Is it well for you to be here? Grieve not too sadly, for none could have died nobler than he died; and in these years that you have been away, I have thought much of him and found him good at heart, and if he did aught wrong 'twas because others wronged him more.'

And while she spoke I thought how Elzevir had gone to shoot her father, and only failed of it by a hair's breadth, and yet she spoke so well I thought he never really meant to shoot at all, but only to scare the magistrate. And what a whirligig of time was here, that I should have saved Elzevir from having that blot on his conscience, and then that he should save my life, and now that Maskew's daughter should be the one to praise Elzevir when he lay dead! And still I could not speak.

And again she said: 'John, have you no word for me? Have you forgotten? Do you not love me still? Have I no part in your sorrow?'

Then I took her hand in mine and raised it to my lips, and said, 'Dear Mistress Grace, I have forgotten nothing, and honour you above all others: but of love I may not speak more to you – nor you to me, for we are no more boy and girl as in times past, but you a noble lady and I a broken wretch'; and with that I told how I had been ten years a prisoner, and why, and showed her the iron ring upon my wrist, and the brand upon my cheek.

At the brand she stared, and said, 'Speak not of wealth; 'tis not wealth makes men, and if you have come back no richer than you went, you are come back no poorer, nor poorer, John, in honour. And I am rich and have more wealth than I can rightly use, so speak not of these things; but be glad that you are poor, and were not let to profit by that evil treasure. But for this brand, it is no prison name to me, but the Mohunes' badge, to show that you are theirs and must do their bidding. Said I not to you, Have a care how you touch the treasure; it was evilly come by, and will bring a curse with it? But now, I pray you, with a greater earnestness, seeing you bear this mark upon you, touch no penny of that treasure if it should some day come back to you, but put it to such uses as Colonel Mohune thought would help his sinful soul.'

With that she took her hand from mine and bade me goodnight, leaving me in the darkening room with the glow from the fire lighting up the sail and the outline of the body that lay under it. After she was gone I pondered long over what she had said, and what that should mean when she spoke of the treasure one day coming back to me; but wondered much the most to find how constant is the love of woman, and how she could still find a place in her heart for so poor a thing as I. But as to what she said, I was to learn her meaning this very night.

Master Ratsey had come in and gone again, not stopping with me very long, because there was much doing on the beach; but bidding me be of good cheer, and have no fear of the law; for that the ban against me and the head price had been dead for many a year. 'Twas Grace had made her lawyers move for this, refusing herself to sign the hue and cry, and saying that the fatal shot was fired by misadventure. And so a dread which was just waking was laid to rest forever; and when Ratsey went I made up the fire, and lay down in the blankets in front of it, for I was dog-tired and longed for sleep. I was already dozing, but not asleep, when there was a knock at the door, and in walked Mr Glennie. He was aged, and stooped a little, as I could see by the firelight, but for all that I knew him at once, and sitting up offered him what welcome I could.

He looked at me curiously at first, as taking note of the bearded man that had grown out of the boy he remembered, but gave me very kindly greeting, and sat down beside me on a bench. First, he lifted the sail from the dead body, and looked at the sleeping face. Then he took out a Common Prayer, reading the *commendamus* over the dead, and giving me spiritual comfort, and lastly, he fell to talking about the past. From him I learned something of what had happened while I was away, though for that matter nothing had happened at all, except a few deaths, for that is the only sort of change for which we look in Moonfleet. And among those who had passed away was Miss Arnold, my aunt, so that I was another friend the less, if indeed I should count her a friend: for though she meant me well, she showed her care with too much strictness to let me love her, and so in my great sorrow for Elzevir I found no room to grieve for her.

Whether from the spiritual solace Mr Glennie offered me, or whether from his pointing out how much cause for thankfulness I had in being loosed out of prison and saved from imminent death, certain it was I felt some assuagement of grief, and took pleasure in his talk.

'And though I may by some be reprehended,' he said, 'for presuming to refer to profane authors after citing Holy Scripture, yet I cannot refrain from saying that even the great poet Homer counsels moderation in mourning, "for quickly," says he, "cometh satiety of chilly grief".'

After this I thought he was going, but he cleared his throat in such a way that I guessed he had something important to say, and he drew a long folded blue paper from his pocket. 'My son,' he said, opening it leisurely and smoothing it out upon his knee, 'we should never revile Fortune, and in speaking of Fortune I only use that appellation in our poor human sense, and do not imply that there is any chance at all but what is subject to an overruling Providence; we should never, I say, revile Fortune, for just at that moment when she appears to have deserted us, she may be only gone away to seek some richest treasure to bring back with her. And that this is so let what I am about to read to you prove; so light a candle and set it by me, for my eyes cannot follow the writing in this dancing firelight.'

I took an end of candle which stood on the mantelpiece and did as he bid me, and he went on: 'I shall read you this letter which I received near eight years ago, and of the weightiness of it you shall yourself judge.'

I shall not here set down that letter in full, although I have it by me, but will put it shortly, because it was from a lawyer, tricked with long-winded phrases and spun out as such letters are to afford cover afterwards for a heavier charge. It was addressed to the Reverend Horace Glennie, Perpetual Curate of Moonfleet, in the County of Dorset, England, and written in English by Heer Roosten, Attorney and Signariat of the Hague in the Kingdom of Holland. It set forth that one Krispijn Aldobrand, jeweller and dealer in precious stones, at the Hague, had sent for

Heer Roosten to draw a will for him. And that the said Krispijn Aldobrand, being near his end, had deposed to the said Heer Roosten, that he, Aldobrand, was desirous to leave all his goods to one John Trenchard, of Moonfleet, Dorset, in the Kingdom of England. And that he was moved to do this, first, by the consideration that he, Aldobrand, had no children to whom to leave aught, and second, because he desired to make full and fitting restitution to John Trenchard, for that he had once obtained from the said John a diamond without paying the proper price for it. Which stone he, Aldobrand, had sold and converted into money, and having so done, found afterwards both his fortune and his health decline; so that, although he had great riches before he became possessed of the diamond, these had forthwith melted through unfortunate ventures and speculations, till he had little remaining to him but the money that this same diamond had brought.

He therefore left to John Trenchard everything of which he should die possessed, and being near death begged his forgiveness if he had wronged him in aught. These were the instructions which Heer Roosten received from Mr Aldobrand, whose health sensibly declined, until three months later he died. It was well, Heer Roosten added, that the will had been drawn in good time, for as Mr Aldobrand grew weaker, he became a prey to delusions, saying that John Trenchard had laid a curse upon the diamond, and professing even to relate the words of it, namely, that it should 'bring evil in this life, and damnation in that which is to come'. Nor was this all, for he could get no sleep, but woke up with a horrid dream, in which, so he informed Heer Roosten, he saw continually a tall man with a coppery face and black beard draw the bed curtains and mock him. Thus he came at length to his end, and after his death Heer Roosten endeavoured to give effect to the provision of the will, by writing to John Trenchard, at Moonfleet, Dorset, to apprise him that he was left sole heir. That address, indeed, was all the indication that Aldobrand had given, though he constantly promised his attorney to let him have closer information as to Trenchard's whereabouts, in good time. This information was, however, always postponed, perhaps because Aldobrand hoped he might get better and so repent of his repentance. So all Heer Roosten had to do was to write to Trenchard at Moonfleet, and in due course the letter was returned to him, with the information that Trenchard had fled that place to escape the law, and was then nowhere to be found. After that Heer Roosten was advised to write to the minister of the parish, and so addressed these lines to Mr Glennie.

This was the gist of the letter which Mr Glennie read, and you may easily guess how such news moved me, and how we sat far into the night talking and considering what steps it was best to take, for we feared lest so long an interval as eight years having elapsed, the lawyers might have made some other disposition of the money. It was midnight when Mr Glennie left. The candle had long burned out, but the fire was bright, and he knelt a moment by the trestle table before he went out.

'He made a good end, John,' he said, rising from his knees, 'and I pray that our end may be in as good cause when it comes. For with the best of us the hour of death is an awful hour, and we may well pray, as every Sunday, to be delivered in it. But there is another time which those who wrote this Litany thought no less perilous, and bade us pray to be delivered in all time of our wealth. So I pray that if, after all, this wealth comes to your hand you may be led to use it well; for though I do not hold with foolish tales, or think a curse hangs on riches themselves, yet if riches have been set apart for a good purpose, even by evil men, as Colonel John Mohune set apart this treasure, it cannot be but that we shall do grievous wrong in putting them to other use. So fare you well, and remember that there are other treasures besides this, and that a good woman's love is worth far more than all the gold and jewels of the world – as I once knew.' And with that he left me.

I guessed that he had spoken with Grace that day, and as I lay dozing in front of the fire, alone in this old room I knew so well, alone with that silent friend who had died to save me, I mourned him none the less, but yet sorrowed not as one without hope.

What need to tell this tale at any more length, since you may know, by my telling it, that all went well? For what man would sit down to write a history that ended in his own discomfiture? All that great wealth came to my hands, and if I do not say how great it was, 'tis that I may not wake envy, for it was far more than ever I could have thought. And of that money I never touched penny piece, having learned a bitter lesson in the past, but laid it out in good works, with Mr Glennie and Grace to help me. First, we rebuilt and enlarged the almshouses beyond all that Colonel John Mohune could ever think of, and so established them as to be a haven forever for all worn-out sailors of that coast. Next, we sought the guidance of the Brethren of the Trinity, and built a lighthouse on the Snout, to be a Channel beacon for sea-going ships, as Maskew's match had been a light for our fishing boats in the past. Lastly, we beautified the church, turning out the cumbrous seats of oak, and neatly pewing it with deal and baize, that made it most commodious to sit in of the sabbath. There was also much old glass which we removed, and reglazed all the windows tight against the wind, so that what with a high pulpit, reading desk, and seat for Master Clerk and new commandment boards each side of the holy table, there was not a church could vie with ours in the countryside. But that great vault below it, with its memories, was set in order, and then safely walled up, and after that nothing was ever more heard of Blackbeard and his lost Mohunes. And as for the landers, I cannot say where they went; and if a cargo is still run of a dark night upon the beach, I know nothing of it, being both Lord of the Manor and Justice of the Peace.

The village, too, renewed itself with the new almshouses and church. There were old houses rebuilt and fresh ones reared, and all are ours, except the Why Not? which still remains the duchy inn. And that was let again, and men left the Choughs at Ringstave and came back to their old haunt, and any shipwrecked or travel-worn sailor found board and welcome within its doors.

And of the Mohune Hospital – for that was what the almshouses were now called – Master Glennie was first warden, with fair rooms and a full library, and Master Ratsey head of the bedesmen. There they spent happier days, till they were gathered in the fullness of their years; and sleep on the sunny side of the church, within sound of the sea, by that great buttress where I once found Master Ratsey listening with his ear to ground. And close beside them lies Elzevir Block, most faithful and most loved by me, with a text on his tombstone: 'Greater love hath no man than this, that a man lay down his life for his friend,' and some of Mr Glennie's verses.

And of ourselves let me speak last. The manor house is a stately home again, with trim lawns and terraced balustrades, where we can sit and see the thin blue smoke hang above the village on summer evenings. And in the manor woods my wife and I have seen a little Grace and a little John and little Elzevir, our firstborn, play; and now our daughter is grown up, fair to us as the polished corners of the Temple, and our sons are gone out to serve King George on sea and land. But as for us, for Grace and me, we never leave this our happy Moonfleet, being well content to see the dawn tipping the long cliff line with gold, and the night walking in dew across the meadows; to watch the spring clothe the beech boughs with green, or the figs ripen on the southern wall; while behind all, is spread as a curtain the eternal sea, ever the same and ever changing. Yet I love to see it best when it is lashed to madness in the autumn gale, and to hear the grinding roar and churn of the pebbles like a great organ playing all the night. 'Tis then I turn in bed and thank God, more from the heart, perhaps, than any other living man, that I am not fighting for my life on Moonfleet beach. And more than once I have stood rope in hand in that same awful place, and tried to save a struggling wretch; but never saw one come through the surf alive, in such a night as he saved me.

PUFFIN CLASSICS

With Puffin Classics, the adventure isn't
over when you reach the final page.
Want to discover more about your favourite
characters, their creators and their worlds?
Read on . . .

CONTENTS

AUTHOR FILE

WHO'S WHO IN *MOONFLEET*

SOME THINGS TO THINK ABOUT . . .

SOME THINGS TO DO . . .

DID YOU KNOW?

GLOSSARY

NAME: John Meade Falkner
BORN: 8 May 1858 in Manningford Bruce, Wiltshire
DIED: 11 July 1932 in Durham
NATIONALITY: English
LIVED: Dorset, Oxford, Newcastle and Durham. John also travelled all across Europe (especially the Balkans), Asia and South America
MARRIED: he did not marry
CHILDREN: he did not have any children

What was he like?

John was a charming, dignified and patient man. To his friends he was an interesting character, full of curious contradictions. He was the son of an English clergyman and had a traditional British education. He loved to learn and was fascinated by antiques and medieval architecture. He also collected rare books and had an obsession for medieval calligraphy. John wrote beautiful and exquisitely decorative script, which was modelled upon the best medieval scribes.

Where did he grow up?

John spent much of his childhood in Dorchester and Weymouth in Dorset. He love for learning developed from an early age and he graduated from Oxford University with a degree in History. John showed no intellectual arrogance and was a loyal and affectionate friend.

What did he do apart from writing books?

After leaving Oxford, John was a tutor to the family of Sir Andrew Noble who ran Armstrong Whitworth & Co. (one of the largest arms manufacturers in the world). John got a job in the company and worked his way up to become a director. His position at Armstrong Whitworth allowed him to travel across the world helping to export warships and armaments. He proved to be an excellent diplomat and was given multiple decorations by foreign governments, including Turkey, Italy and Japan. However, John never lost his scholarly mind. He loved being in Constantinople, Florence and especially Rome, where he frequently visited the Vatican Library and struck up a friendship with the Pope.

Where did John get the idea for Moonfleet?

John drew inspiration from his own childhood experiences. The geography of *Moonfleet* reflects the landmarks and landscape of Dorset and the Isle of Wight, where John grew up. It is a tale of smuggling, royal treasure and shipwreck, and reflects many features of John's own travels and experiences. Although a work of children's fiction, the novel mirrors some aspects of John's own life, including the name of the main character.

What did people think of Moonfleet when it was first published in 1898?

The book proved extremely popular among children from its first publication; its sense of adventure and gripping storyline perfectly captured young imaginations. *Moonfleet* continues to be widely read to this day and is studied in many schools.

What other books did he write?
John published guide books, historical essays and poetry, but his three published novels were his greatest successes. He wrote a fourth novel but it was lost on a train and never rewritten. John also filled over forty notebooks with comments and analysis (all in Latin) of Vatican manuscripts.

John Trenchard – a fifteen-year-old orphan who is taken under the wing of the local innkeeper, Elsevir Block. John attends lessons given by Parson Glennie and through these meets Grace Maskew, the local magistrate's daughter. John is determined to find 'Blackbeard' Mohune's cursed diamond, and falls in with a gang of smugglers, led by Elsevir and Ratsey. John is arrested and sent to prison. He escapes and flees the country but years later returns to Moonfleet to marry Grace.

Elsevir Block – the gruff landlord of the local inn who keeps himself to himself. Elsevir is heartbroken by the death of his son at the hands of Maskew, the local magistrate. Elsevir gives John a room at the inn and becomes a father figure to him, finally giving up his life for John's.

Colonel John 'Blackbeard' Mohune – buried in the Mohune family crypt under the church, he is said to have been an evil man who squandered the family fortune. To make amends on his deathbed he left his ill-gotten treasure – a diamond stolen a diamond from King Charles I – to the poor. But he died before handing it over, so no one knows where the diamond is hidden. Moonfleet legend has it that Mohune's ghost wanders at night and the mysterious lights in the churchyard are said to be due to his activities.

Ratsey – the sexton of Moonfleet church, Ratsey was once a mason and carves the lettering on the tombstones. He is a close friend of Elsevir Block and always kind to John.

Reverend Mr Glennie – the local clergyman who also teaches in the village school. He is friendly to John and treats him as an equal.

Mr Maskew – the unpopular local magistrate. A widower, he lives with his young daughter, Grace, in the large but ill-kept manor house. During a struggle with Elsevir Block, Maskew is shot dead by the soldiers but it is John who gets the blame.

Krispijn Aldobrand – a well-known Dutch diamond merchant who dupes John and Elsevir out of the diamond. On his deathbed he begs forgiveness and in his will bequeaths his entire fortune to John.

Grace Maskew – the magistrate's daughter and John's childhood sweetheart. She becomes a rich young lady, having inherited her father's money, and keeps a light in her window for John's return from his years in exile.

Miss Jane Arnold – John's aunt and only living relative. She throws him out when he comes home drunk, but gives him his late mother's prayer book in the hope that he may mend his ways.

Which is your favourite episode in the story and why?

Why do you think Elsevir is kind to John?

Do you think John 'Blackbeard' Mohune's ghost really haunts the village?

Despite being written over 120 years ago, *Moonfleet* has remained in print and is as popular today as when it was first published. What do you think are the classic qualities that have helped to make the book so appealing to each new generation?

Stories about shipwrecks and smuggling have always been popular. Can you think of five other books, films or television programmes with a similar theme to *Moonfleet*?

Choose an exciting scene from the story and turn it into a comic strip. For example, the episode when John hides from the smugglers behind Colonel Mohune's coffin in the vault of Fleet Church.

Create a map of Moonfleet using details from the text, such as the churchyard close to the sea, the Why Not? inn and John's aunt's cottage.

A Hollywood studio has asked you to make a new film of *Moonfleet* . . .

- What would your costumes and sets look like?

- How would you go about turning the novel into a film script?

- Who would you cast as your main characters?

The Dorset coast has a long tradition of smuggling, and it was the nearby village of East Fleet by Chesil Beach that provided the setting for J. Meade Falkner's novel. In 1955 *Moonfleet* was made into a film called *The Smugglers of Moonfleet*, and since then there has been several other adaptations. See if you can find a copy of the original film to watch and then compare it to the book. Which do you prefer and why?

One of the most famous smugglers operating along the south coast of England in the eighteenth century was Isaac Gulliver. He became known as a gentle villain because he claimed to have never killed one man during his smuggling career. Use the internet and library to see what else you can find out about this notorious smuggler.

- Smuggling was a very risky business! In the eighteenth century the entire Dorset coast in the south of England was a smuggling hot spot. It was easy to bring boats into hidden coves to unload a cargo, avoiding customs duties (the tax paid on the import of goods). Spirits such as brandy and gin, and other goods – like tea, tobacco, spices and silk – were then sold for a big profit.

- If you were caught smuggling you would be hanged or deported to one of the British penal colonies, such as Australia.

- Smuggling still happens today though it tends to be more than just food and drink which is transported illegally – now technology, like DVDs and mobile phones, are often smuggled across borders.

- In 1906 the famous author Rudyard Kipling wrote a poem called *A Smuggler's Song*.

- It was not only men who were involved in the eighteenth-century smuggling trade. The earliest recorded female smugglers were Anne Bonney and Mary Read who began trading in counterfeit goods before becoming full-blown smugglers. After a career of seafaring crime, they went on the run. They were eventually captured and ended their days in prison on the island of Jamaica.

GLOSSARY

almshouse – a house built and run by charities to provide accommodation for the poor

appellation – the name or title that a person or place is given

assizes – courts held in the main county towns and presided over by visiting judges from the higher courts based in London

bulwark – a solid, upright, fence-like structure along the sides of a boat's deck

buttress – a support, usually made of stone, that supports a wall

cipher – a secret system of writing; a code

cognizance – knowledge or understanding

cutter – a small, fast, rigged sailing boat belonging to a ship

duchy – an area of land that is ruled by a duke or duchess

excise – a tax, or duty that the government of a country puts on particular goods, such as alcoholic drinks

felon – a person who has committed a crime

Hollands – a strongly-flavoured Dutch gin

ketch – a type of sailing ship that has two masts

laggard – a dawdler or straggler

Low Countries – a low-lying region along the coast of western Europe, consisting of Belgium, the Netherlands (Holland) and Luxemburg

lugger – a small working boat, rigged with a lugsail

matchlock – a mechanism on an old type of gun, which held the wick or cord for igniting the powder in place

pinnace – a small boat carried on a large ship used to transport goods and people from the ship to the shore

posse – a group of people who have been brought together, usually to enforce the law

If you have enjoyed *Moonfleet* you may like to read *Treasure Island*, by Robert Louis Stevenson, in which young Jim Hawkins finds himself the owner of a map to hidden treasure . . .

1

The Old Sea Dog at the 'Admiral Benbow'

Squire Trelawney, Dr Livesey, and the rest of these gentlemen having asked me to write down the whole particulars about Treasure Island, from the beginning to the end, keeping nothing back but the bearings of the island, and that only because there is still treasure not yet lifted, I take up my pen in the year of grace 17—, and go back to the time when my father kept the 'Admiral Benbow' inn, and the brown old seaman, with the sabre cut, first took up his lodging under our roof.

I remember him as if it were yesterday, as he came plodding to the inn door, his sea-chest following behind him in a hand-barrow; a tall, strong, heavy, nut-brown man; his tarry pigtail falling over the shoulders of his soiled blue coat; his hands ragged and scarred, with black, broken nails; and the sabre cut across one cheek, a dirty, livid white. I remember him looking round the cove and whistling to himself as he did so, and then breaking out in that old sea-song that he sang so often afterwards:

> 'Fifteen men on the dead man's chest –
>   Yo-ho-ho, and a bottle of rum!'

in the high, old tottering voice that seemed to have been tuned and broken at the capstan bars. Then he rapped on the door with a bit of stick like a handspike that he carried, and when my father appeared, called roughly for a glass of rum. This, when it was brought to him, he drank slowly, like a connoisseur, lingering on the taste, and still looking about him at the cliffs and up at our signboard.

'This is a handy cove,' says he, at length; 'and a pleasant sittyated grog-shop. Much company, mate?'

My father told him no, very little company, the more was the pity.

'Well, then,' said he, 'this is the berth for me. Here you, matey,' he cried to the man who trundled the barrow; 'bring up alongside and help up my chest. I'll stay here a bit,' he continued. 'I'm a plain man; rum and bacon and eggs is what I want, and that head up there for to watch ships off. What you mought call me? You mought call me captain. Oh, I see what you're at – there'; and he threw down three or four gold pieces on the threshold. 'You can tell me when I've worked through that,' says he, looking as fierce as a commander.

And, indeed, bad as his clothes were, and coarsely as he spoke, he had none of the appearance of a man who sailed before the mast; but seemed like a mate or skipper, accustomed to be obeyed or to strike. The man who came with the barrow told us the mail had set him down the morning before at the 'Royal George'; that he had inquired what inns there were along the coast, and hearing ours well spoken of, I suppose, and described as lonely, had chosen it from the others for his place of residence. And that was all we could learn of our guest.

He was a very silent man by custom. All day he hung round the cove, or upon the cliffs, with a brass telescope; all evening he sat in a corner of the parlour next the fire, and drank rum and water very strong. Mostly he would not speak when spoken to; only look up sudden and fierce, and blow through his nose like a fog-horn; and we and the people who came about our house soon learned to let him be. Every day, when he came back from his stroll, he would ask if any seafaring men had gone by along the road. At first we thought it was the want of company of his own kind that made him ask this question; but at last we began to see he was desirous to avoid them. When a seaman put up at the 'Admiral Benbow' (as now and then some did, making by the coast road for Bristol), he would look in at him through the curtained door before he entered the parlour; and he was always sure to be as silent as a mouse when any such was present. For me, at least, there was no secret about the matter; for I was, in a way, a sharer in his alarms. He had taken me aside one day, and promised me a silver fourpenny on the first of every month if I would only keep my 'weather-eye open for a seafaring man with one leg', and let him know the moment he appeared. Often enough, when the first of the month came round, and I applied to him for my wage, he would only blow through his nose at me, and stare me down; but before the week was out he was sure to think better of it, bring me my fourpenny piece, and repeat his orders to look out for 'the seafaring man with one leg'.

How that personage haunted my dreams, I need scarcely tell you. On stormy nights, when the wind shook the four corners of the house, and the surf roared along the cove and up the cliffs, I would see him in a thousand forms, and with a thousand diabolical expressions. Now the leg would be cut off at the knee, now at the hip; now he was a monstrous kind of a creature who had never had but the one leg, and that in the middle of his body. To see him leap and run and pursue me over hedge and ditch was the worst of nightmares. And altogether I paid pretty dear for my monthly fourpenny piece, in the shape of these abominable fancies.

But though I was so terrified by the idea of the seafaring man with one leg, I was far less afraid of the captain himself than anybody else who knew him. There were nights when he took a deal more rum and water than his head would carry; and then he would sometimes sit and sing his wicked, old, wild sea-songs, minding nobody; but sometimes he would call for glasses round, and force all the trembling company to listen to his stories or bear a chorus to his singing. Often I have heard the house shaking with 'Yo-ho-ho, and a bottle of rum', all the neighbours joining in for dear life, with the fear of death upon them, and each singing louder than the other, to avoid remark. For in these fits he was the most over-riding companion ever known; he would slap his hand on the table for silence all round; he would fly up in a passion of anger at a question, or sometimes because none was put, and so he judged the company was not following his story. Nor would he allow anyone to leave the inn till he had drunk himself sleepy and reeled off to bed.

Treasure Island is available in Puffin Classics